PRAISE FOR J. R. WARD AND HER
BLACK DAGGER BROTHERHOOD SERIES

'Frighteningly addictive'
Publishers Weekly

'J. R. Ward is a master!'
Gena Showalter, *New York Times* bestselling author

'J. R. Ward is the undisputed queen ... Long live the queen'
Steve Berry, *New York Times* bestselling author

'Fearless storytelling. A league all of her own'
Kristen Ashley, *New York Times* bestselling author

'J. R. Ward is one of the finest writers out there – in any genre'
Sarah J. Maas, No. 1 *New York Times* bestselling author

'Ward is a master of her craft'
New York Journal of Books

'Now here's a band of brothers who know
how to show a girl a good time'
Lisa Gardner, *New York Times* bestselling author

'This dark and compelling world is filled with enticing
romance as well as perilous adventure'
Romantic Times

'The Black Dagger Brotherhood owns me now.
Dark fantasy lovers, you just got served'
Lynn Viehl, *USA Today* bestselling author of *Evermore*

J. R. Ward lives in the South with her incredibly supportive husband and her beloved golden retriever. After graduating from law school, she began working in health care in Boston and spent many years as chief of staff for one of the premier academic medical centres in the nation.

Visit J. R. Ward online:

www.jrward.com
www.facebook.com/JRWardBooks
@jrward1

By J. R. Ward

The Black Dagger Brotherhood series:
Dark Lover
Lover Eternal
Lover Awakened
Lover Revealed
Lover Unbound
Lover Enshrined
Lover Avenged
Lover Mine
Lover Unleashed
Lover Reborn
Lover at Last
The King
The Shadows
The Beast
The Chosen
The Thief
The Savior
The Sinner
Lover Unveiled
Lover Arisen
Lassiter

The Black Dagger Brotherhood:
An Insider's Guide

The Black Dagger Brotherhood:
Prison Camp
The Jackal
The Wolf
The Viper

The Black Dagger Brotherhood World:
Dearest Ivie*
Prisoner of Night*
Where Winter Finds You
A Warm Heart in Winter

The Black Dagger Legacy series:
Blood Kiss
Blood Vow
Blood Fury
Blood Truth

The Lair of the Wolven series:
Claimed
Forever

Novels of the Fallen Angels:
Covet
Crave
Envy
Rapture
Possession
Immortal

The Bourbon Kings series:
The Bourbon Kings
The Angels' Share
Devil's Cut

Firefighters Series:
The Wedding From Hell:
The Rehearsal Dinner*
The Wedding From Hell:
The Reception*
Consumed

ebook novella

J.R. WARD

DARIUS

PIATKUS

PIATKUS

Previously published in 2022 in audio format by Simon and Schuster Audio
First published in physical format in the US in 2023 by Gallery Books
An imprint of Simon & Schuster, Inc.
First published in audio format in Great Britain in 2022 by Piatkus
This physical edition published in 2023 by Piatkus

1 3 5 7 9 10 8 6 4 2

A CIP catalogue record for this book
is available from the British Library.

Hardback ISBN 978-0-349-43863-4
Trade paperback ISBN 978-0-349-43864-1

Printed and bound in Great Britain by Clays Ltd, Elcograf S.p.A.

Papers used by Piatkus are from well-managed forests
and other responsible sources.

Piatkus
An imprint of
Little, Brown Book Group
Carmelite House
50 Victoria Embankment
London EC4Y 0DZ

An Hachette UK Company
www.hachette.co.uk

www.littlebrown.co.uk

To you, and your mate.
In so many ways, you were what started it all.

GLOSSARY OF TERMS AND PROPER NOUNS

abstrux nohtrum (n.) Private guard with license to kill who is granted his or her position by the King.

ahvenge (v.) Act of mortal retribution, carried out typically by a male loved one.

Black Dagger Brotherhood (pr. n.) Highly trained vampire warriors who protect their species against the Lessening Society. As a result of selective breeding within the race, Brothers possess immense physical and mental strength, as well as rapid healing capabilities. They are not siblings for the most part, and are inducted into the Brotherhood upon nomination by the Brothers. Aggressive, self-reliant, and secretive by nature, they are the subjects of legend and objects of reverence within the vampire world. They may be killed only by the most serious of wounds, e.g., a gunshot or stab to the heart, etc.

blood slave (n.) Male or female vampire who has been sub-jugated to serve the blood needs of another.

the Chosen (pr. n.) Female vampires who have been bred to serve the Scribe Virgin. They are spiritually rather than temporally focused, and meet the blood needs of unmated members of the Brotherhood, as well as Brothers who cannot feed from their *shellans* or injured fighters.

chrih (n.) Symbol of honorable death in the Old Language.

cohntehst (n.) Conflict between two males competing for the right to be a female's mate.

Dhunhd (pr. n.) Hell.

doggen (n.) Member of the servant class within the vampire world. *Doggen* have old, conservative traditions about ser-vice to their superiors, following a formal code of dress and behavior. They are able to go out during the day, but they age relatively quickly. Life expectancy is approxi-mately five hundred years.

ehros (n.) A Chosen trained in the matter of sexual arts.

exhile dhoble (n.) The evil or cursed twin, the one born second.

the Fade (pr. n.) Non-temporal realm where the dead re-unite with their loved ones and pass eternity.

First Family (pr. n.) The King and Queen of the vampires, and any children they may have.

ghardian (n.) Custodian of an individual. There are varying degrees of *ghardians*, with the most powerful being that of a *sehcluded* female.

glymera (n.) The social core of the aristocracy, roughly equiv-alent to Regency England's *ton*.

hellren (n.) Male vampire who has been mated to a female. Males may take more than one female as mate.

hyslop (n. or v.) Term referring to a lapse in judgment, typically resulting in the compromise of the mechanical operations of a vehicle or otherwise motorized conveyance of some kind. For example, leaving one's keys in one's car as it is parked outside the family home overnight, whereupon said vehicle is stolen.

leahdyre (n.) A person of power and influence.

leelan (adj. or n.) A term of endearment loosely translated as "dearest one."

Lessening Society (pr. n.) Order of slayers convened by the Omega for the purpose of eradicating the vampire species.

lesser (n.) De-souled human who targets vampires for extermination as a member of the Lessening Society. *Lessers* must be stabbed through the chest in order to be killed; otherwise they are ageless. They do not eat or drink and are impotent. Over time, their hair, skin, and irises lose pigmentation until they are blond, blushless, and pale eyed. They smell like baby powder. Inducted into the society by the Omega, they retain a ceramic jar thereafter into which their heart was placed after it was removed.

lewlhen (n.) Gift.

lheage (n.) A term of respect used by a sexual submissive to refer to their dominant.

Lhenihan (pr. n.) A mythic beast renowned for its sexual prowess. In modern slang, refers to a male of preternatural size and sexual stamina.

lys (n.) Torture tool used to remove the eyes.

mahmen (n.) Mother. Used both as an identifier and a term of affection.

mhis (n.) The masking of a given physical environment; the creation of a field of illusion.

nalla (n., f.) or *nallum* (n., m.) Beloved.

needing period (n.) Female vampire's time of fertility, generally lasting for two days and accompanied by intense sexual cravings. Occurs approximately five years after a female's transition and then once a decade thereafter. All males respond to some degree if they are around a female in her need. It can be a dangerous time, with conflicts and fights breaking out between competing males, particularly if the female is not mated.

newling (n.) A virgin.

the Omega (pr. n.) Malevolent, mystical figure who has targeted the vampires for extinction out of resentment directed toward the Scribe Virgin. Exists in a non-temporal realm and has extensive powers, though not the power of creation.

phearsom (adj.) Term referring to the potency of a male's sexual organs. Literal translation something close to "worthy of entering a female."

Princeps (pr. n.) Highest level of the vampire aristocracy, second only to members of the First Family or the Scribe Virgin's Chosen. Must be born to the title; it may not be conferred.

pyrocant (n.) Refers to a critical weakness in an individual. The weakness can be internal, such as an addiction, or external, such as a lover.

rahlman (n.) Savior.

rythe (n.) Ritual manner of asserting honor granted by one who has offended another. If accepted, the offended chooses a weapon and strikes the offender, who presents him- or herself without defenses.

the Scribe Virgin (pr. n.) Mystical force who is counselor to the King as well as the keeper of vampire archives and the dispenser of privileges. Exists in a non-temporal realm and has extensive powers. Capable of a single act of creation, which she expended to bring the vampires into existence.

sehclusion (n.) Status conferred by the King upon a female of the aristocracy as a result of a petition by the female's family. Places the female under the sole direction of her *ghardian*, typically the eldest male in her household. Her *ghardian* then has the legal right to determine all manner of her life, restricting at will any and all interactions she has with the world.

shellan (n.) Female vampire who has been mated to a male. Females generally do not take more than one mate due to the highly territorial nature of bonded males.

symphath (n.) Subspecies within the vampire race characterized by the ability and desire to manipulate emotions in others (for the purposes of an energy exchange), among other traits. Historically, they have been discriminated against and, during certain eras, hunted by vampires. They are near extinction.

talhman (n.) The evil side of an individual. A dark stain on the soul that requires expression if it is not properly expunged.

the Tomb (pr. n.) Sacred vault of the Black Dagger Brotherhood. Used as a ceremonial site as well as a storage facility for the jars of *lessers*. Ceremonies performed there include inductions, funerals, and disciplinary actions against Brothers. No one may enter except for members of the Brotherhood, the Scribe Virgin, or candidates for induction.

trahyner (n.) Word used between males of mutual respect and affection. Translated loosely as "beloved friend."

transition (n.) Critical moment in a vampire's life when he or she transforms into an adult. Thereafter, he or she must drink the blood of the opposite sex to survive and is unable to withstand sunlight. Occurs generally in the mid-twenties. Some vampires do not survive their transitions, males in particular. Prior to their transitions, vampires are physically weak, sexually unaware and unresponsive, and unable to dematerialize.

vampire (n.) Member of a species separate from that of *Homo sapiens*. Vampires must drink the blood of the opposite sex to survive. Human blood will keep them alive, though the strength does not last long. Following their transitions, which occur in their mid-twenties, they are unable to go out into sunlight and must feed from the vein regularly. Vampires cannot "convert" humans through a bite or transfer of blood, though they are in rare cases able to breed with the other species. Vampires can dematerialize at will, though they must be able to calm themselves and concentrate to do so and may not carry anything heavy with them. They are able to strip the memories of humans, provided such memories are short-term. Some vampires are able to read minds. Life expectancy is upward of a thousand years, or in some cases, even longer.

wahlker (n.) An individual who has died and returned to the living from the Fade. They are accorded great respect and are revered for their travails.

whard (n.) Equivalent of a godfather or godmother to an individual.

INTRODUCTION

My name is Darius, son of Marklon. I was sired of the Black Dagger Brother Tehrror, and born in 1618 by the human calendar. I died in 2005.

If I had a gravestone, those would be the sum of my identity descriptors and the numerical fences that corralled the events of my life upon the earth. They are at once the most essential details of my autobiography, but also the least significant things you will know of me.

Let me share with you the most important sentences:

When I first met her, I did not know she would be my one true love.

When I fell in love with her, I did not know she would bear me a daughter on her deathbed.

When I died, more than twenty years later, it would be while trying to save the life of our young. On a rainy night.

When the tears I could no longer shed fell from a disinterested Caldwell sky.

Those are the real details of me.

As a keeper of diaries, I wrote down the events of my life in a compulsive fashion, even though I rarely reread them and was well aware the Chosen in the Temple of the Sequestered Scribes were doing a far better job at the recording. Looking back on it, I wonder whether I'd sensed my destiny all along and that was why I took to ink and page. In marking my present, it's possible I was trying to take some control over the future that I could feel coming for me, the brief sunshine that was followed by so many years of dark suffering looming just under the surface of my conscious mind.

But if that was the case, how stupid. Penmanship, no matter how fine, has never been as persuasive as prayer. And prayer is no guarantee of happiness or salvation, either.

Given my grieving, you might ask if I would have chosen a different path, if I'd have denied or avoided my destiny if I could have. It would be more courageous, more admirable, to clothe myself in the armor of "absolutely not." But that's just an easy virtue signal—as well as a claim no one can refute because nobody else is in my head, in my heart.

The honest truth is more nuanced, more complex. In the moment my path collided with my female's, before everything started, yes, I probably would have taken another route: If the second before we met, I would have known what I had to face, I'd have balked.

There. I admit it.

That's just the survival instinct at work, though. Noth-

ing more than a reflex to avoid pain that fires in a nano-
second and is untempered by higher purpose and reasoning.

It is a truth, but not *the* truth.

One night after I first met my female, I knew over
Campbell's tomato soup and Wonder Bread toast that I
would never leave her. And even after she told me to go . . .
and then after she died in my arms . . . I never left her. I've
taken my beloved everywhere with me, hoping that through
my eyes she could see the beautiful thing we made together
and know our daughter is safe.

I'm a male who keeps his promises.

In my female's last moments, when she knew she wasn't
going to survive, she asked me to watch over our daughter.
She made me swear that I would guard our young. I would
have done that anyway, but as it was the one and only way I
was able to honor my mate, that vow became my connection
to her and my reason for living.

I stopped writing anything down about my life after
that night. But there were other recordings, photographs
now, no longer my words, that documented my time. I
amassed a collection of hundreds of pictures of our young,
and I framed them so that those moments I could not be by
our daughter's side in person were preserved forever for my
heart. From a distance, from the oculus of a camera lens held
by another, I witnessed her maturation. Raised as an or-
phan, she was never alone, my loyal butler doing the daylight
shift and I, myself, on the nighttime watch. Wherever she
was, in the orphanage or out on her own in the world, we
were never far from her.

She could not know the truth of who her father was,

however. Half-breeds are rare, and although being a human is not safe, existing as a vampire is downright dangerous. Further, I always had the hope that her *mahmen*'s genes would prevail and she would never go through the transition.

That was another prayer not answered.

As our daughter's time for the change approached, after years of mere worrying, I became terrified. To see any vampire through their first feeding is perilous. To get a female with mixed blood through it? There was only one male she could take from and have her best chance at surviving.

Only one purebred vampire left on the planet.

Except it was like turning her over to an undertaker. Who kept his business going with black daggers and throwing stars.

It was at this critical juncture in her life that death came for me in the form of a car bomb, leaving our daughter not just undefended, but on the precipice of a life-altering, mortally dangerous change she didn't even know was on her horizon.

So of course, I had to find a way to come back.

When my time to enter the Fade came, I struck a bargain with the Scribe Virgin, the *mahmen* of the species, and I returned to the earth in a different form for a different life . . . with the same purpose.

And so it has been, for these most recent years, me peering through new eyes at the beautiful proof that I had known love.

Unlike my destiny, our daughter has had much joy: a King who loves her, a son to call her own, a protected home, and an extended family. Everything I could have wished for her has come true, and if the cost of such a fate required my sacrifices?

One does everything for one's children.

Yet as time has changed her, it has also changed me. The foundational role of a parent is to usher their progeny into adulthood, to make sure they are set and settled, prepared to carry the torch forward past the lives of those who created them. Of late, I am beginning to think my purpose for her has been served—and the more this feels true, the more the pain of who I miss, who I am separated from, who I long for, is growing intolerable.

With the same compulsion I previously focused on my present, I now find myself returning to the past and reliving the origin story of our daughter. But it's not about the young.

It's about my female. Myself.

Through the course of my recollecting, I am compelled to get each and every detail of our love story right. I want all the words we shared relived with their proper tone and inflection. I want the glances, the touches, the heartbeats, cataloged. I want even the scents right.

I have to remember everything.

It's the only way I can decide whether it is finally time to release myself of my duty upon the earth . . . and try to find my love on the Other Side.

If she'll have me, that is.

Perhaps this story of mine will at long last lead to a happily ever after.

Or maybe I was wrong about everything.

And nothing awaits me in the Fade.

DARIUS

CHAPTER ONE

May 1981
Caldwell, NY

Darius, begotten son of Tehrror, forsaken son of Marklon, decided to drive into town the night his destiny came to claim him. Two weeks before, he had directed his trusted, elderly *doggen*, Fritz Perlmutter, to go to the BMW of Caldwell dealership and accept delivery of a brand-new 735i. The car had been ordered about six months before, and although vampires did not celebrate the human Christmas holiday, as its arrival date drew nearer, Darius knew all about sugarplums dancing in the head.

The sweet anticipation had been an antidote to so much dread and duty in his life, and the wait had been interminable. There had even been a delay or two, the production in Germany hitting a snag, and then the cross-Atlantic shipping taking longer than scheduled. But then, *finally*, the call had come in, and when Darius had returned home after a weekend away of fighting, covered in black blood that smelled like baby powder, with a gunshot wound through the meat of his upper left arm, Fritz had whipped open the back door and proclaimed that "she is being prepared and is ready to be gathered tomorrow afternoon!"

Darius had stood there on the kitchen stoop like a big dummy, his sluggish, exhausted brain failing to process whatever news had made his butler light up like a streetlamp. And then it had sunk in. Talk about your second wind.

As a *doggen*, Fritz could go out into the spring sunlight, and given that he was the most faithful servant on the planet, he had been as excited as his master when he'd headed off twelve hours later to pick up the new car. The last sixty minutes or so of patience had been a slog of centuries-long duration, and Darius had churned through the time pacing in his subterranean bedroom, circling his desk, his bed, his seating area. The hearth. The bath. Rinse and repeat.

Fritz had come down to report she was safely on the premises as soon as he'd gotten home, but given that the gracious Federal mansion had a detached garage, there had been no way to go see the car until the sun was under the horizon. That it was spring in upstate New York meant there had been another forever-wait, and Darius had wished, even though the nicer weather was more enjoyable, that the calendar had been closer to December 21.

Hell, in winter, he could have gone to the dealership himself.

And then it was time.

Bursting out of the back door, he had all but skipped

across the asphalt court. Fritz had deliberately closed up the garage bay, and Darius had twitched through the final thirty seconds as his butler had scooted in and hit the opener.

The panels rising and revealing the BMW, inch by inch, had been like opening a present, and there had been no disappointment. The bronze metallic paint had gleamed, and those four headlights had stared back at him as if the thing were alive. Initial shock and awe over, Darius had prowled around the sedan, trailing fingertips on the cool steel, on the smooth glass, on the hood, the roof, the boot.

And it drove like a dream.

Which was why a vampire like him, who could dematerialize anywhere he wanted, chose to take the long way home sometimes . . .

As he passed through a part of town congested by newly constructed developments of mid-market apartment buildings, he turned up the volume on the stereo so Supertramp could tell him more about lonely days and lonely nights. He didn't need the primer. Sure, he had no wife at home, but he did feel like a piece of furniture in his own life: When he was fighting *lessers*, those pale, soulless killers who hunted vampires, he was as animated as they came; inside of himself, though, he had become an inanimate object. He'd noticed this fossilization about a year ago, and ever since then, he'd been trying to figure out exactly what his problem was. A rereading of his diaries, whereupon he'd probed the fact patterns of his life as if he were a disinterested third party instead of the main character, had yielded nothing of note.

And endless, contemporaneously penned entries detailing the fact that he was rereading his diaries hadn't gotten him any further.

Then again, maybe it was because he already knew what ailed him and he just didn't want to look at all that he couldn't see ever changing.

His cycles of days and nights were always the same: Fighting. Eating. Sleeping. Feeding in a chaste way from a Chosen. Doing it again. And again. And again. As the pinwheel of time continued to spin, and humans went in and out of different fashions, fads, and presidents, he was the trudging same. Not even the noble purpose of his existence— saving the vampire race from the Lessening Society and protecting the King who refused to lead—was enough to relieve the rote detachment that blanked him like anesthesia.

And this was why he not only needed a nice new car, but had to drive the thing.

Running his hand over the top of the steering wheel, he breathed in deep. He didn't require a vampire nose to appreciate the rich perfume of hand-tooled leather, that delicious new-car smell—

As he rounded a turn in the road, the movement came at him from the left, the streak the kind of thing that his peripheral vision caught and his hair-trigger instincts reacted to without any conscious thought on his part. In quick coordination, he punched the brake pedal and yanked the wheel to the right. The tires did their best to find purchase, squealing in their slow-down efforts, but there was too much mass, too much acceleration. A sickening jolt of impact registered, and then the BMW veered off the four-lane road and jumped the curb.

The tree in his headlights was enormous.

The biggest arboreal anything he had ever seen.

Then again, when you were about to crash your brand-new BMW, that did lend a certain distortion to things—

Boom!

Like a bomb going off, the impact was loud and had shock waves. As his ears rang, he was thrown forward and the steering wheel punched back, defending its territory with the stiff arm of its column. A flop of the head later and he was close as his own nose to the windshield before a boomerang effect snapped him back into his seat.

At which point he smelled gas, heard hissing, and started cursing.

As his eyes focused, he found that the trunk of the maple was just about centered between those two sets of headlights, like the blue-and-white hood ornament was a target. And what do you know, that badge was now halfway up into the engine block.

With a deflation characteristic of people who find themselves in the crosshairs of chaos theory, he opened his door. The damage had not extended back far enough to affect its release, hinges, or panel, and glancing into the interior as he got out, he closed his lids against how pristine everything remained in the cockpit, the dash and seating still so fresh and new. When he was ready, he turned to—

The fact that mid-pivot he caught sight of the unused seat belt seemed like a tap on the shoulder from Fate, a little reminder that this time—*this* time—he'd gotten away with it, but in the next accident, his head was going right through that safety glass.

Maybe he should buckle up in the future—

Freezing in his tracks, he caught the scent of fresh blood, and as he ripped his head around, he saw the human woman lying in the center of the four-lane street on the yellow line. She was tucked into a ball, crumpled as if by a fist, and he had an instant impression of a blue skirt that was the color of a morning glory, and a white blouse that was untucked. A red sweater was tied around her waist. The shoes were brown with no heels. No stockings.

She wasn't moving.

Oh, God, he'd hit someone. That was what the jolt had been.

Darius bolted across the two lanes he'd been traveling on. As he knelt down, he touched her shoulder. "Madam?"

No response. Then again, he'd felt the impact even inside the car, had heard the terrible sound.

"Madam, I'm going to roll you over."

With gentle hands, he unfurled her tight contraction, and as she flopped half onto her back, he didn't like the way her head was so loose on the top of her spine. The moan was good, though. It meant she was alive.

"We need to get you medical treatment." He glanced back to his car, which turned out to be at the tree line of a park-like area. "And I have no transport to offer—"

"Help . . ." she whispered. "He's going to hurt me . . ."

A cold rush hit Darius on the crown of his head, and he bared his fangs. "What did you say?"

When she just mumbled, he looked across the other two lanes. A short-stack, inter-connected collection of apartment buildings was set back from the street on a rise, with a stretch of grass separating them from the road. There were lights on inside almost all of the units, but no one was out on any of the balconies, and there were privacy blinds drawn across every window—

Another flash of movement.

In the breezeway of one of the building blocks, a figure ran out of the shadows—and then jumped back into the darkness as if they didn't want to be seen. Given the shape, it was clearly a male, and Darius flared his nostrils, scenting the air.

"Please, don't let him get me," the woman said in a reedy voice. "He's going to kill me."

CHAPTER TWO

Patricia Wurster didn't like her name. Had never liked it. Not the first part, especially if it was shortened to the dreaded Patty, and not the second part, especially when she'd been in elementary school and gotten called The Worst. The middle wasn't all that bad, though—

"Anne . . . my name is Anne."

As she spoke hoarsely, she was responding to a question directed to her, but she couldn't figure out why she was introducing herself . . . or to who? Opening her eyes, she got no clues because everything was dark—and yet she wasn't alone. Someone was holding her—

"Nice to meet you, Anne."

The voice was deep, a man's, and she instantly loved the sound of whoever it was. The syllables were so low and rolling, and that accent was certainly European, although she couldn't quite place it to a specific country . . .

Where was she? As the thought occurred, she decided she was in a bed, but not her own. This mattress was too hard and too small. And while she tried to figure out why she was so cramped, she wished the man would ask her another question because she preferred him talking to the weird delirium she was in. Maybe he could go the what's-your-sign route. Or want to know her height and weight, like she was at the doctor's. How about a quick algebra equation—

Bump!

The bed under her hit something, and the jostling that came with the impact rattled every bone in her body. As pain set up shop in little campfires that burned in her legs, her arms, and one shoulder in particular, she wondered why a mattress would hit a speed bump—wait, what was that subtle whirring in the background?

"I'm in a car," she mumbled.

"Yes," replied that male voice. "I'm taking you to the hospital."

Annnnnd that was when it all came back. In a series of flash card images, like her memory was dealing out the fact pattern of the evening on a tabletop, she remembered everything—

Anne went to sit up in a rush, but all kinds of things stopped her: those little flames flaring into bonfires, a cramped backseat . . . and a heavy but kind hand urging her to lie down again.

"We're almost there—"

"I have to go—"

Her words were cut off as panic took over, and she went on a messy scramble, shoving at whatever came into range—

"Fuck!" came a high-pitched squeak.

As she shrank away, the driver of whatever car she was in cranked around the headrest. Talk about a taxi driver. He was at once balding and in need of a haircut, the frizzy stripe at ear level and the patch-island at the top totally out of control. And he was not happy. His face was fleshy and round as a basketball, and his expression was the kind that usually went along with a flare-up of gout.

"Everybody okay back there?" he asked in an annoyed Jersey accent. "I'm not drivin' fast enough for ya?"

What was that guy from *Taxi* doing driving her anywhere—

"I'm not Danny frickin' DeVito. Jesus."

Guess she'd spoken that out loud.

The guy snapped his head forward. "Why the hell does everybody say that? I'm better-lookin' than . . ."

As he worked out his ego problems in the front seat, Anne glanced over . . . at . . . the . . .

All of her thoughts stopped, and not like a train that gradually slowed down: Her cognition slammed into a brick wall. Talk about better-looking than. The man sitting on the other side of the bench seat was worthy of the cover on a Johanna Lindsey novel. Dressed in black clothes, with a broad chest and shoulders, his body seemed to fill the whole car, and his face transfixed her. Classically handsome, with dark hair that was trimmed tightly, he would have drawn anybody's eyes.

But he was not any happier than the driver, and the reason was obvious. He had both palms pressed into his crotch, and a wince carved into his striking features—and just as putting your hands up to your throat meant you were choking in any language, he was making the universal signal for holy-hell-you-just-nailed-me-in-the-nuts.

"Oh, my God," she said. "I'm so sorry."

She reached out, but wasn't sure where to touch him. And boy, that fuzzy feeling in her head was totally gone now.

Nothing like corking a stranger in the hey-nannies to perk a girl up—

"You're sorry," the driver snapped. "I'm sorry I got two strangers in my backseat, no frickin' clue why I'm going to the hospital, and a headache like I been on a bender to the Poconos."

Anne lowered her voice. "I really am sorry."

The man with the proverbial privacy issues opened his eyes. As the peachy glow from a sodium streetlight flared through the windows, his irises were a resonant blue, like a clear autumn sky. He also had dark lashes that were long and brows that she was willing to bet had a natural arch when they weren't in a grimace.

"It's okay," he grunted with his accent. "Now I can sing the Leo Sayer parts."

His smile wasn't a big one, but the lift to his lips was endearing, taking all that manly-man and giving it a hint of the boy he had once been.

"What happened—" She glanced around. "I mean, what's happening?"

"You don't remember?" He rearranged himself on the

seat and swiveled his hips a little, like he was trying to assess whether things were still attached. "You were hit by a car—"

All at once, the flood of memories returned again and the pain in her body exploded, as if her recollection was a second impact.

"We're almost to the emergency room," the man next to her said.

"And then I'm out," Danny DeVito-esque announced from up front. "I don't know how in the hell I got involved in—Jesus, this headache. Either one a' ya moochers gotta aspirin?"

Anne focused on those beautiful blue eyes. "You were driving the BMW. I saw through the windshield right before I was hit . . . it was you."

The man nodded. "I didn't see you coming. And when I finally did, I swerved but it was too late."

Searching his face, she wondered what she'd said to him at the scene. Whether she'd told him why she'd been running across the road.

"I can't go to the hospital," she said quietly.

"Does he work there?"

She closed her eyes and tried on some denials. Then lost what little energy she had for putting up a brave front. "No, but he has my purse, so I have no money on me."

"I'll cover the costs of your care."

"No, you won't—"

"You need to be checked out. And the accident was my fault."

"It was not. I bolted into the street in the dark." She pounded on her sternum with what was, admittedly, a weak fist. "Besides, I'm breathing and I have a heartbeat. The rest I can walk off—"

"Look, lady," the driver cut in as he glared into the rear-view, "you're gettin' out at the hospital. I ain't goin' this way because I wanna. What ya do once ya there, I don't give a crap, but that's where ya road ends."

On that note, there wasn't any more conversation. Then again, they didn't have much farther to go. St. Francis Hospital appeared on the right, its blocky building surrounded by a three-hundred-and-sixty-degree parking lot. The ER was around to the far side, and Not-Danny DeVito cut off a station wagon to get onto the lane that went right up to its covered entrance.

"Now get outta my car," he said as he hit the brakes.

Anne opened her mouth to argue, but not with him. Her problem was with her fellow backseater. Here was not the place, however—not that any debate was going to go much better out on the curb, but at least she could hope for a less hostile peanut gallery there.

Reaching for the door handle, she popped the thing and extended a bare foot. With a frown, she tried to remember . . .

"I'm missing a shoe."

"Let's just get you looked at." The man next to her opened his side. "We'll worry about shoes afterward."

Before she could think of a response, he was standing in front of her and offering his hand. When she merely stared at his palm, the driver chimed in.

"Jesus, just get outta my car. Let him help ya already."

"I don't need to be here," she muttered as she grabbed ahold of what was being put forward.

Anne was pulled out gently—and as she wobbled and fought another tide of pain, she thought, wow, the man was tall. And then, as he bent down to give some money to the grumbling Samaritan, she couldn't stop her eyes from a quick review of his body.

Which pretty much proved there was no brain damage, right? If she was busy checking out the attributes of a perfect stranger, she had to be—

Okay. Well. The bottom half of him was just as good as the upper half, his thighs stretching the fabric of his black pants, his posterior region filling out the seat of those—

Anne snapped back to attention as the car she'd been rescued in took off with a squeal of rubber.

"I'm just going to get a taxi now," she said as the man turned to her. "A real one, that is."

"I thought you had no money."

"At home, I have an emergency twenty tucked into my mother's *Fannie Farmer Cookbook*."

He blinked. Like he'd never heard of such a thing. Or maybe cookbooks in general.

Hard to imagine the confusion was about currency.

"Come on." The man squeezed her hand and tucked her arm through his. "This won't take any time at all—"

"It's an emergency room. We're going to be here forever. And I don't—"

He looked into her eyes so deeply that everything stopped for her, including whatever argument she'd been making. As well as her lungs. And definitely her heart.

"Twenty minutes ago," he said, "I had to pick you up from

the middle of the road and put you in that backseat. I bet you don't remember much of the trip here, and yes, I realize you don't want me to pay for anything, but I cannot live with myself if I've left you on the side of the road to die."

"You didn't leave me and I'm not dying."

"If I don't get you through those revolving doors and into the hands of a doctor, you're just going to go home. So it's constructive abandonment."

"I won't go home, I promise."

"You're not a good liar."

"Yes, I am." As his left eyebrow arched, she cursed. "I mean, I'm not lying."

"So where else will you find a doctor this time of night."

As a long, tense moment gouged in between them, Anne was vaguely aware of people coming out of the ER's entrance. Going in the entrance. Coming out. Going in. Like the universe was on his side and trying to provide her with a visual demonstration of how the place worked.

"Please." His eyes roamed her face, and she wondered what he saw. "You need to do this for my peace of mind, okay?"

"You don't owe me anything."

"That's not how common decency works. Let's just make sure nothing is broken and then we'll go our separate ways. You'll never have to see me again."

Now why would that strike her as a loss, she wondered. He was a perfect stranger—

"Whoa! I got you," he blurted.

"What—"

And that was when the world went around in circles, the concrete underfoot turning into decking on a boat in high seas.

As Anne weaved on her feet, strong arms shot around her, and she was back where she started, once again up on the solid wall of a chest that made her feel safe.

Even though she didn't know this man from a hole in the wall.

Maybe she had been knocked senseless, after all.

"I've got you," he said softly. "You can trust me."

CHAPTER THREE

As Darius waited on the far side of a screen of privacy draping, he pulled at his jacket to make sure his autoloaders weren't showing. Then he glanced around on a reflex that had developed over centuries of fighting. This part of the ER's treatment area had a dozen or so examination bays, each station separated by these bolts of dull green curtains that were closed if the bed was occupied. The center aisle created by the layout was a highway for gurneys, medical staff, and equipment, and there were all kinds of patients and family members floating around the periphery.

Nothing threatening, anywhere, and no one paying much attention to him. He was just another kibitzer.

Things had to stay like that—

"Okay, you can come back in."

Ducking through the drapes, he made sure that the part in the fall closed properly in his wake, and he found himself bracing his shoulders as he looked up.

Patricia Anne Wurster, or Anne, as she'd introduced herself, was back on the bed, but the thing had been jacked forward to a ninety-degree angle, so it was as if she were sitting up. She looked . . . well, like she'd been hit by a car. Her long, dark hair was tangled. There were bruises on her face and a nasty scrape over her left eye. And one arm was raw like it had been worked over with sandpaper.

God, he could have killed her.

Trying to forget all the might-have-happened's, he glanced at her change of clothing. The blue-and-pink hospital gown she was now wearing dwarfed her, the collar hanging loose around the base of her throat, the sleeves billowing. Blankets had been pulled up to her waist, and she worried their hems with pale, blunt-nailed hands.

He thought of her lying in the middle of that road. Then he remembered when she'd come to in the back of that car. And finally he concluded . . . not for the first time . . . that she was captivating in a way that had nothing to do with being beautiful, and everything to do with being *her*.

Which, of course, didn't make a lot of sense. But what part of this evening had anything to do with logic?

"I don't know how we got this room so fast." She tugged the thin covers higher. "Guess we hit things at just the right time."

Can we please not use the H-word, he thought.

"Guess so." He took a seat in one of two plastic chairs. "Maybe our luck is changing."

"Considering your car got wrecked and I'm in a hospital johnny, I think that would be a good thing."

As he stared at her, he wanted to smooth the loose brunette hair back from her face. "Hopefully the doctor will be in soon."

"You don't have to stay," she said. "I mean, you were worried I'd walk, but I'm all registered and stuff. I'm in the system until they let me out."

"There's still a bill involved." He put up his hands. "If you'd rather me hang out in the waiting room or something—"

Overhead, a canned voice announced: "Dr. Peters, line two. Dr. Peters, line two."

"No, it's all right." Anne fiddled with the blankets some more. "As long as I'm, you know, not naked or anything—"

"Oh, yes. Obviously, I wouldn't stay when they examine you—"

They both stopped short. Laughed awkwardly. Looked elsewhere.

Darius cleared his throat. "Is there anyone I should call? For you, I mean."

"No." The answer was quick. "Thank you."

"Parents?" he prompted.

She shook her head. "No."

When she didn't expand on the details, he was tempted to get into her mind and access the information for himself. But an invasion of privacy was still wrong even if the person didn't know they'd been violated.

"I'm okay, though," she tacked on. In the way people did when they were lonely, and a little afraid, and didn't want anybody to know.

She wasn't looking to him to solve anything, however. Then again, what was he to her, motor vehicle assaults aside.

While Darius kept staring at her, he wondered whether the red patches on her neck and the side of her face were from the accident . . . or from the man who had so clearly been chasing after her.

So can I take care of whoever was trying to hurt you? he wondered as the curtain was pushed back.

"Hi, I'm Dr. Robert Bluff—"

The physician who stepped into the bay stopped dead. And he had reason to.

Well, hello there, my friend, Darius thought as he looked at the guy.

Or male, rather.

The vampire in the white coat had hazel eyes and dark hair, and a face with the kind of symmetry and features that equated to a conventional standard of attractiveness. He was also equally surprised to see another member of the species. Meanwhile, Darius didn't personally recognize him—and surmised for the male to be working here, with whatever degrees and credentialing he had to have to get that "M.D." stitched after his name, he must be a half-breed who could go out in the sunlight and who had worked his way up the human ranks.

Mind control and manipulation were good tools one-on-one, but they couldn't be used to snow an entire community of humans over a long period of time.

As the male tried to hide the alarm he was clearly feeling,

Darius thought back to the way things had been in the Old Country, when there had been a proper King and court, when there had been a strict division between humans and vampires. Now? In the New World? Standards were more loose, as long as you weren't a member of the aristocracy.

Maybe the male was antsy because he had blood ties to the *glymera*? As a half-breed he couldn't be in it officially, of course, but he was certainly looking like he'd put his foot in a pile out on the proverbial lawn.

The doctor cleared his throat. "Ah . . ."

Not interested in creating any problems, Darius nodded curtly, acknowledging the fact that, yup, they were both who they were, but nope, he wasn't going to do anything about it.

The doctor took a deep breath and turned to his patient. After he tugged at the lapels of his white coat, he did another round of throat clearing. "As I was saying, I'm Dr. Bluff and I'm going to take care of you. Do you want to tell me what transpired tonight, Patricia?"

"I go by Anne, actually. It's my middle name."

The partial vampire smiled at her without flashing fangs, assuming he had any. "Anne, please call me Rob. Now, what happened? I know you already told triage, and your intake nurse, but I'd like to hear it for myself."

Anne looked down at where her hands had twisted around themselves. "It was an accident. I crossed the street without looking and it was dark." She nodded in Darius's direction. "He wasn't speeding or anything. It was all my fault."

Darius frowned, but kept quiet. He wanted to bring up the other half of the truth, that she'd been chased, but he figured the medical types would find all her injuries, even if they didn't know the why's of her entry onto the roadway.

"So you were hit by a car."

"Yes, but as I said, it wasn't his fault. There's no reason to get the police involved or anything."

Dr. Bluff nodded. "And I understand you came in here on your own."

"Sort of." Her anxious eyes shot over to Darius. "He carried me in, I think."

"Okay." Dr. Bluff got a stethoscope out of his white coat's pocket. "While I listen to your heart and lungs, and check your pupils, I hate to ask the unoriginal question, but where does it hurt?"

As the male plugged his ears with his instrument and leaned over the bed, Anne started going through the rest of the spiel she'd shared two other times. On the sidelines, Darius closed his eyes and listened to the rise and fall of her voice. The words she spoke were simple ones, rarely anything multi-syllabic, and certainly nothing terribly complicated in terms of translation. They focused him like a laser, however.

On her. And whatever she wanted, needed.

Ordered him to do.

"You're not going to pass out, are you?"

Darius popped his lids. The other vampire in the room was right in front of him, face banked with panic. Like the last thing he wanted were all of the physical anomalies of the species showing up during the treatment of what was supposed to be just another queasy bystander.

"No, no, I'm fine."

A knowing look came into the male's eyes. "I'm going to order some X-rays of her right shoulder and her right lower leg. I'm also going to have to perform a full physical exam. Unless you'd prefer me to have a female doctor do it?"

"Oh, it's fine," Anne said from over on the bed. "I'm not shy."

The other vampire didn't acknowledge his patient's consent. Instead, he waited for permission to proceed . . . as was the way when any healer dealt with a bonded male and his female: No one wanted the kind of trouble that arrived swiftly and surely if the protective instinct of a male was triggered.

Clearly, the doctor thought some of the story was a ruse.

And besides, Darius hadn't bonded.

"Um . . . hello?" Anne prompted. "You boys finished making decisions for me, or are you expecting me to wait a little longer while you figure out my consent?"

As Darius glanced over to the bed, he couldn't explain to her why the deference was being paid. And in any event, she wasn't his mate—

"Yes, a female doctor would be best," he heard himself say. And then he switched into the Old Language. "*And I shall be right on the other side of that thin curtain during the exam.*"

"*But of course, sire,*" Dr. Bluff replied with an incline of the head. "*We shall not have it any other way. Are there any other special provisions you require for her?*"

Darius could feel the woman's eyes narrowing on him. *"No, that is all."*

"She shall be treated with the utmost consideration."

"She better be," he growled.

✦   ✦   ✦

A mere half hour later, Anne and her bed were wheeled back into her little green-draped subdivision. And what do you know, the man with the blue eyes and the big body was just where she'd left him, waiting on that flimsy plastic chair like a dog at the front door during a workday.

"Dr. Bluff will be back in very soon," the orderly said. "You good?"

"Yes, thank you."

The guy nodded. "You take care now."

And then she and her mystery man were alone again. As she glanced over at him, she had a feeling he was trying not to stare at her, and there was the temptation to think it was because he found her alluring in some way.

Yeah, because this hospital gown really brought out the red in all of her bruises.

"Did they treat you in an acceptable manner?" he asked as he continued to focus on the floor.

He had the strangest way of putting things, so formal, so precise.

"They were great, thanks. Although I think I glow in the dark now from all the X-rays." She pulled her blankets up a little higher. "I really can't believe how quickly this is going."

When he just nodded, Anne reached up and probed the

white bandage that was over her eyebrow. A female doctor had come in and listened to her lungs and checked her stomach and torso for problems, and then, when there had been a short wait for the X-ray machine to be free, the woman had cleaned and covered anything that required a clinical-grade Band-Aid.

"Were they gentle with you?"

She turned her head on the thin pillow. The mystery man who seemed to be orchestrating the whole ER visit had crossed his legs knee to knee, and had one long, elegant hand hanging off his thigh, his perfect posture turning that flimsy chair into a throne. Unsurprisingly, his profile was every bit as good as the head-on of his face, his nose a straight shot down from his brows, his jaw strong, his broad shoulders and pronounced upper arms the perfect frame to it all. Even though his hair was dark, he had no five-o'clock shadow, and she wondered if his chest was bare or—

Flushing, she looked away. Then she rearranged herself on the hospital bed with a groan. Things were already stiffening up on her, her muscles tightening, certain joints locking into place. Likewise, contusions were settling in for a duration on what felt like most of her body, the focal points of soreness like bad-apple roses, all thorns.

"Who are you?" she blurted. "To this hospital, I mean."

There was a pause. "Just another onlooker."

"You know the doctor, though."

"Not really."

She had to glance back at him. "What was the language you spoke to him in? I didn't recognize it."

"It's just an obscure European dialect. It doesn't matter."

"So how did you know he'd speak it?"

Before he could reply, the curtain was pulled back, and Dr. Bluff stepped in. "Everything looks good." He focused on the mystery man. "Nothing is broken. I think she'll have some lingering swelling and soreness—"

"Hey, Doc," Anne interrupted. When both men looked at her in surprise, she smiled tightly and gave them a little wave. "When you're reporting the results of my X-rays, I'd appreciate it if I'm the one you're giving them to."

Dr. Bluff blinked. Glanced at the man.

When the man nodded, the doctor came up to the foot of the bed. "I'm sorry I focused on your husband. Of course, you're right."

Anne sat up a little higher, ignoring the way her shoulder thumped with pain. "He's not my husband."

"I—all right then." Dr. Bluff shook his head like he was confused, but not going to dwell on business that was none of his own. "At any rate, we don't see any fractures or misalignments. Your vitals are great, your wounds attended to. I'm comfortable releasing you with just a light pain reliever. But if you experience any double vision, nausea or vomiting, new or worsening headache, or any other symptoms that concern you, I want you to get in touch with your doctor or come back here."

"I don't have a physician."

"Then you need to return to St. Francis and ask for me." Dr. Bluff glanced back at the man. "I'll take care of her. Don't you worry."

Okaaaaaay, she was really ready for the day when adult women weren't treated like children.

"Great," she muttered. "I appreciate it."

"You're welcome," Dr. Bluff murmured to the man with a little bow. "I'll just go write a prescription and she can be on her way."

After the doctor left, Anne closed her eyes in frustration, but decided to move on from being treated like a child—because she had a bigger problem than the kind of benevolent misogyny she dealt with at work. Or in her neighborhood. Or out in the world, in general.

"I don't have my purse," she said to herself. "So I don't have my keys ... my ID ..."

"I am so sorry. I didn't see anything in the road—"

"No, it's because I left it in his ..." She went to rub her face and poked herself in the bandage, right where it hurt. Cursing, she put her head back and stared at the ceiling. "This night just keeps getting longer, it really does."

"Where did you leave your things?"

"Back with him."

As a strange sound weaved around her bed, she looked over to it. The man's brows were down low, and his eyes gleamed with something that she couldn't define—no, wait. She knew what it was.

She wasn't threatened by the fury, however.

In a low voice, he said, "I'll get your things back from whoever, wherever. Just say the word and it is done."

The words were spoken quietly, but somehow, the lack of volume made them scarier than if he'd yelled them. And as much as it didn't reflect well on her character, she entertained a brief, but very vivid, fantasy of this man she didn't know at all showing up on the doorstep of a man she'd thought she'd known very well.

"It's okay," she murmured. "I'll take care of myself."

The curtain pulled back again and Dr. Bluff reentered. "All right, here's the prescription. It's just a little Tylenol with codeine to help her sleep. Take as needed. She should expect to feel pretty sore for the next couple of days."

As he went to give the slip to the man, there was another exchange in that language she couldn't translate—and then the man who'd been sitting with her frowned and leaned forward in the plastic chair. With a shake of the head, the doctor put his hands out as if he were insisting—after which Anne's mystery man got to his feet and offered his palm. As they shook, that slip changed possession.

"You take care," Dr. Bluff said to her. "You're going to be just fine."

Gritting her teeth, Anne didn't respond to the doctor leaving, even though that was rude. What did it matter, though. He wasn't going to get a *pater familias* personality transplant just because she wasn't polite to him, and she needed to save her energy for part II of this nightmare.

"I'll just wait outside for you," the man told her. "While you change."

"Fine." God, she was tired. "I mean, thanks."

Except instead of leaving, the man came over to the bed. "I'm serious about getting your stuff back. I'll take care of it."

She looked up at him, measuring those powerful shoulders. Those strong arms. Meanwhile, the sounds of the emergency room were a helluva soundtrack, the urgent footfalls, whispered exchanges—and quiet weeping across the aisle—like a destiny foreshadowed. Waiting for her like a stalker who'd been denied this night, but was coming back for her on another.

And meanwhile, vengeance was standing right in front of her, at her beck and call.

Anne focused on his eyes, which had gone midnight in color. "It must be nice to be able to . . . handle things."

"Just say the word."

Her heart skipped a beat. God, she really wanted to let him loose. Like he was a bullet from a gun or a dog from its handler. But violence never solved anything, and more to the point, she wasn't looking to become an accessory to murder.

Because that was what the man was offering her: Some things didn't need words.

Yet she still was not afraid of him.

Anne took a deep breath—or tried to. When a band of pain took the place of her rib cage, she coughed out, "I thought once you knew I was okay medically we were done."

"I only want to see this through."

As images of gravesites flashed before her eyes, she plugged back into reality and shook her head. "I told you before, I'm not your problem. Besides, don't you have a car to take care of? It was a nice one, if I remember. The last thing I have a clear memory of is the BMW hood ornament. Well, that and the sound of it crashing into something."

"I can get another sedan. There isn't going to be another you."

When there was a beat of silence, he tilted his head—and made her think of a German shepherd: big, fierce . . . and endearing.

"Why are you looking at me like that?" he asked.

"Do you want me to be honest?"

"Always."

"I can't decide whether you're a savior . . . or a case of out of the frying pan, into the fire." Pushing the blankets off, she shuffled her legs over the side of the hospital bed and looked down. "I think I lost a shoe, didn't I. I seem to recall that all of a sudden."

"I didn't have time to look for it. I'm sorry."

She stared at her bare feet for a moment. Then glanced over to the chair next to the one he'd been in. When she'd changed into the hospital johnny, she'd folded her clothes and put them on the orange plastic seat. The lone surviving L.L. Bean penny loafer seemed like a commentary on not just the last couple of hours, but her life as a whole.

"I really liked those shoes, too."

"I'll find it for you."

Flexing her feet, she felt a tightness in her right calf, as well as an ache in her hip and some numbness in her knee. It was a good thing, she decided, getting those X-rays, even if the doctor had been patronizing.

"I'll get dressed now," she said.

"I'll be waiting for you just outside."

Anne watched as the draping swung back into place behind him, and the way the heavy fabric undulated made her think of a flag in a lazy wind. And then as she looked at her clothes again, the sounds and smells around her returned, like the knob on the hospital had been turned back up: The hushed crying across the way was still ongoing.

A spear of fear went through her. Things could have ended very differently in her case—except no one would have been crying for her. In fact, she had to wonder who would have claimed her body. She had a couple of cousins in Vermont. Maybe they'd have taken care of things?

Or maybe she'd have wound up on that island off of NYC where they buried the unclaimed. Did they do that anymore . . . or was she confusing an historical article she'd read on the train with current practice—

"Dr. Peters, paging Dr. Peters," came from the overhead speaker. "Please come to the triage station."

Dr. Peters had had a busy night. Someone always seemed to want him.

Sliding off onto the cool linoleum, she winced and hobbled over to the chair. As she took off the johnny, she shivered, and she tried to be quick about the redressing. Her hands were sloppy, though, and her shoulder was more of a problem than she'd have thought, especially with the bra. And jeez, her body was a patchwork quilt with all of the gauze patches on various impact areas.

Eventually, she managed to get dressed, but it was weird. Her clothes seemed to fit differently, the skirt and shirt like a stranger's even though they were the same things she'd put on hours ago. She was also a little cold, but there was no way in hell she was going to try and get her red sweater fully on. With the stiffness continuing to intensify, she'd have to cut herself out of the pullover by the time she got home and tried to get into bed—

As she went to tie it around her waist, she froze. Smudges of blood marked everything she had on. There were tears in her clothes, too.

And only the one shoe.

Steeling herself, she picked the thing up and pulled back the curtain. The mystery man was standing at the split and facing outward, like he was a bodyguard. And as he immediately turned around, he took her elbow.

Like he was worried he might have to sweep her off her feet again.

"How do we check out?" she mumbled as she did her best to keep her own balance.

"It's all taken care of."

Thinking back to that exchange before the doctor had departed, she had a feeling that "Rob" had refused to charge them—

All of a sudden, an emergency exploded down at the far end, the curtain agitating around the last treatment bay across the aisle, the booties and scrubs-clad calves of doctors and the white skirts of the nurses shifting around as people traded places at the bed. On the floor, blood-stained tufts of discarded gauze and sponges bounced like grim little balls, a reminder of how some things could not be fixed.

"Come on," the man said in a low voice. "Let's go."

Relying on his arm and moving slowly, Anne allowed herself to be led out into a broad corridor that dissolved into the registration desk, triage area, and waiting room. As it was just before midnight, the glass windows that ringed the open lobby were like the surface of a piano, glossy and black, the whole world blocked out by the night, a secret that seemed threatening.

"I'm going to be okay," she said hoarsely.

"Of course you are."

At least one of them believed her, Anne thought as they continued along, the halting and the lame-ing only on her side of their marching band. Meanwhile, people wilting from wait looked over from rows of seats that were screwed down into the floor, their envy that she'd been processed as palpable as their exhaustion.

And just as she'd clearly jumped the line and gotten preferential treatment, now there was no paperwork or dis-charge payment collected from her. It was like she'd won the ER lottery in too many ways to count, but she was too tired to argue the manufactured good fortune anymore.

Not that the man at her side would be willing to explain any of it.

At the entrance, the automatic whirring doors paddled in their glass-and-steel corral like a bread mixer, and she was glad that the man fed her into them. She was struggling with focus, although not because of any head injury. At least she didn't think it was a concussion.

Nah, it probably is a concussion, she thought as she touched the bandage at her temple.

Oh, wow. It was raining lightly and things had gotten chilly in the way spring could sometimes.

"Jesus. Took you long enough."

Anne blinked. Off to the left, a maroon sedan was parked at the curb and running, its taillights glowing red, a little drift of exhaust curling from its tailpipe. The driver from before was leaning out his window, his thick neck straining as he looked back at her like she was a pickpocket who'd taken his wallet. His tufts seemed even more frizzy, as if he'd been rubbing his head with a static balloon.

"Will ya get in already? He gave me a hundred-dollar bill, not ten of 'em."

Anne turned to her mystery man. "What is—"

"You can trust him." The man went over and opened the rear door. "He'll take you anywhere you want to go."

As a way to buy time, she took a quick inventory of her assets, which included such high-flying extravagances as one shoe, clothes with blood on them, and absolutely no money or ID on her—

"Look," Danny DeVito-esque said, "I got a daughter 'bout ya age. I ain't gonna do nothin' but take ya home. I swear."

The driver made the sign of the cross, kissed his fingertips, and motioned to heaven. "My motha would kill me. Okay? Okay."

"Go," the mystery man said softly. "You'll be safe with him."

Anne looked up, way up, at the stranger who had been there for her more than anybody else had in a very long time. "What about the bill."

Her words were quiet, and had nothing to do with what was really on her mind. She had spent most of the last two hours trying to get rid of the guy, but now that the time to go their separate ways was here? She couldn't believe she didn't even know his—

"What's your name?" she blurted. How could she not have asked this before?

"He's frickin' Santa Claus, whaddaya want. Are ya coming or going?"

"Call me St. Nick," the man said with a small smile. "And take care of yourself."

This was it? Really? She might have just met him, but she felt like she'd known him for years.

Definitely a concussion, she decided.

"Thank you," she whispered.

"For hitting you with my car?" He lifted his hand, like he was going to touch her—maybe on the shoulder or to brush her hair back. But then he dropped his arm. "I'm just glad you're okay."

Anne glanced at the driver, who was drumming his fingers on the top of a steering wheel covered with a fuzzy grip. Then she looked back at the man.

"Thank you," she said. "I mean, okay. I mean . . . goodbye."

She put her palm out.

"Goodbye," the mystery man said as he took a step back from her.

As it was impossible for things to get any more awkward, she rubbed her hand on the seat of her skirt and turned away. Getting into the backseat, she reached for the handle to pull the door shut, but the man closed her in himself.

Her last image of him was as Not-Danny DeVito hit the gas and shot them away from the curb. Cranking around, she looked through the back windshield, through the rain-streaked glass. The man stayed at the entrance and watched the car go with arms crossed over his chest, seemingly unaware, or uncaring, that his hair was getting wet. His jacket, too.

"So where to, sweethaht."

Anne pivoted around and met the driver's eyes in the rearview.

"Listen, I'm a licensed driver." He popped a piece of gum in his mouth. "So don't worry about the storm. Now where ya live?"

He seemed a little more relaxed—well, that wasn't the word for it. Polite, maybe? Okay, fine, at least he wasn't biting her head off.

"Do you know that man?" she asked.

"The one with all the bright ideas? Nope. But I recognize Ben Franklin's face anywhere."

As they came up to the traffic light that governed the inflow and outflow of the hospital site, she forced her head to get with the program.

"I need to . . ." She cleared her throat. "I have to stop somewhere first on the way."

"Of course you do," the driver griped as the light turned green.

"To the left," she cut in before he could make the demand. "And I'll direct you."

"Greeeeat." He put a pack of Wrigley's over his shoulder. "Gum?"

"Don't mind if I do," she said as she took one of the foil-wrapped lengths. "Oh, it's my favorite flavor."

"Mine, too," he announced. "You need some heat back there?"

"No, I'm fine. And I really appreciate you taking me home. Your daughter's lucky she has a father like you, willing to help a stranger."

His eyes whipped up to the rearview and narrowed. After a moment, he grunted and shrugged. "Ya know what. You and me? We're gonna get along fine, girl."

Her hands shook as she slid the strip of gum from its green sheath. "Thank you."

She just needed to get her purse back. Then . . . it was all over, the whole nightmare was done. No more ties, no more reason for contact.

Staring out the window, she put the gum in her mouth and started to chew. She took little note of the streetlamps or the few cars that traveled with them on the road. The image of that mystery man standing outside the emergency room's entrance was like a filter brought down between her and the rest of the world.

Of all the things that had happened tonight, he felt like the most important.

Which made no sense at all.

CHAPTER FOUR

I t's this first building," Anne said as she sat forward on
the seat. "Here."

The driver turned into the development's shallow
cul-de-sac. "This one?"

"Yes, on the right." Anne took her one shoe and slipped
it on her foot with a grunt. "I won't take long."

The ring of multi-unit, three-story apartment buildings orbited a common area of porte cocheres. Glancing
over the lineup of cars and trucks, the sight of a brand-new
white Datsun gleaming in the security lights made her
stomach roll.

At least he wasn't parked outside her house.

"This won't take long," she repeated as she glanced to
the second floor.

His lights were on. God, could she do this?

As she popped her door, she glanced to the rearview. "You won't leave, will you?"

The driver met her eyes and opened his mouth like he was going to say something "smaht." Then he frowned. "You want I go witchu?"

"No. It's better if it's just me. You know."

"Okay. I ain't leaving. Don't worry. And if you need me, you just hollah."

"Thank you."

When he nodded like they had a pact, she decided that she was going to have to recast her dim opinion of the human race.

Shutting the car door, she looked down. The foot that had the shoe was fine. The bare one was wet and cold on the damp asphalt. For a split second, she wondered if she shouldn't go out to the street and search for what she'd lost . . . but then she realized that what she was really missing was courage, not anything from a retail store.

Staring up at the apartment she had run from, she started forward and stumbled on the curb. The walkway to the exposed, common-use stairwell was a short one, and her breath grew tighter as she got closer to the three levels' worth of doors. She told herself she had a witness with a bad attitude and a loud mouth, and there were people around—

The sound of a dog barking froze her at the base of the concrete-and-steel steps. Glancing up through the slats of the balustrade, she could just see the top jamb of his door. That dog of his weighed a good fifty or sixty pounds. She'd already gotten away from the apartment once tonight. Why was she doing this—

"Because it's my purse," she whispered. "It's *mine*."

To give herself time to find a little spine, she focused out the far side of the open breezeway. The light fixtures overhead turned any vista of the four-laner they'd come in on into the same kind of black hole that had waited outside the ER's entry.

Releasing her hold on the banister, she walked around the base of the stairs. The breezeway led out to a lawn-covered knoll that drifted down to the road, and as she stepped off the concrete, the trees of the public park were a blur in the rain. She had to walk some distance until her eyes could adjust to the dimness, her bare foot registering the springy padding of the cold, wet blades of grass.

There it was. Directly across from her.

Off the shoulder, grille into a tree.

The BMW was where it had been left, and she entertained a thought that she'd just wait right here until the tow truck came—then she'd cop a ride to whatever body shop it was taken to. After that, she'd air-dry and drink bitter coffee and reread the same hunting and fishing magazines until it was fixed.

Finally, after the repairs were done, its owner would come to claim the vehicle, and she would be there to ask him what his name really was—

Anne went to push her sodden hair back and bumped into the pad of surgical gauze again. The shot of pain took her back to the moment when she'd gotten free of the apartment. She'd raced down the stairs, her wild momentum and lack of coordination banging her body between the concrete wall and the balustrade. At the bottom, she'd just blindly bolted.

It could have been into the parking lot. Could have been out to the street.

Could have been to the edge of the world.

She'd never considered knocking on any of his neighbors' doors for help. She'd just wanted to get away from him . . . so she'd broken out into a run and ended up right in the road. The squeal of those tires had been like her scream. At least she assumed she'd screamed.

When you were hit with a car, didn't you scream?

Turning back to the breezeway, she locked her eyes on the underbelly of the stairs and knew it was time she faced—

Something off to the side on the lawn caught her attention. It was a scatter of debris . . . little objects that glowed in all of their wrong-placedness.

"Are those my sunglasses?" She glanced around. But like there was anybody standing beside her who could answer that?

Going over, she knelt down with a grimace. Her knock-off Ray-Bans had been mangled, the cheap drugstore earpieces bent out of place, one of the tinted insets falling free of its fake gold frame as she picked the aviators up.

Anne rubbed her thumb over the scratched lens that remained. Then she stretched her good arm out and picked up the next thing of hers—her little makeup bag. The scent of flowers rose up as she opened what had been zipped tight. Her cheap lipstick had been ground all over the inside, and she jerked her finger out as the shattered glass of her blusher's compact mirror nipped her.

Her purse was three feet farther over, and she picked it up by one of its handles. The thing was in tatters, so ripped apart that she could see through it in places. Something had been used to destroy the fake leather—a knife . . . maybe a pair of utility scissors?—and a piercing sensation went through her chest. Sure, the bag had been cheap to begin with, another knockoff that was pleather rather than anything remotely cowhide. But it had been hers, and she'd bought it only a month ago in JCPenney—

Anne grimaced. *What was that smell?*

The whiff of urine made her jerk the thing away—and that was when she saw her wallet over by the bushes. Like the purse, it had been torn apart, the cash taken, the change purse emptied. She handled it with her thumb and forefinger and got a nose-full of the same stink that was on her purse.

Her credit card and her ID were out of their slots.

Making a sweep of the area, she collected what else had been hers: the soft container of Kleenex that was damp, her mini-hairbrush . . . a couple of receipts that were soaked, fortunately just by the dew on the grass.

The muffled sound of his dog barking again jerked her head up.

She'd never gotten along with that animal. It hadn't liked her from the get-go and clearly that was among the first warning signs for the whole relationship. She should have followed her instincts instead of wasting eight months of her life to confirm what she'd guessed pretty much on their second date—

"I got this grocery bag here."

She wheeled around. The stubby, cranky, tufty car driver was standing in the breezeway, holding out a paper bag with the Grand Union logo on it. In the harsh lighting, he looked like a J. R. R. Tolkien troll who'd turned into an unexpected protagonist.

"Put your stuff in here," he said as he stepped onto the lawn. "And then let's get you to a dry place. You look a mess."

"Thank you."

Meeting him halfway, she disappeared her purse and her wallet into the folds of the bag, and then flinched as the driver laid his hand on her good shoulder.

"I'll take ya home. Unless you wanna talk to him?"

"How do you know it's a man," she mumbled.

"You sayin' it ain't?"

Looking at the stairs, she shook her head. "The talking part didn't go well the first time tonight. I don't think a second try will improve things."

"Come on then."

Memories of the argument eclipsed the world around her, and the next thing she knew, she was back in the maroon sedan and giving directions to her house. She was impressed she knew the way. She felt as though her mind were misfiring, an old jalopy that needed not just a tune-up, but a replacement engine.

She'd never felt so alone.

But better than in bad company.

✦   ✦   ✦

Darius followed the maroon car all the way to Anne's house.

He kept up with its progression in distances of a quarter mile, dematerializing and re-forming on the roofs of minimalls and stores—even a box van parked in a metered spot.

In all instances, he stayed out of the way of headlights, streetlamps, and any kind of security lights. He was of the night, traveling through the damp May air, a ghost who lived and breathed.

When the car finally stopped in front of a little house on a street of little houses, he perched behind the chimney of the Cape Cod across the street, his breathing even and slow, but his body tense.

As Anne emerged from the backseat, he approved of the fact that the stocky driver got out from behind the wheel and walked her to her door. On her front stoop, they shared words that did not carry all the way up to him, but going by the way her head lowered and she held that paper bag of her things in tight hands, she seemed both resolute and exhausted.

The driver waited until she was safely inside, the red-painted door shut tight, a light flaring, soft and yellow, inside.

The man who had been such a grudging help hesitated as if he were worried about her. Then he shoved his hands in the front pockets of his pants and stomped off, his perma-frown back in place, that not-half-bad heart clearly heavy under all the gruffness.

After the car took off, Darius stayed where he was. Anne was moving around her home, other lights coming on behind the privacy curtains. The fact that no one could see inside was a good thing. He didn't like the idea of her being both undefended and highly visible.

Although undefended and not highly visible wasn't much better.

It was hard to leave. But he had a job to do.

The return trip to that development of apartment buildings was the work of a moment as he had no reason to take
the dematerialization in stages. Resuming his corporeality
on the lawn where she'd picked up her stuff, he looked back
at his car on the far side of the road—and promptly forgot
about the BMW he'd loved so much for such a short time.

Stepping into the building's central pass-through, he
took the stairs two at a time. On the second floor's landing,
he did a roundabout at the four closed doors and the three
welcome mats. He approached the apartment that didn't
have anything at the foot of its entry.

He knew he had the right one because this was where
she had stared as soon as she'd gotten out of the car.

Curling up a fist, he knocked on the door.

The barking from inside the apartment was immediate,
and a sharp male voice responded in a harsh tone. A good
minute later, things were opened.

The human on the other side was about six feet even,
with some manner of light-colored eyes and a hairline that
was clearly a little farther back than it had been in his college
years. Given his slightly pinched features and trim torso, he
was good-looking in the way someone who was almost
handsome beat out another guy who was solidly average—
and his pale gray suit and pink tie were all *Miami Vice* without a beach. Or the Testarossa.

"Who the hell are you—"

Darius locked a grip on the front of the man's throat and
pushed. As the guy tap-danced backwards, his arms pin-
wheeling, his mouth dropping open, the door shut on its
own and a brown dog in a crate started to bark.

Darius glanced over at the mutt and bared his fangs—which took care of the noise: The canine instantly submitted to the alpha animal in the room, going down on its belly and putting its head between its paws.

Gagging and choking filled the audio-void.

Slam!

The impact of its owner's back meeting the far wall of the living area cut off all the defensive flapping and slapping. Still, Darius banged that spine again. And again—

Something fell off a shelf. A book or, no, it was a photograph in a frame.

The dog whimpered as Darius finally cut it with the knock, knock, knockin' on heaven's door, and as he let off a little on the squeeze, a deep breath was dragged in. On the wheezing exhale, he put his face forward so that he was nose to nose with his prey. No talking. Instead, he went into the frontal lobe and probed all kinds of memories.

What he saw made him go back to the full-squeeze, his grip getting so tight that the bright red flush and the goldfish gaper of a mouth took on comedy-trope levels. Or horror ones.

Pulling out of that brain, Darius wanted to bare his fangs a second time—and sink them into the piece of shit's jugular.

Instead, he kept his voice low and deep. "You know Anne?"

Clicking of the tongue. Snuffling. Gulping.

And if those eyes bulged any further, they were going to pop out and turn into projectiles Darius was going to have to duck.

He relaxed some of the pressure again. "Patricia Anne Wurster. You know her."

"Wh-wh-wh-what—yeah, yeah, I do—"

"You leave her the fuck alone from now on. I catch you anywhere around her, even walking on the same side of the street downtown, I'm going to handle you. Are we clear? You don't go near her, you don't call her, you don't send her a letter or a carrier pigeon. No contact, not after tonight, if you want to stay alive."

The man pulled in some air. "Who are you?"

"I'm her fairy godmother, that's who I am. And I will beat you to death, do you understand." As those eyes went wide again, Darius got even closer. "I will kill you with my bare hands and they will never find your body. You have *no* more business with her. Nod if you understand me."

"Wh-what-what—"

Done with the conversation, Darius picked the man up by that throat and threw him across the room. The dead-weight asshole landed half on, half off the sofa, the resulting crack suggesting some vertebra or another was protesting a serious misalignment—and wow, looked like gravity worked on hose bags: The aftermath slide-off-the-padded-arm was as close to boneless as an adult male anything could get, the torso rolling over listlessly, upper limbs flopping, legs tangling, until there was a bump on the carpet.

Darius stalked over to the guy. In the ordinary course of things, when humans and vampires mixed, the fanged side of the equation scrubbed any memory of the interaction. Staying under the radar was always the prime directive. Or almost always.

Amnesia was not how shit was going to go tonight.

Squatting down, Darius relocked on that throat. "I will kill you, do you understand. And I will do it slowly."

"Who . . . are you," came the hoarse response.

"Not what you have to worry about. You want to stay alive, you will never fuck with Anne Wurster again. Now nod, or I'm going to make you respond in the affirmative, and you're not going to like how that feels."

The response was vigorous, like the guy had been asked if he wanted a winning lottery ticket. An all-expenses-paid vacation to the Caribbean. A new car.

"Good."

Darius released his hold and straightened. Then he looked around. The apartment was navy blue and nasty neat, everything in its place, not a newspaper on the coffee table, a stray dish in the galley kitchen, a pee spot on the rug from the dog—

He went over and picked up the photograph that had fallen off its shelf. It was an artsy shot, a black-and-white of a snowed-in field.

"You took this picture?" Darius asked.

The guy pushed himself up a little. Slipped as his hand skidded out from under. "Y-yes. I did."

"You like photography, then."

"Ah, yes—"

Darius snapped the frame in half, the glass shattering in his grip and cutting into his palm. Letting the fragments fall to the carpet, he shook out the fragile, glossy print.

The apartment wasn't all that big, so it was a short trip over to the four-top of gas burners in the kitchen. Cranking the one in the front right on, he glanced back at Bruce Allen McDonaldson Jr.

The guy was just sitting on his ass, his suit jacket wedged up under his armpits, his pink tie over his shoulder—his eyes blinking myopically at some middle distance in front of him. Which was what bullies did when they picked on the wrong person and got their nuts slapped by someone bigger and stronger than they could handle.

"Hey, Brucey," Darius called out as he snapped his fingers.

The guy's head came up and around like he'd been trained.

Even with the counter and the sink between them, Bruce had a clear visual shot to the stove, and as his eyes focused properly, Darius lowered the picture into the flame. When the thing was properly burning at the corner, he brought the Kodak-candle back over to the amateur Helmut Newton.

Dropping down onto his haunches, he squared up the photograph between their faces so that he was staring through the hungry curls of orange and yellow. Then he unfurled his dagger hand and put the little bonfire in his open palm. The pain as his skin burned along with the image was a sweet sting that sharpened his purpose, his commitment.

Not that he needed help with that.

On the far side of the tiny fire, the human's eyes were bugging again—and then there was nothing but gray and black ash, and the smell of chemicals and flesh.

Still maintaining eye contact, Darius put his fore- and middle fingers into the ashes, pushing the soot around until the pads of both were black as night.

Meanwhile, Bruce looked like he was going to piss himself—

Oh, wait. He already had.

Darius switched into the Old Language: "*Upon my honor, and the honor of mine bloodline, I mark you as my prey and no other's, barring the will of the King I serve.*" He drew an X over one of the man's fluttering eyelids. And then the other. "*Should you violate your vow unto me, you shall know agony the likes of Dhunhd and beyond under mine hand and mine dagger. So I voweth this night and evermore, in the name of the great Virgin Scribe.*"

Darius marked an X over the man's mouth as well, and went back to English. "I will come for you, out of the darkness. You won't see me until it's too late. And I'm going to make you suffer."

That last word was drawn out until it was a growl, deep in his chest.

Rising to his feet, he loomed over the man. He would have taken the sonofabitch's life right then and there if he could have. He wanted to see those eyes go dark as the inside of a grave. But he knew Anne wouldn't approve of the killing. She would want the man to be given a chance to go in peace. Besides, if Bruce were to disappear tonight, she would know who did it and blame herself.

And someone would need to take care of the dog—

"That's her fucking shoe," Darius said abruptly.

The errant loafer was on its side, by the dog's water and food bowls. Teeth marks punctured the leather of the upper part as well as the sole, and the penny was missing from the band in the front.

Darius picked up her property and went over to the door. Opened things back up. Took one last look at the terrified bag of carbon-based molecules who had three crude Xs on his pasty white face.

Sprawled there in his disarrayed, Don Johnson duds, Bruce looked like he'd been in a bar fight. And had lost.

"Try me," Darius said softly. "Please. I want to kill you so badly right now I can taste your blood on my tongue."

Stepping out of the apartment, he made sure the door closed quietly. Because really, once you've marked a man for death, did you have to be loud about your departure?

Descending the stairs, Darius fantasized once again about ripping the throat that had been in his palm open with his fangs. The specificity of the vision and the relish that accompanied it belied his fundamentally pacifistic-leaning temperament. Unlike so many in the Black Dagger Brotherhood, he was a vampire who was violent only when necessary.

But if anyone wanted to hurt that woman?

They were asking for a very messy corpse.

CHAPTER FIVE

At the end of the following day, Anne reflected that public transportation in any city was always a Venn diagram, an if-this, then-that cobble-together of predetermined routes that had as much to do with efficiency as a mouse in a maze. Sitting three rows behind the bus driver, she stared out a cloudy window. She had about eight minutes left with this leg of her journey. And then about six minutes of walking.

To get to Bruce's.

Moving her second-best purse higher on her lap, she swayed in the bench seat she had to herself, and winced as her bad hip was forced to bear more than half her weight. The pit in her stomach got worse as the bus trundled on, and when they arrived at her stop, she thought she was going to throw up as the brakes squeaked. Out of the dozen

or so people riding with her, she was the only one who dis-
embarked, and she pulled her light coat closer as she emerged
onto the sidewalk. Left in the dust, the sweet smell of diesel
made her nose tickle as the rest of the passengers were taken
farther down the line.

Over to the west, the low sun glowed warm and beautiful at the horizon, and she told herself it was a good omen.
In reality, it probably didn't mean a thing.

God, she wasn't sure she had the energy to do this. In
addition to her normal responsibilities at work, the day had
been full of people asking her to explain her injuries. She
hadn't known what to say, and the half-truth that she'd
shared with almost everyone had been an exhausting repeat
to pull out of her conversational pocket over and over again.

She'd only told the whole story to two people . . . one of
whom had been a mistake. So the entire firm probably knew
everything by now.

Well, everything except for her mystery man. She'd kept
him totally to herself.

But she couldn't worry about office gossip. No, she had
other things on her mind right now.

One that note, she set off at a limp, and focused on the
park that was on her side of the roadway. The tree line kept
backing away and coming forward again, the rise and fall as if
the collection of maples and oaks were inhaling and exhaling
and the cement pavers she was on were its rib cage. Through
the pale green new growth, she could see bike riders pedaling
along a winding path just inside the city acreage's limits, and
way off in the distance, pedestrians were taking breaks on
blankets and playing with dogs.

She envied them their easy lives, even though they were strangers and she knew none of their details.

Then again, that was how window-shopping other peoples' destinies worked, right?

She stopped when she got to the set of tire tracks that jumped the curb, cut across the sidewalk, and scored the grass in a twin set of deep ruts. The tree that had been impacted was no more than ten or fifteen feet away, the fresh scars in its trunk like gouges in flesh. Pivoting to the road, she pinpointed where she and the BMW had shaken proverbial hands. It was where the skid marks started.

Crossing the street, she stepped over the black rubber stains on the dotted white line separating the outgoing lanes . . . and then she did the same at the yellow double stripe in the center. After that, she navigated the incoming lanes, and then finally the grassy rise up to Bruce's building. Entering the breezeway, she felt herself clutch her handbag like there was a weapon in it. Which, of course, there wasn't.

Out on the far side, in the parking area, his white Datsun was in its spot.

Closing her eyes, she put her hand on the stairwell's balustrade—

Up on the second floor, a door opened and someone with hard-soled shoes exited an apartment. There was a muffled slam and then the jingle of keys.

Swallowing through a dry throat, Anne backed up onto the doorstep of the building's first unit—

The waft of perfume was so strong that she had to rub her nose to clear a sneeze, and then a pair of ankle boots came down the steel steps. The blond woman in a bright blue coat walked off without realizing Anne was there, her confident strut taking her out into the parking area on a strident beat. The fact that she got into a red Chevy Chevette that had rainbow stripes down both sides seemed right, and as she drove off, Anne felt another flash of envy.

Surely that kind of self-assurance was Teflon to a bad day's worth of crap falling on your head.

Going back over to the stairs, she ascended in an awkward shuffle, feeling like her hip was going to lock up at any moment. At the second-floor landing, she went over to Bruce's door, straightened her jacket, and tucked her purse into her side under her arm. Like she was both at a job interview and about to get mugged.

She knocked. And stepped back.

Clearing her throat, she wondered whether doing some vocal warm-ups would help "Give me back my ID and credit card" come out with more conviction. Maybe she just needed ankle boots and half a bottle of Giorgio. And a blond wig—

Frowning, she stepped forward and knocked again.

Then she looked around, like that was going to change anything.

"Bruce," she said, "I know you're in there. I just want my—"

The door opened a crack, the security chain preventing it from going very wide. "Here. Take them."

From out of the slit, her ID and her MasterCard flittered down to the concrete.

"Don't come back," he said. Then he slammed the door shut.

The sound of the dead bolt getting thrown was such a surprise that Anne just stood there and blinked. Last night, he'd been all about boasting how he didn't need her or "that fucking law firm" anyway, that he was making some big changes thanks to an important opportunity, and that she was nothing more than a secretary who wasn't going to keep up with him.

Oh, and he'd also told her she was making the biggest mistake of her life.

After which he'd come at her physically.

Memories of the hatred in his eyes snapped her back to attention. Scrambling to pick up the piece of plastic and the laminated picture of herself, she hit the stairs on a hustle. The irony that the man who'd lost it on her the night before had just shut her out like she scared him was rich. Then again, Bruce had proven to be unexpected in a lot of ways, none of them good.

As she reached the lower level, she went out the far side of the breezeway and hobbled back down toward the road. The ruined purse and wallet she could get over easily enough, but she hadn't been looking forward to tangling with Master-Card for a replacement. At least there was no way he'd have made any purchases on her account. He didn't look like an Anne—

Across the street, a silver car with tinted windows had pulled over to the shoulder at her accident's impact site, its hazards blinking. Close by, a man with a mustache and a plaid sport coat was taking pictures of everything from the marks on the curb to the gouges in the grass to that poor tree.

Anne told herself to leave it alone. That BMW and its owner were none of her business, even if she had thought of little else during the day—

Of course, she went right over.

The man lowered his camera. "Can I help you?"

"I was just . . . ah . . ." She searched his face, trying to read his expression. His dark eyes and straight mouth gave nothing away. "I guess there was an accident here, huh."

"Yup."

"Are you . . . with the police? Or something."

"Detective Gonzalez." A badge was taken out of the breast pocket and flashed. "Do you live in this neighborhood?"

As the man's stare shifted to the cul-de-sac's entrance, Anne shook her head. "No. I just stopped by . . ." To get her ID and credit card back. From a man who'd attacked her. "I just was seeing a friend real quick."

"Oh, okay." There was a pause. Then the detective frowned and indicated the skid marks with his camera. "Do you know anything about what happened here?"

The image of the man who had helped her to the ER became so clear in her mind that she felt as though he'd stepped in beside her.

"No, I don't."

The detective reached into his jacket again and took out a business card. "Well, if you remember something, call me."

"I said I didn't know—"

"Take this anyway."

She reached out and didn't like the fact that her hand trembled. "Thanks."

"You all right?"

"Oh, yes." She ducked the card into her coat pocket. "Sure. Yup."

"Your head okay?"

"I'm sorry?"

He pointed with the camera again, like the thing was so much an extension of him that he was used to treating it like a hand. "You've got a bandage on your temple."

Anne touched her forehead lightly—and decided she really wouldn't make a very good criminal. "Oh. It's nothing. I slipped and fell. In my own bathroom."

The detective smiled with that hard-line mouth, but not his keen stare. "That happens. After all, most accidents occur in the home."

"Do they? I didn't know that. Well, I've got to go catch the bus."

"Okay. Feel better."

"You, too. I mean, I will—I mean, thanks."

As she turned away, the detective said, "I didn't catch your name."

"Anne." She glanced over her shoulder. "Anne Wurster. Do you want my address, too?"

"Nope. When I meet someone new, I just like to make introductions. Hope your head heals fast."

"It doesn't hurt."

"And that limp of yours, too."

Mumbling something, anything, Anne hurried away, being conscious that yes, she actually was favoring that bad side, wasn't she.

The rest of the way back to the bus stop was a blur. The only good news about the detective being on-site at the crash was that she didn't worry so much about a white Datsun coming after her. Sure, Bruce had told her to stay away, but he lied. About everything.

When she got to the bus stop, no one was inside the Plexiglas box, and she took a seat on the wooden bench, wincing as her hip sent out a protest. Putting her head in her hands, she felt like the world might be spinning, and as she got nauseous, she straightened back up and tried to find something to distract herself.

People hadn't been kind to the bench, carving names and initials into the wooden slats, the scars of true-love hearts and "4evas" marring the weathered horizontals. Like-wise, there were scratches all over the clear plastic panels that bordered the concrete slab, and as daylight dimmed, the headlights of approaching cars turned things milky white.

Like she was sitting in a cloud.

She thought of the man with the beautiful eyes who had done what he could to make things right. It seemed strange to miss someone she didn't know.

Shifting her weight to relieve the pressure on her pelvis, she knew she was going to need another round of aspirin to-night, and figured tomorrow she was probably going to be even more sore. She'd always found two days after an injury was the worst—Wurster—for swelling and pain.

She didn't even know his name.

Probably should have taken a page out of the detective's book and made a proper introduction, huh.

"Crap," she muttered.

◆   ◆   ◆

Down in the basement of Darius's home, in the master suite, there was a whole lot of pacing going on. Fully dressed for war, with weapons holstered on his chest and backup ammunition strapped to his hips, he made yet another loop around his antique desk . . . then crossed the Persian carpet and passed by his bed . . . and ended the circuit with a swing by the closed door to the stairwell.

No new territory. And he made the trip again.

He was retreading the behind-the-desk stretch when a soft knock brought his head around. "Yes?"

Except he knew what it was. He could scent the—

The heavy wooden panels opened. Fritz, butler extraordinaire, was standing out in the shallow hall at the base of the stone steps. In between his hands, a sterling-silver tray that was polished to a high sheen supported a cloche-covered, traditional First Meal of eggs, toast, sausage, and hash browns. There was also plenty of fresh coffee and orange juice, because the *doggen* never forgot the beverages.

Like Darius, the elderly male was dressed for his work, the formal black suit and tie, and spit-and-shine black shoes, what he always wore until Last Meal, when he changed into black tie and tails. As well, the worry etched into his wrinkled face was a perennial part of his uniform: In spite of being the very personification of perfect service, he was always anxious, as if dire consequences were about to land like a piano on his head.

And currently, Darius knew what the problem was, but he couldn't help the male.

"Sire." The butler bowed low over the food he had so lovingly prepared. "Upon your desk?"

"Thank you, Fritz."

The *doggen* walked across and placed the tray on the blotter. Then he stepped back, straightened his formal jacket, and stared at the floor.

"He's not going to eat anything," Darius said gently.

"But mayhap if I were to ask him—"

"Do you honestly want to wake him up?"

"Mayhap you could, sire?" The old male trembled at the temerity of asking his master for aid of any kind. But according to his entrenched, traditional dictate of serving whoever stayed the day, he was stuck between a real rock and a hard place. "He is much, much less likely to kill you, sire."

The latter was tacked on with a shot of hopeful optimism, although it was hard to say whether that was tied to Darius acquiescing to the request . . . or living through the proposed interaction.

Darius shook his head. "I don't want to give him any excuses not to come here. At least we know where he is when he's across the hall."

The pair of them looked out of the master suite. On the far side of the shallow space, the door to the guest quarters was closed tight—and considering what was inside, the chamber should have been triple locked. Chained. Barricaded.

Which was what you did to keep monsters away from the general public.

"Shelter is all we can provide him," Darius said.

"I wish there was more, sire." The *doggen* bowed again, and then changed the subject with a palpable resignation. "Your car is in the garage. You did not provide me with instructions as to whether it should be repaired or sent to the junkyard. So I thought it best to keep the remains on-site until you decide."

Like it was a dead body—and the whole autopsy thing was up in the air.

"Thank you, Fritz." God, he'd forgotten all about the BMW. "I'll deal with it later."

"As you wish. Is there aught more I may do for you?"

"No, I'm fine."

The *doggen* headed for the doorway. Pausing in between the jambs, he said absently, "I had a mind that we could serve lamb for Last Meal?"

Darius shook his head. "He's not coming back at the end of the night. He never stays two days in a row."

"But of course." The exhale was an expression of grief and regret. "Please summon me if there is aught I may do."

"I shall—and Fritz?" As the *doggen* looked over his shoulder, Darius wished he could have embraced his faithful servant. Given the *doggen* code of conduct, however, such a display of emotion would cause total paralysis on the butler's part. Maybe even cardiac arrest. "It's not your fault, okay? And there's nothing you can do. Try not to take things with him personally."

"Thank you, sire. I shall endeavor to heed your advice."

With a final bow, Fritz stepped out—although there was another pause at the base of the stairs as if he were struck anew by his inability to serve the brother who slept the dreamless sleep of the vengeful behind that heavy door.

"Go on, Fritz," Darius ordered.

The butler did as instructed, mounting the lantern-lit stone steps that wound their way up to the first floor of the mansion. When footfalls sounded overhead, quiet and as ever respectful, Darius did some pining of his own.

Without conscious command, his own feet took him out of his private quarters and across the little open area. Standing in front of the stout oak panels, he considered the truism that leaving bears unpoked was a jolly good idea—

He reached forward and took hold of the latching mechanism.

Without making a sound, he lifted the pin from its seat and pulled on the grip. The weight of the door was such that he added his shoulder into the effort, but contrary to its ancient and dungeon-worthy appearance, there was no vampire-worthy creak of the hinges.

Flickering light from the stairwell's lanterns pierced the chamber's darkness, illuminating the figure lying on the red-and-black bedding platform with a tentative glow.

As if even flame was afraid of the male.

Wrath, son of Wrath, the last purebred vampire on earth, the heir to what was, under his tenure, the unclaimed throne of the species, lay fully clothed and facedown across the king-sized bed, his long black hair a shroud that covered his face. He was so tall that his lower legs hung free off the side, and so broad that he filled the space between the stacks of soft pillows and the folded duvet at the footboard. He hadn't even taken his steel-toed boots off, the soles flashing Darius their heavy tread.

And he was armed, even at rest: In his left hand, a silver

throwing star was locked in a tense grip, and though Darius couldn't see the right side of things, he was willing to bet there was a dagger hilt in the other palm.

The war with the Lessening Society's pallid, soulless killers had gone on for too long, the vampire community struggling to survive against the Omega's legion of slayers, the Black Dagger Brotherhood their first, and only, line of defense. And Wrath had clearly found a fight or two before crashing over day. The baby powder smell of the enemy's blood saturated the chamber's air, but that wasn't the only scent. Wrath had been freshly injured—

"What."

Darius took a deep breath. "Just checking to see if you're alive."

"What time is it?"

"Do you want me to go get Marissa? Do you need to feed?"

Though posed as questions, they were actually statements. Clearly, the male needed to—

Wrath's head lifted and slowly turned to look over his hulking shoulder. With the hand that clasped the deadly martial arts weapon, he swept a fall of black hair out of his face, those sharp points of the star oh-so-close to tender areas. Not that he seemed to care.

Pale green eyes with tiny pupils stared myopically across the chamber. "Time."

"You've got a good two hours still," Darius lied. Because if he told the brother that there were only about fifteen to twenty minutes left before it was safe to go out, Wrath would leave now and to hell with the nuclear sunburn.

That head went back down and the rib cage expanded and contracted.

"You're always welcome here," Darius said.

When he didn't get a response, he glanced around the familiar room. Over on a side table, three mismatched, lidded jars were in a cluster. One was blue and shiny but cheap, the kind of thing you'd find at a neighborhood store or on a home goods shelf at Sears. The other two were old, the patina of age dulling enameled contours that had been hand-, not machine, made.

"Do you want me to take these to the Tomb?" Darius asked.

"It'll save me time."

"Okay. I'll go for you later."

Not that the King who would not lead cared much about the tradition. No doubt he only captured the jars of his kills when it was convenient—and regarded putting them in the Black Dagger Brotherhood's sacred ante hall with the thousand or so others a waste of time.

"You know," Darius hedged, "Fritz can make you anything if you want to eat. In fact, if you wouldn't mind indulging him, it would go a long way toward . . ."

Toward what? he wondered as he let his voice trail off.

There was no response again, but Wrath wasn't sleeping, and it was doubtful he'd resume any kind of slumber. Then again, for the most part, the brother was fueled by the powerful accelerant of hatred, requiring minimal sustenance, blood, or rest to keep going.

Giving up, Darius backed away and closed the door.

For a moment, he considered just chucking everything

and heading out himself. But then he looked into his chamber at the food that had been prepared for him.

With a sense of foreboding for the species, he went to his desk, sat down, and put the damask napkin in his lap. Picking up a sterling silver fork, he lifted the cloche and started to eat. In spite of the dire realities of the war, he found his motivation to hunt *lessers*, kill them, and take their jars ebbing.

Then again, he had something else on his mind.

Or someone, rather.

Shit.

CHAPTER SIX

Yes . . . that's right. A BMW, off the road at Ashley Park—" As Anne spoke into her phone receiver, she walked over to the stove, the curlicue cord expanding from its wall-mounted unit. "Oh, okay. No. That's it. Sorry to bother you. Thanks."

Lowering the harvest gold handset from her ear, she stirred her Campbell's tomato soup. Then she returned to the built-in desk, hung things up, and bent over her yellow pages. Two more tow services to call and it was almost seven o'clock. Taking the receiver back off its cradle, she dialed the seven digits for Salvatore's Towing. When there was no answer, she moved on to the last entry, T & T Towing 24 Hrs.

No answer.

Maybe it was a sign.

"But it was already after five when I started," she said as she went over and put two pieces of Wonder Bread in her toaster. "Lot of places had front offices that were closed."

And it wasn't like the man had pushed the car home.

Tomorrow. She'd call the others that hadn't picked up again tomorrow.

When things were warm enough in the pan, she poured some of the soup into a bowl, hit the toast, and grabbed a plate out of her cupboard along with some butter from the fridge. After things popped, she sat down at her table, forgot a spoon for the soup, got back up again—

"Oh, my God!" she shouted as she jumped.

Someone was standing right on her little back porch. Just on the far side of her sliding door. The hulking shape was nothing but a shadow because she hadn't turned on her security fixture—

Knock. Knock. Knock.

Blindly throwing her hand out for the phone, she tried to remember what the number of the police station was. She should have *known* Bruce would do this. That he couldn't possibly let things end where they had—

Was that her missing shoe?

"Anne. It's me."

For a moment, the muffled words didn't register. She was too distracted by the voice. That deep, low, beautifully accented voice.

"I don't mean for this to be awkward or anything," the man from the ER said through the glass. "But I knocked on your front door a couple of times, and when you didn't answer, I just—well, I wanted to bring this back and I was worried—"

Anne bolted around her table, unlocked the door, and yanked it open.

And there he was. The man she had thought of all day long . . . as well as throughout the night before when she hadn't slept.

He was just as she remembered. Well, maybe a little taller, a little broader, a little more . . . astounding.

"I'm sorry," he said softly in that accent of his. "I remembered your address from when you checked in at the emergency room and thought you'd want this back and—"

"I'm so glad you're here," she choked out.

There was a pause. "You are?"

When she nodded, he stared into her eyes as if he'd forgotten how to speak . . . or maybe had heard words he hadn't expected.

"Sorry," he murmured. "I'm just . . ."

"What?" she whispered.

"Here. Your shoe."

As she took the loafer back, she cradled it to her chest like he'd returned a lost pet in the middle of an ice storm.

"Do you want to join me?" She stepped back and indicated the flimsy table with her free hand. "I just made some soup. It's nothing fancy."

Well. If that wasn't the lamest offer he'd ever get. Like asking a tiger whether it would care for a salad. Or maybe a Tic Tac.

"I'd love to come in," he said. "Thank you."

As he entered her house, she remeasured his body in her peripheral vision—while trying not to make like she was doing a corporeal inventory on the poor guy. Except then she dropped all pretense and simply stared at him.

"Hi," he said with a gentle smile.

"I didn't think I'd ever see you again."

In the pause that followed, she had the strangest feeling he wanted to hug her. Which was fine. She wanted to hug him, too. This all felt like a reunion of two people who had been separated by vast time and distance.

Instead of a mere twenty-two hours and however many Caldwell miles.

"Did you sleep at all?" he asked.

"No." For someone who didn't talk a lot about herself, he was amazingly easy to be honest with. "And not just because of the soreness."

"Racing thoughts?"

"All night long." No reason to mention it had been because she'd been consumed with memories of him. This wasn't a deposition—

"Deposition?" he asked.

Oh, crap. She'd said that out loud. "Um . . . I had dreams I was in court. When I finally fell asleep."

"That's too bad. And you weren't even the one behind the wheel." He shrugged. "Still, a brush with death will make your mind do crazy things."

Focusing on his clothes for the first time, she had a thought that he looked like a soldier, just without any U.S. military insignia on his heavy leather jacket. Those were definitely combat boots on his feet, however . . . and she had to wonder what the bulges under his arms were and what was inside all the pockets of his black pants.

"It's okay, Anne," he said quietly. "I'm not here to hurt you."

"I know you aren't." How she was so sure of that, she . . . well, she wasn't clear on that part. But down to her soul, she was certain he would do her no harm. "You'd never hurt me."

"Never."

After a silence that seemed to vibrate, she said something about soup or food again and he said something like "That'll be fine" or "That'll be great." And then she was over at her refrigerator listing its meager contents like she was declaring them at customs after a European vacation.

Why couldn't she have gone shopping after work? Or anytime this friggin' week?

This was a man who needed more than hot liquid tomatoes for dinner.

"I'm really fine." He sat down across from her place setting. "I'm grateful for whatever."

Anne closed the fridge's door and wondered what kind of cologne he was wearing. It was positively . . . delicious—what was she doing? Oh, right.

"Wonder Bread and butter as a side it is," she said.

Anne gave him the other half of what was in the pan, started some more toast just like her own, and brought his bowl over. He didn't start eating, or even lift the spoon she gave him, until she sat down and resumed her own Campbell's thing, and she couldn't help but notice that he had perfect table manners.

While they ate, the silence between them was almost

tender. And weaving in and around the quiet were currents she didn't want to look too closely at.

At least for her there were currents—

Pop! went the toaster.

Anne was the only one who jolted at the sound. And as she got up, she blurted, "I think my ex would have killed me last night."

As the man's eyes narrowed, she couldn't believe what had come out of her mouth. Then again, she'd been so desperate not to think of things like the size of his shoulders . . . or whether he was looking at her . . . or how his mouth seemed very . . .

Yes, all of those things had to be kept good and hidden. And God knew there was no better brick wall than Bruce.

"Tell me what happened," her mystery man prompted as she put his toast on a plate and buttered it. "I know I'm a stranger, but sometimes it's good to just say things out loud. I know I wish I had someone to talk to a lot of the time."

How was this big, beautiful man lonely, she wondered as she brought over the carbs.

"You don't have a—" As she put things in front of him, she fumbled over the word "wife." "You live alone?"

"I live with an old friend."

She sat back down. "Oh."

"He's taken care of me and whatever house I've lived in forever."

"Oh?" she said with a shot of relief.

"Tell me about your ex."

Ducking her eyes, she stirred the cooling, congealing

tomato soup around her bowl . . . and tried not to think about how in the right light, it looked like blood.

"I, ah, I met Bruce about ten months ago. I do payroll processing at a law office. My job's about as exotic as this toast." She took a bite of her second piece of toast. "He came in to apply for a position as a paralegal and he got lost. It's a big place, you know, our offices downtown. Four floors, seventy lawyers, support staff of over a hundred."

She paused as she remembered that first meeting, Bruce in his dark blue suit, his hair all combed back, a briefcase in his hand. His tie had been so straight, the press in his slacks so starched, his shoes buffed to a high polish. He'd seemed focused and directed. Determined and intelligent.

A man with a horizon, as opposed to the dead end she was in.

"Thinking back on it, I realize now . . ." She shrugged. "Well, it doesn't matter. He ended up on the wrong floor, and stopped by my desk to ask me for directions. I took him to my boss, who's head of HR, and on the way, he told me he was in law school at SUNY Caldwell. Starting his third year. Looking at the paralegal thing like a paid internship. I didn't expect to see him again, but after he was finished with the interview, he came back and told me he thought he'd nailed it.

"A week or two later, we ran into each other on the elevator. He told me he'd gotten the job and asked me out for coffee. That's how it all started." She pushed her bowl away. "The women in the secretarial pool kept telling me I was so lucky, and I did wonder why me. There were better options, you know what I mean? But he wanted me."

The man across from her murmured something. But when she glanced up, he shook his head like he wanted her to move along with the story.

"I think my cheering section was part of the problem." She wiped her mouth with a paper napkin and sat back in her chair. "I guess sometimes when you think nothing is ever going to change . . . you take what comes your way, especially if it's backed up by a bunch of people telling you to go for it because of how good it is."

"When did things start to go wrong?"

Anne frowned and tried to find the right words. "I ended up in a labyrinth of deception. And the punch line was that the lies were the best part of the relationship." She glanced across her table. "It was all bullsh—crap. He was married, for one thing. He has two kids, for another. He wasn't in law school, wasn't even trying to get into law school. And his coping mechanism for dealing with the stress of living a fake, made-up life was a pathological need for order and discipline. I was part of that. Or I was supposed to be. I wasn't as good at taking orders as he thought I'd be."

"If he loved you, he should have—"

"It wasn't love. For either one of us." She cleared her throat. "The whole thing came out because his wages this month were garnished for failure to pay child support. Like I said, I'm in charge of payroll for the firm, and I couldn't believe it when I saw the decree from the court. After stewing about what to do, I went to one of our attorneys for advice, and he got a private investigator to look into Bruce. Within twenty-four hours, there was a whole dossier on him." She shook her head. "I read it through twice, and then had to excuse myself to go throw up in the bathroom. Good thing it was after hours."

Pausing, she went to rub the ache behind her eye and bumped into that bandage for the hundredth time. With a wince, she put her hand in her lap. "After I left the building last night, I went over there to let him know I wasn't going to see him anymore—but I wasn't going to bring anything else up. The relationship wasn't working for me even apart from everything I'd learned and I'm pretty sure he was aware of it. What I didn't know was that the dossier had also been shared with HR. The attorney I'd gone to had taken the investigator's report to my boss and they'd fired Bruce for lying about his credentials at the end of the workday. I had no clue I was walking into . . . a storm."

"What exactly happened?"

Anne closed her eyes. "He blamed me for everything—because he'd guessed that the garnishment of the wages had tipped me off and I'd reported it. But his ranting was so much more than that. He railed against the law firm, and talked about some new opportunity that was going to transform him. And then he just snapped. He grabbed me around the throat." Her hand crept up to her collarbones. "He was red in the face and vacant in the eyes, so furious that I didn't think he was even seeing me. And what he was saying . . . I was terrified. He started out yelling at me, but then it all morphed . . . he was screaming about how he was going to have power, too. He was going to be bigger and stronger than everybody. Like he was a villain in a superhero comic book. It was a total break with reality, but given all his lying? The delusion was totally him."

The man across from her frowned, one of his hands curling up in a fist. "How did you get away?"

"I kneed him in the nuts—" She winced. "Jeez, I kind of did that to you last night as well, didn't I. In that backseat. It's not a hobby, I promise."

The man laughed a little. Then lost any semblance of levity. "I'm sorry you had to go that route, but I'm glad you did."

"With him, you mean. Not you."

Only the hint of a smile touched his mouth. "That's right."

Anne looked out of the slider, at the darkness that didn't seem so threatening at the moment because of who she was with.

"I truly thought Bruce was going to kill me." She frowned and shook her head. "He hadn't gotten physical before, but his temper was never far below the surface. Like, he'd get so frustrated if something in his condo got moved. If the dry cleaners didn't add enough starch to his shirts. If I was late because the bus was delayed. He walked a tightrope of flipping out, but if you lead two lives, you're juggling a lot, right? I mean, a deserted wife and two kids in Buffalo? A law school you aren't going to?"

She thought back over the previous months. "And then he was always making like he was a big man and getting angry because no one knew it. At work, he was so jealous of the full-blown attorneys, especially the partners. Then we'd be in his car, stuck in traffic, and he'd be checking out the makes and models of the vehicles around us, rattling off how much they cost, what their options were, why his was better.

On the weekends, he'd drag me to open houses at properties he couldn't afford, and trespass onto the grounds of golf courses he wasn't a member of. I mean . . . it was so messed up, in retrospect, but when you're in something, you don't notice what you've become accustomed to."

There was a moment of silence. Then the man nodded. "Truer words have never been spoken."

She went to brush a strand of hair from her eyes, but caught the movement before she poked herself in the bandage again. "When I went over there today—"

"Wait, what?" The man sat up straighter. "You went to see him? Did you take the police with you?"

"No, I didn't. But there were plenty of people around, plenty of daylight left—and he'd kept my credit card and my ID. I needed them back."

"You should have called me."

She would have, she realized. If she could have.

"I don't even know your name," she said softly as she stared into his blue eyes—and then she looked away. "Anyway, he wouldn't even open the door for me. It was like . . . he was scared or something. I got my card and my ID back, though. He pushed them through the crack by the jamb."

"Good," the man said tightly. "That's good. Don't go there again."

"I have no plans to, trust me." Taking a deep breath, she tried to look more collected than she was feeling on the inside. "You know what they say . . . that which cannot continue, will not. It is done."

As she picked at the last of her own toast, she felt him staring from across the table—and it was the oddest thing.

Though he was focused on her, she had the sense he was somewhere else in his mind.

Then he abruptly seemed to snap back to attention. "That's right about things ending. That's . . . exactly right. And you don't have anything to worry about, anymore."

She wasn't so sure about that, although she hoped he was right. Then again, it was easy for a man who was as muscular as he was to say she shouldn't be concerned. At least Bruce was barred from the law firm's building downtown, however—and the attorney who'd hired the private investigator had said that Anne could call for more help, day or night.

Still, people did crazy things.

"It's going to be fine," she told herself in a voice that was supposed to be firm.

◆   ◆   ◆

She didn't believe things were going to be fine. Not at all.

As Darius went back to the soup in his bowl, he wanted to tell Anne exactly why she could take that piece of shit Bruce off her proverbial plate. But he didn't want her to think that she was trading one hotheaded volcano for another.

Not that Darius was in line to be chosen—

With an inner curse, he glanced down at the toast she'd made him . . . and couldn't wait to take another bite just because her hands had touched the bread.

Oh, noooooo, he wasn't looking to be next up in her life. Not at all. He was just sitting in her kitchen, sharing the human version of Last Meal, prepared to murder her ex and defend her to the death.

Just a friendly little visit, really.

After he rolled his eyes at himself, he looked across the table again—and became instantly transfixed by the woman who, to him, was achingly beautiful in her blue sweater and her gray sweatpants and her bedroom slippers. Anne's hair was pulled back in what appeared to be a corporate-America bun, but wisps had come free of the twist, the dark, silken hairs curling up around her face. Her eyes were tired, and he hated that bandage at her temple . . . hated, too, the way she moved stiffly and with caution, as if lots of things hurt. But she wasn't complaining.

No, she only wanted to fill his belly and share what she had with him.

"This soup is delicious," he said.

"You have low standards."

"Not at all."

No offense to Fritz's venerable French training, but this soup-and-toast routine was the best meal he'd ever had. And dearest Virgin Scribe, what he really wanted was to feed her from his dagger hand, off a plate he had piled high with food he had hunted for her. And he wanted to do this in a secured home, built on a defensible position. With an Army anti-tank gun within easy reach.

"Seriously, thank you," he murmured. "For this."

Her brows arched. "You're welcome. I mean, it's nothing special."

It is to me, he thought.

Abruptly, she smiled again. "Can you believe I still don't know your name? Clearly, it's not St. Nick—"

"Darius." He placed his dagger hand over his chest and

inclined his head. "I am pleased to meet you, Anne. And I should have introduced myself about twenty-three hours ago."

Except back then, he'd been thinking there was never going to be any more contact between them. So what was the point.

Now, however, he'd evolved to thinking there *shouldn't* be any contact.

Progress, thy call sign was self-deception.

"That's a nice name," she said. "It's old-fashioned. It suits you. Is it okay if I ask you what you do?"

"You can make any inquiry of me you wish." He smiled, even though he didn't like fudging his truth. "And I'm a security guard."

"Oh? Like for a building or a mall?"

"Private security, actually."

"A bodyguard?"

Well, yes, if Wrath ever decided to assume the throne, and the Brotherhood returned as a personal guard unto the King.

"Pretty much." He leaned into the table. "That's why I'm going to give you my number. If you ever feel threatened, you can call me. I have some background and experience when it comes to protecting people—and of course, there's always your police, too. You should never hesitate to call them, either."

"Was that fancy BMW your boss's car?" Anne put her hand up to her mouth. "Oh, God, are you in trouble at work? I'm so sorry I ran into your—"

"No, I'm not in trouble." God, he hated not being totally

honest with her. "And it was worth it. Meeting you, I mean. Well . . . not like that. Crap—I'm babbling."

Anne opened her mouth. Closed it. Lowered her eyes.

"Sorry," he said remotely. "I don't want to get creepy on you."

"You're not. And if I'm honest, I don't quite know how to handle . . . this." She frowned and wiped her hands on her napkin. Even though they were clean. "I mean, not that this is a *this*. You coming here tonight, I mean. Like, anything date-ish, or anything—you know what, I need to shut up, too."

"No, you don't. I always want to hear what you're thinking."

She flushed and looked away, as if she didn't want him to know how much that pleased her. "But you just brought my shoe back. That's why you're here. That's the purpose. Right?"

In the silence that followed, he studied her downturned face, memorizing the curve of her lips, the lashes that hid her eyes, the flush on her cheeks.

"It's not just about the shoe, Anne."

As her stare flipped back to his, he spoke slowly so that there was no risk his accent would get in the way of his meaning. "I know you've just gotten out of a really bad situation, so I'm not asking for anything other than a little time to get to know you. But blind luck put us both on that road at that moment. Don't you think that might mean something?"

Of course, blind luck had also brought her a fucking psycho with an upward-mobility fixation and a wardrobe out of a Florsheim ad.

Also a round of X-rays.

"I'm not going to push you," he murmured. "I'm not like him."

"Oh, you are definitely not like Bruce." She shook her head. "He never said thank you, and he never brought me a shoe."

"Next time I'll show up with something even better."

"I'm not really a flowers person." She flushed again. "Sorry, that's not really romantic of me, is it. And maybe you aren't thinking in those terms—"

"I was thinking socks, actually." As Anne laughed, he knew it was the best sound he would ever hear. "Maybe it'll be a set of tubes. Could be tennis with the little balls at the heels. Hand knit or machine washable? I'm going to leave you guessing in hopes the mystery keeps you interested."

She threw her head back and outright giggled—until she grimaced and put her hand on her side. "Oh, jeez, I'm going to have to take it easy over here. Or you're going to have to be a lot less charming."

Sitting back in her modest house, in her modest kitchen, at a small table in a little alcove . . . Darius realized that he suddenly, and most unexpectedly, had the whole world in front of him.

He really did.

"I wish I could stay longer," he whispered.

There was a pause. Then in a rueful voice, she said in an equally soft way, "And I wish I had another shoe for you to bring back."

CHAPTER SEVEN

As Anne arrived at her desk the following morning, her telephone was already ringing. Launching herself into her chair, she nearly knocked over her office plant to catch the call.

"Hello, this is Anne—"

"Mr. Thurston wants to see you upstairs in his office."

As the voice of the senior partner's secretary speared into her ear, she kept the groan to herself. Miss Nancy Martle was over fifty, married to her job, and built like a battleship. In her gray suits and her fifties-era cat-eye glasses, she would have been considered a stereotype if she didn't inspire fear in just about everyone. Including the attorneys.

"When would he like—"

"Now."

The call was cut off and Anne hung up her end. Glancing

around, she saw other members of the support staff finding their seats at their desks, putting down purses, taking off coats. Everyone was female except for two supervisors who were men, and the rows of workstations were kitted out with identical accessories—single rolling chair, single visiting chair, wastepaper basket, phone, typewriter, and a coat stand. Overall, the wide-open space sparkled with cleanliness and efficiency, everything white and chrome. Then again, Beckett, Thurston, Rohmer & Fields invested properly in their facilities, even for the little people—

"You still hurting bad?"

As the question was posed, Anne snapped to attention. "Oh, Penny, hi."

"So how are you?" Her next-door neighbor shrugged out of her incredibly pink coat. "You don't look good."

Try facing Mr. Thurston on an empty stomach. Hell, make that Miss Martle.

"I'm fine, Penny. Thanks. I just have to go upstairs."

"Oh, check you out." The woman hung her blinding outerwear on a hanger on her stand. "Fancy. You getting promoted or something?"

The girl was in her mid-twenties, but looked older because she had Tammy Faye makeup and a bottle-blond bleach job on her bobbed hair. With her too-bright, too-tight, always-Easter-Sunday clothes, she was a cartoon character who'd been colored in by an exuberant, if sloppy, hand.

"Nothing like that." Anne grabbed a steno pad, even though she hadn't been asked to bring one. "I'll be right back—"

"You're going in your coat?"

"Huh—" Anne flushed and took off her jacket. "Sorry, I'm a little distracted."

Penny's heavily penciled eyebrow jogged up into her glossy forehead. "You get back with Bruce or something? Please tell me that's a no."

Of all the people she worked with, *why* had she told Penny the whole story? She might as well have put a notice in the *Caldwell Courier Journal.* "Ah, no. It's not . . . Bruce. I have to go, be right back."

Anne all but bolted for the elevators, and as she ran off—or tried to, what with the aches that were still hanging in—she had the sense that there were eyes on her. Except she was used to that. Ever since word had gotten out that she was dating Bruce, she'd been a topic of conversation. *Thanks, Penny.* And now with her own blabbermouth, she'd made herself even more visible. Surely, though, someone else in the firm could date somebody who seemed on the surface to be too good for them only to have the guy get canned for faking his résumé? It could happen . . . right?

Then again, maybe she and Bruce had set such a high standard for gossip it was never to be repeated.

Talk about your professional accomplishments.

At the bank of elevators, she hit the up arrows on both sides of the short hall, and she was lucky that there was a *bing* almost immediately. Hopping into a car full of suits and ties, she shuffled off to the side and kept her head down and her eyes on the marble floor.

Lot of wingtips. Lot of deep-voiced jocularity about golfing at the club, and whiskey, and that cart girl who really knew how to polish balls.

Naturally, the hale-and-hardies rode up to the twenty-ninth floor, and also unsurprisingly, they got off first, elbowing for position as if the evacuation were a race. No one held the doors for her, and she had to catch the brass and mahogany panels before she was locked in and sent all the way down to the lobby.

The reception desk and waiting area for the main attorney floor and its boardrooms was directly ahead, and the brunette-haired woman in charge seemed to have been chosen as a piece of art that could answer a telephone. Tall and slender as a model, she was wearing a black suit that coordinated with the black-and-gold color scheme of the decor, and the ceiling light above her was angled down like she was a painting. Still, her red-lipped smile seemed sincere, and her eyes were not judgmental in the slightest as Anne cautiously approached.

"Mr. Thurston is waiting for you." The woman indicated the way to her left with a manicured hand. "Would you like me to have a coffee brought to you?"

"Oh, no. No, thank you. No."

"Go right down."

"Thank you."

The firm's Big Wig waiting area was like a hotel lobby, full of modern marble sculptures and padded leather chairs, and its view of Caldwell's twin bridges was beautiful, especially on a sunny May day. The fresh flowers in crystal vases were a nice touch, too, the flares of pastel yellow and pink adding discreet pops of color.

Passing by a lineup of high-end conference rooms, Anne came to a second reception zone that was smaller, but no less formal, and there was Miss Martle, sitting at her desk like a sentry in front of a military garrison. The woman was on the phone, speaking quickly and with force, and as she held up her forefinger for Anne to wait, you had to wonder if the thing was loaded and what kind of range it had.

Miss Martle ended her call. "You may go in. He's off his line now."

Anne's eyes shifted to the open doorway beyond. "Thank you."

Approaching the corner office, her feet made no sound on the thick carpeting, and she could smell fresh coffee and something cinnamon, as if there were a cook somewhere making the partners their breakfasts to order.

It's a different world, she thought as she stepped inside what was considered hallowed ground.

Silhouetted against the view of Caldwell's other half, sitting behind a desk the size of a king-sized bed, Mr. Thurston was white-haired and distinguished in his pin-striped suit, looking as if a Supreme Court justice and a Wall Street tycoon had had a love child.

The man glanced up from an orderly stack of documents and removed his tortoiseshell reading glasses. "Miss Wurster. Sit down."

"Thank you, sir."

Closing the distance, she lowered herself into an oxblood leather seat across from the man. The royal-blue-and-gold office was so vast that it had its own meeting table, as well as a bar and what had to be a private bathroom off in the corner. Mahogany shelves filled with leather-bound books covered all the walls, except for a six-by-six area reserved for a full-length oil painting of a man who looked so much like Mr. Thurston that he had to be the man's father or grand-father.

They had the same icy blue eyes.

And wow . . . Bruce had painted his apartment the exact shade of this navy color, hadn't he.

When there was a soft click from behind, Anne twisted around to find that they'd been shut in together.

"I understand there has been some unpleasantness," Mr. Thurston said. "How are you feeling."

Totally not surprised the man knew about the whole thing—because nothing escaped him if it involved his firm—Anne raised a hand to her temple. She'd replaced the hospital's bandage with a couple of Band-Aids, and she was hoping to go without them entirely soon.

"I am fine, sir." She went back to clutching her steno pad. "Thank you."

"I never did care for that McDonaldson character. Saw right through him. Glad he's gone."

"Yes, sir."

"There's a reason that we don't encourage interoffice dating." This was said with censure, as if she were Eve with an apple, as if she had courted trouble and shouldn't be surprised when it came to her. "It's really not appropriate, but you young people have different ideas of things."

"We disclosed our . . . we did go to human resources. Per the employee manual."

The *hmrph* that came back at her could have meant a lot of things, none of which were complimentary. "Enough about that." Mr. Thurston linked his fingers together over the case work he'd been reviewing. "We, the firm, want to make sure you're taken care of."

"I'm sorry, sir?" Outside the office, a phone rang softly. "So I'm not fired?"

Mr. Thurston waved his reader glasses. "Of course not. You've never caused any trouble outside of this McDonaldson business."

Between one blink and the next, Anne relived the feel of Bruce's hands locked on her throat, and saw his screaming, furious face inches in front of her own. The temptation to point out that being assaulted by a man whose lies had been exposed wasn't something she had "caused" stung.

"So we'd like to give you a thousand dollars."

Anne lifted her brows and tilted forward in the chair. "Excuse me?"

Mr. Thurston smiled like a king sparing the life of a serf. "I know, it's a lot of money. But this firm cares about its employees. We understand that there was a visit to the hospital for your very minor injuries and we want to help with your medical bills. We know that we're being too generous. People first, though. It's our slogan."

No, Anne thought. *The firm's slogan was* Integrity, Excellence, Legacy.

"I don't need any money," she said. "I just want to keep my job."

Mr. Thurston's hand moved to rest on a piece of paper . . . and what looked like a corporate check.

"Your job is safe." That self-satisfied smile came back,

the one that was an internal reflection of his belief that he was superior to most people, and yet not without a heart. "We just want to make things easy on you."

Anne's eyes lingered on the check. She couldn't read the writing from here, but it wasn't blank and the blue sprawl on the signature line was no doubt Mr. Thurston's.

"Is there a problem, Miss Wurster?"

"I don't need any money, thank you." She got to her feet. "I'm very grateful, however. I'll just go back to work now."

Those pale blue eyes narrowed on her, a mask coming over the man's features, locking all that patrician down— which gave her a sense of exactly how good Mr. Thurston was at his job at the negotiating table.

"You must have a lot of savings," he murmured, "to turn down our generosity."

"Thank you for thinking of me."

"Well. I'll just keep this here." He tapped the check and the piece of paper. "But only for a day. I am not going to talk you into accepting the goodwill of your employer."

Foolish girl, the tone implied. *You foolish, silly little girl.*

Anne looked past the man to the view. Out on the Northway, morning rush hour traffic was backed up on both sides of the river, the lines of cars crawling toward clogged exit ramps and crowded surface roads.

"Miss Wurster?"

"Thank you, Mr. Thurston," she said quietly. "Have a good day."

She turned away without a dismissal, and felt a cool wave of disapproval escort her out the door. On the far side of the inner sanctum, Miss Martle was on the phone again, but the woman's eyes snapped up from her desk and focused on Anne's hands.

As a flare of surprise registered on that disapproving cat-eye-glassed face, Anne wanted to go home. And as she went back through the main reception, got to the elevators, and hit the down arrow, she wondered if she had the guts to put the lobby to good use and walk away from the building, tossing the steno pad in a municipal garbage bin—

"*Psst.*"

Anne glanced to the right, to the head of a back hallway that accessed the service facilities and freight elevators. "Hello?"

"It's me, Charlie."

"Charlie—"

"Shh." A disembodied hand shot out and its forefinger crooked at her. "C'mere."

Anne glanced at the receptionist, who had her phone up to her ear and her eyes down on whatever she was writing.

"What's going on," Anne murmured as she scooted out of view.

R. Charles Byrnes III was a Mr. Thurston in training, with the same bone structure, same Brooks Brothers wardrobe, probably the same family tree, if you went back seven generations of white bread. The difference was thirty years and maybe a little bit of true conscience, although whether the latter would last as time went on, who knew. The guy had it now, though, and that was why she'd gone to him when she'd found out about the wage garnishment.

Plus Bruce had been his paralegal.

"Did you take the money," he demanded as he brushed back his thick blond hair.

She did a double take. "Excuse me?"

"Tell me you didn't take the money and you didn't sign anything." As she struggled to follow, he got impatient, but kept his voice hushed. "That's why I saw you walking into Thurston's office, right? The full story is out—not by me—and he wants to pay you off."

"Ah—he said the firm would like to take care of my medical bills."

"Did you take it?"

"Oh, I don't need the money—"

"It's not about the cash to them. They want you to sign a release. McDonaldson was an employee and so are you. That asshole might have attacked you off-site, but the partners are not going to want trouble in the press or with their blue-chip clients because a hire they failed to do proper due diligence on assaulted one of their backroom girls. They'll throw a little cash your way in the hopes this will go away, but you need to hold on for more—"

He stopped talking and looked over his shoulder as a uniformed maintenance worker came out of the stairwell.

In the pause, Anne felt compelled to lean back and check to make sure the Brooke Shields at the reception desk was still busy and no one was by the elevators. Yup. All clear.

"Listen, I appreciate your concern," she said when they had some privacy again. "But—"

"You're going to want a twenty-times multiple of what-

ever their first offer was. At least. If you were my client, I'd
go for fifty times over."

As her brain got scrambled, she thought absently that
Charlie's upset seemed very honest.

"I'm not going to take their money. I'm fine." She
frowned as he glanced across his shoulder again. "Why are
you talking to me at all if it makes you so nervous?"

The man's eyes returned to her and locked in on her
banged-up temple. "Because it's wrong, what happened to
you when you went to Bruce's, and on top of that, the firm's
trying to screw you over to their advantage. The way I see it,
you've been hurt enough, and someone needs to give you
some good advice."

Anne glanced down at her steno pad. "But Mr. Thurston
didn't ask me to sign anything."

"You didn't take the money yet. Don't kid yourself. He's
going to be back and he will force your hand."

"Then fine. I'll do whatever they want, I don't care. I just
need to keep my job."

A hand rested lightly on her shoulder. "Consider this advice from a friend, okay? I'm loyal to this place as long as
they're playing fair, but they aren't with you. You've got
leverage. You need to use it. This is a cold, hard world, and
money makes a lot of things easier."

"Thanks," she said. "I, ah, I have to go—"

"And there's one other thing."

"What."

He tilted to the side and looked around her. "Meet me
down by the loading dock, six o'clock tonight. I want you to
take a look at something." When she hesitated, he rolled his

eyes. "I'm a happily engaged man, and I'd be a fucking fool to mess that up. Just meet me out back, okay? Six o'clock. I can't go into it here."

Charlie gave her shoulder a little squeeze and then hustled away.

As Anne watched him go, she knew she was not going to be anywhere in the building or outside of it at six p.m.

She had a date tonight.

CHAPTER EIGHT

S o we're clear? You know what to do?"

As Darius spoke up, he was inspecting his reflection in the gold-leafed mirror over his bathroom sink, and he was not satisfied with what was staring back at him. His hair was still damp from his shower, and it was a little long, in his opinion—but no time for Fritz to give him a trim now. He'd also managed to nick himself while shaving, and couldn't wait to get rid of the piece of toilet paper he'd tacked onto his chin to stop the bleeding. And he wasn't sure about the outfit.

"Oh, yes, sire." The *doggen* bowed in the background. "I understand my duties."

"Good."

"And the meal has been prepared as you requested."

"Thanks, Fritz." He turned around. "How do I look?"

Fritz clasped his hands in worry. Then the butler blinked a couple of times as if he might be having a stroke.

"Spit it out," Darius muttered. "I command you to speak."

"Ah . . . forgive me, sire. But it was my understanding that you have a guest of the female persuasion coming this evening?"

"That's the plan."

"And might I extrapolate, based upon the detailed instructions you provided me concerning the finer points of the meal and the dessert—indeed, this house as a whole—that you wish to impress this female?"

"Yes." He glanced down at his black-on-black ensemble. "I really want her to—well, have a good evening."

"May I please speak with a bit of candor, then."

Darius fought the urge to curse. "If you don't, I'm going to put my head through this mirror."

"Sire, I would not advise that. I fear that I would have to wrap your face in bandages, and I am not certain I have sufficient Neosporin—"

"What is wrong with my clothes," he demanded. "*Now.*"

The old *doggen* sprang into motion, rushing to the carved wardrobe that filled most of one of the bedchamber's walls. "Mayhap I might suggest"—he opened both of the doors—"one of these suits. I would think a double-breasted gray, paired with a cheerful tie, and a—"

"No, I can't do formal. This isn't a formal thing."

"Oh." The butler paused. And then seemed to fall into a sartorial mourning as he slowly closed the doors. "Well. Then."

The *doggen* turned around and presented a forcibly pleas-ant expression. "You have achieved a perfect casual effect. And those slacks are most flattering, as is the turtleneck."

Darius yanked the shirt out of the waistband. "I look ridiculous, don't I. Like someone held my head and dipped me into a vat of black paint."

"I'm not certain that would be possible, sire."

"I'm speaking in a figurative sense."

"I was thinking more the issue of consent—"

Gong!

The pair of them whipped their heads up to the ceiling.

"*Shit*, she's early," Darius said as he checked his watch. "She was supposed to come at seven thirty. I can't go up there, it's too light out."

"It cannot be her, sire. 'Tis too light for any vampire."

"She's not one of us, Fritz."

There was a pause. "A human, then?"

"No, a toaster oven in heels." As the butler's brows went into his hairline like he was struggling with a mental picture, Darius wiped the air with his dagger hand. "Just go up there and get her inside."

He needed to put some shutters on this house, maybe ones that could be dropped electronically, all at once.

"But of course, sire!" The *doggen* bowed low and raced for the stairwell, speaking over his shoulder. "I am eager to welcome a guest into our home—*your* home, rather."

As the butler hit the first stone step, Darius said sharply, "Fritz."

The loyal servant jerked to a halt, pivoted on a dime. "Yes, sire?"

Darius stared across at the elderly male, taking in the formal black tie and tails, the white hair that was set perfect as a cap, the wrinkly face that was somehow undiminished by age. As Darius thought of all the years they had been together, going back to that estate in the Old Country, he realized he couldn't imagine life without the butler.

"It's *our* home, Fritz. Yours and mine. I would appreciate it if you referred to this abode properly."

Fritz flushed and looked a little wobbly. Then again, *doggen* did not handle praise or honor well, and to that point, the only way Darius could have gotten away with what he'd said was phrasing things as he had, as an order.

"Yes," Fritz said roughly. "Of course."

"Now go answer the door."

"Shall I bring her down here?"

"I don't know." Darius glanced around. "I mean, it's a bedroom. I don't want her to think . . . well, you know."

The *doggen* smiled wisely. "But of course. I shall welcome her properly into our house up above, sire. And we shall wait upon you."

◆   ◆   ◆

Well . . . she had double-checked the address. This had to be Darius's house.

Darius's boss's house, rather.

Anne took a step back. And then another. Over the glossy black door, the correct number was displayed in gleaming brass numerals, and she knew the street was the right one.

And PS, what a house. When he'd said it was white with black shutters, she'd expected something fairly fancy given that whoever owned the place had a full-time security person—and also because she knew the neighborhood from the society articles in the *CCJ*. But this mansion . . . was like something that belonged on *Dynasty*. Set away from the road, the gracious antique had all the lines and craftsmanship of an authentic construction that was a century or two old, yet it, and the property it sat on, were maintained to a scrupulous degree. No chipping paint, no dirty windows, no cracks in the asphalt on the driveway, no bushes or blooming fruit trees out of order.

In the early-evening light, the lawn looked like it had been mowed . . . and then vacuumed—

The door opened.

What was on the other side shouldn't have been a surprise.

Still, Anne rubbed her eyes just to see if things were a figment of her imagination. Nope. It was as if the Queen of England had come for a visit and left her butler behind: Though the silver-haired man in traditional uniform was clearly elderly, he gave off the air of being a model of efficient servitude, his carriage that of a thirty-year-old soldier, his arms and white-gloved hands down at his sides, his chin up and eyes alert.

Except . . . he was smiling at her?

"Mistress," he said with warmth. "Welcome."

And then he bowed.

Anne glanced behind herself. You know, in case some visiting dignitary had arrived and was coming up the steps.

"Um, hello?" She refocused on the man. Butler. "I'm not sure if I'm at the—"

"You are most expected, do come in." The butler stepped back and indicated the way inside with a gracious motion. "We are most pleased to have you."

Clasping that second-best purse of hers, she entered the house. Her first impression was that it smelled like fresh roses—oh, right, there was a vase of about a hundred and fifty of the by-any-other-names right over there. Her second impression, as she looked to the left and saw a parlor, and then to the right to check out a formal dining room, was that the place was like a museum, the collection of antiques and rugs and furnishings like nothing she had ever seen outside of a magazine.

"May I take your coat, mistress?"

Was she even wearing one, she thought in a daze.

"Ah, yes, please." She shrugged out of the lightweight jacket. "Thank you."

Wonder if he'd ever hung up anything that had been bought off the rack. On sale. At Casual Corner.

And that accent of his. Just like Darius's.

"If you would be so kind as to follow me."

"Okay."

The butler looped her flimsy outerwear over the crook of his arm and walked farther into the house, passing a staircase that clearly led to heaven, its red-carpeted steps and carved balustrade begging for a woman in a gown and diamonds to drift down them.

The living room—no, it had to be called a parlor, too, right? Or a drawing room? Jesus, where was she?—in the back was even more impressive, the rich wood paneling and leather furniture suggesting that it was for gentlemen to smoke cigars in after the dessert course. And was that . . . ?

Across the way, taking up most of a wall, an oil painting of a king in an ermine-trimmed robe was staring out of a gilded frame with haughty self-possession. The rendering had clearly been done by a master, the eyes so lifelike, she felt as though she'd better curtsy or run the risk of being guillotined.

". . . mistress?"

She spun around. "I'm sorry. I was just—that's quite a painting."

"It is, is it not." The butler gave her a gentle smile. "Darius is attending to some business at the moment, but he will be right with you. Would you care for a libation?"

Tilting forward, she frowned. "I thought I was free to go?"

"I beg your pardon?"

"A liberation?"

"I've never heard of that cocktail?"

"Cocktail?"

As they both went quiet in confusion, she wondered where Darius was. Maybe he could help save this conversation? Or at least add a couple of responses not phrased as questions.

"A drink, madam?" The butler made a pinch, extended his pinkie, and mimed sipping from a wineglass. "Perhaps you would like one?"

With a curse, she would have V-8'd her forehead, but she was still healing. "Ah, just water, thank you."

The old man seemed crestfallen, as if he had missed a

chance to show off his bartending skills—and something about the sincerity of the reaction made her want to relieve the suffering she didn't quite understand.

"Actually, how about some . . . orange juice?" she hedged.

"Oh, marvelous choice!" He clasped his gloved palms together as if she had just called his infant grandson a Rhodes Scholar. "I shall hand squeeze it—and perhaps we should add a bit of mandarin to enhance the flavor profile?"

"I—you know, I'm going to rely on you to make that decision."

"Right away!"

The butler went off with a spring in his step, and somehow his unadulterated joy at having such a modest duty made her feel more comfortable in the fancy house than anything else could have. Glancing around, she wondered what kind of "business" Darius was handling. Hopefully, nothing dangerous—

Click.

Whrrrrrr.

Like something out of a James Bond movie, the painting of the monarch was moving on a slide along its wall, revealing . . . a spiral stone staircase that was lit with gas lanterns?

Anne glanced around and wondered if she should call for the butler. But given that he was in charge of the place, chances were good he wasn't going to be surprised.

Drawn forward by the mystery, the darkness, the flickering light, she leaned in and looked down the descent. The steps were worn and very old, and with the curve, she couldn't see where they led—

Anne?

At first, she thought she was hearing things. But then her name was spoken again. "Anne . . . ?"

"Darius?"

It was a night for questions, she thought. And also, wasn't this how horror stories got started? A woman with no family being called by a relative stranger down a creepy set of steps into the earth?

Where there were, like, monsters waiting to eat her or something.

"Anne, can you come down here?"

She glanced at the portrait in its new position. Then looked back to the churning lanterns. The sense that her life would never be the same if she took the first step was so profound, her body weaved back and forth.

Except then she realized . . . the course of things had already changed for her.

Irrevocably.

"Yes," she whispered. "I can."

CHAPTER NINE

At the bottom of the curving staircase, Darius had one hand on the rough wall and the other on insanity's proverbial shoulder. All he wanted to do was rush up to the woman who was at the top of the steps, but it just wasn't safe. He and Fritz always left the drapes open around the house, the better to fit in among humans, and there was still enough light in the sky to blind him. Maybe even smoke his skin.

And he didn't want Anne to see that.

So here he was, stuck underground, dying to get to her—but all he could do was try to entice her down a set of stone steps that no doubt looked like something out of a Vincent Price—

"I'm waiting for a drink," came her voice again.

He closed his eyes, partially because he loved the sound

of her. And partially out of frustration for how the Scribe Virgin had chosen to tie the hands of her one and only creation.

"Fritz will bring it down for you," he said roughly. "And I'm sorry about this, I'm just working on something here."

As he spoke the lie, everything he wasn't telling her crashed into his conscience. Except there were rules, old rules, that needed to be adhered to even in this New World where no one was willing to lead.

And just maybe . . . he didn't want to see the expression on her face when she learned the truth of what he was.

Shit—

"What is this place?"

The sound of her footfalls barely carried over the soft hissing of the gas lanterns, but he could hear her coming down to him, slowly, steadily—and then he caught her scent.

Closing his eyes again, he breathed in, drawing the fragrance of fresh meadow flowers into his nose, his soul. Even though he had seen her just the night before, it felt like a lifetime since he'd—

And there she was, rounding the curve, the restless, banked flames playing over the face that he had visualized in his every waking moment and throughout his dreams. Oh, wow, she had worn her hair down for him, the naturally highlighted brown length flowing free and shining off the crown of her head—and her clothes were what he had come to expect, simple and perfect, a loose linen skirt and a bright white button-down, coupled with a coral sweater tied around her shoulders.

She looked bright and sunny, even though it was early evening.

"Hi," he said as she stopped a couple of steps higher than him . . . so that their faces were on the same level.

Her smile was shy. "Hi."

Annnnnnd then they just stared at each other. Which made him feel less like a letch: As long as she was looking at him in the same way, then consuming her with his eyes seemed less inappropriate.

"I'm sorry if this is weird." Wait, that was what he'd said to her last night, right? "Jesus, I'm like a broken record, aren't I."

"What is this place?" She indicated the stairwell. "I mean . . . that painting, these steps, the lanterns? I feel like I'm in a Vincent Price movie."

"That's exactly what I was worried about." He shook his head. "You have nothing to fear here, I promise you."

It wasn't like she was standing in front of Dracula, or anything.

Fuck.

"It's okay." She smiled in a way that reached her eyes and warmed them. "Now that you're here—I mean, I'm here with you—I mean—"

"Now that we're together."

"Yes," she murmured. "That's right. Everything's okay now."

As he felt a wave of heat hit his face, it was like he'd never been alone with a female before. Sure, he was nothing on Rhage's level when it came to the opposite sex, but he was not unfamiliar with these things. He had even had two young outside of proper mating who had tragically died centuries ago.

When it came to Anne, however, he . . .

His eyes dropped to her mouth. And all he could think of was kissing her.

Except as he glanced back into his own chamber, he knew she deserved more respect than to be alone with him where his bedding platform was, especially given where he was in his head. What the hell had he thought they were going to do down here? Stand at the base of the stairs until sunset?

Well, as she said, at least they were together.

As if on cue, she leaned forward and looked into the darkened guest suite, where Wrath sometimes slept.

"What an incredible place," she murmured. "This house . . . is amazing."

"Let me show you around."

Darius led the way into the other chamber because it was the better of the two options. And though there was no indent where the King had lain across the bed, he smoothed his hand over the duvet anyway.

"Is this where your boss stays?" she asked as she walked around and looked at the landscape paintings that were supposed to take the place of windows. "It certainly seems very secure."

"Yes, this is his room." He cleared his throat. "Well, when he's here. Which isn't as often as I'd like."

"You're close to him, then? As a friend?"

"No one is close to him. But I'd like to earn my keep."

With a nod, she went by the desk that was kitted out with a plume and an inkpot, as well as stationery. Not that anyone would be using any of it.

Picking up a sheet of the paper, she frowned. "What's this?"

Crossing the room, it was no sacrifice to get close enough to peer over her shoulder. "Hmm?"

"This . . . it's writing, isn't it?"

Her thumb passed over the engraved heading that spelled out Wrath's royal lineage in the Old Language, the listings of the father of the father of the father . . . going back generations, and yet the symbols were all the same because all the Kings of the species had been named Wrath.

The same sequence was tattooed on the insides of the current Wrath's forearms, with the females of the bloodline also included—and between one blink and the next, Darius saw the flesh, rather than the paper.

Back when he'd been younger and more idealistic, he'd known with certainty that all Kings would carry that name. That the *Dhestroyer* prophecy would be fulfilled and the *lessers* and their evil master eliminated. That his generation of the Black Dagger Brotherhood would finally usher in a peaceful future, that their hard graft in the war would be rewarded with a victory earned upon the honor and the legacy of the brave dead as well as the courage and commitment of the living.

It had been a long time since he'd believed any of that fantasy.

Now, he saw not just a King who would not lead, but no more Kings, ever: There was no possibility for any offspring to come from the current Wrath because though he was promised unto a female of worth, he refused to lie with her—and with him ending the most important bloodline of them all, it was not hard to extrapolate that there was no future for the race, either. And then there were the problems within the Brotherhood. There was no cohesion among its current members, no coordination of effort, no way to get backup if you needed it. Therefore, this era of what had once been the best line of defense against the enemy wasn't winning the war with the Lessening Society; hell, they weren't even holding ground. They were losing.

Where exactly did anyone think all of this was heading? A King who refused to unite the species, a foe with endless inductees, and a dwindling number of brothers, as no one was bothering to develop and replenish any of the membership . . .

"Are you okay?" he heard Anne ask from a vast distance.

She was right, he thought. Just as she'd pointed out the night before, it had all happened so incrementally that the now-inevitable culmination wasn't something he or anybody had noticed.

Until this precise moment.

"I think . . . I'm going to sit down."

At least that's what he thought he said. Abruptly, he couldn't feel anything in his body, much less hear what was coming out of his mouth. All he knew was that if he walked quickly enough across the chamber, he'd make it to Wrath's bed before he fainted.

And crushed the woman who he sensed was following him—

The mattress arrived just in time. As his legs let go, the softness came up to greet him, and on the bounce, it dawned on him that this was how Wrath must do it, just fall onto the bed face-first. A collapse. Like dead weight.

Like a corpse.

"Darius? Darius . . . talk to me."

Small, strong hands rolled him over, and then Anne's visage appeared before his own, her silken hair falling forward in dark, fragrant waves, her lips moving, though he couldn't hear anything she was saying.

He really wanted to listen to her. His ears weren't functioning, however—and she seemed frantic with his lack of response. To make sure she knew he was conscious, he reached up and drew his fingers through the wavy brunette lengths that trailed forward, a bridge between the two of them.

"I would always touch you thus," he said in the Old Language. "Oh, lovely female, so full of beauty and grace . . . I fear thou art mine pyrocant, sent to warm me with a fire that could as easily destroy me."

For a reason that he did not understand, her quiet gasp broke through his deafness. And then she withdrew sharply.

Shifting his eyes to the door, he saw Fritz standing in the guest chamber's open doorway, a glass of what appeared to be orange juice in one hand . . . and an expression as if he had seen a ghost on his hangdog face.

Oh. Anne hadn't been the one to gasp at what he'd said. That had been his butler.

Well, at least she didn't understand the mother tongue.

His admission was the kind of thing that would no doubt scare her off.

+ + +

"I can't understand anything he's saying," Anne implored the butler. "Can you ... is he okay?"

As she knelt on a bed the size of her living room—bent over a man who had gone white as a sheet in front of her and then face-planted—she was prepared to call an ambulance. Or maybe his employer had a private doctor? Meanwhile, over in the open doorway, the old man seemed so shocked, he was totally frozen.

Fortunately, he snapped into action.

"Here," he said as he rushed forward with the juice. "Perhaps this shall revive him."

Refocusing on Darius, she was relieved to find his eyes open and locked on her. The pupils seemed okay, but what did she know? And was he babbling or speaking in that other language?

"I think we need a doctor—"

"Lift him, mistress," the butler said. "I shall offer this unto his mouth."

Shifting her position, she tucked her legs under her and propped Darius's head in her lap, making sure his chin was tilted so he could drink. Then the butler put the glass up to those lips, and when a sloppy hand tried to bat it away, she captured the palm.

"Please," she said, "drink."

Instantly, Darius complied, as if he had been taking orders from her his whole life, and as he swallowed, his Adam's apple undulated under the tight, high collar of his turtleneck. She quickly glanced down his body. His slacks were of a fine material that draped his thighs and calves, and the belt he wore was of good leather locked by what appeared to be a polished gold buckle. Somehow, she wasn't surprised he was dressed in all black. It seemed to be his wardrobe staple, and he did look good in it.

Still, things seemed funereal given his current state.

"He hasn't been eating enough," the butler said as he backed off with the glass. "He has been very tense of late."

She glanced at the elderly servant. "It sounds like he has a stressful job."

"Very, mistress."

"So his boss is difficult?"

The butler put the glass back to Darius's mouth, and when nothing happened, Anne commanded, "Drink."

Orders were followed again, his lips drawing in for a sip once. Twice. A third time. Until the glass was more than halfway consumed.

"So his boss is hard to work for?" Anne prompted as she looked into the deep blue eyes that stared back at her, the dark lashes setting off the resonant hue.

Yet she wasn't sure what he was seeing.

The butler released a long, slow breath. "His . . . boss, as you say . . . has broken his heart. There is nothing sadder than a leader who refuses to lead, especially if he is sought by his . . . well, by those in his employ, as it were."

"I'm sorry to hear that," she murmured.

She and the butler both fell silent—just in time for the man between them to announce, "I'm not dead, you know."

The voice was strong, the syllables forceful, and Anne

had to smile a little. "I figured that, given you've had half my OJ."

"Well, you told me to drink."

Without thinking, she stroked Darius's face, her finger-tips running from his cheek to his jaw. "Yes, I did."

As his eyes drifted to her mouth, a flush warmed her body. And then the butler was saying something about bringing dinner down here on trays. And Darius was saying something back, like yes, please.

And then they were alone.

"I think you need a doctor, not dinner," she said.

"Let's start with the latter, and then we'll debate about the former, deal?"

"I'm not sure I agree."

"Fritz can set us up over there," Darius countered. "At the desk. And you can monitor me the whole time."

"Or . . . maybe I can just feed you right where we are." When his eyes flared, she shook her head. "No offense, but I don't want to have to try to pick you up off the floor. At least if we're here, you're safe because gravity already owns you."

"I'm fine—"

"Sure you are."

"No, really—"

As he went to sit up, she settled him back down just by putting a hand on his chest. "Stay."

When he complied, it wasn't lost on her that they had done this the night before last, just with the roles reversed. It was also very clear that he was choosing to stay where he was, because he was more than strong enough to get up off the bed if he wanted to.

"I like the idea of paying you back." She ran her fingers through his hair. "It feels fair, even though I don't . . ."

"Don't what."

"I don't want you to suffer."

"I'm not."

She wasn't sure that was true. Not eating well? Because of stress? Still, sometimes the kindest thing you could do for someone was let them keep the illusion they were presenting—

Wait a minute. Was she stroking his hair? Why, yes, she was.

"I'm sorry," she said as she flushed and took her hand away.

"Don't stop," he whispered. "You're healing me every time you touch me."

Instantly, the two of them seemed to lock into place with each other, the connection invisible, but powerful enough to make her feel like nothing else existed. And given what had been going on in her own life lately, what a relief to take a break from the chaos. The fear.

"Anne . . ."

Riding a wave of undefined emotion, she had to look away, her eyes traveling over to those landscape paintings that hung on the black stone walls, and the old-fashioned wardrobe that was no doubt full of suits, and the formal desk where that stationery with the beautiful writing was.

"This is like another world," she said hoarsely. "Down here."

When she felt her hand get squeezed, she realized she was still holding his palm in her own. And maybe she should have been shy or embarrassed about the contact, but as with when she'd smoothed his hair, she wasn't. This house, the butler, the whole thing was so far out of her normal life . . . that it made her feel like she was in a dream.

And she could use a good fantasy right about now.

"Just you and me." He squeezed her hand again. "Tonight, let's just be . . . you and me."

"Are you sure you're okay?"

"Positive. I missed a meal . . . or two. That's all. Don't worry about it."

The next thing she knew, the butler was coming back into the room, with what appeared to be a sterling silver tray layered up with a dozen sterling silver serving dishes. Somehow, the old man kept the load steady.

"Here," she said, "let me help—"

Pressure on her hand kept her in place, and Darius said in a hiss, "Oh, God, no, don't. He doesn't like to be helped."

"But—"

When Darius shook his head like he was trying to keep her from volunteering for a quicksand bathtub, all she could do was sit back as the butler placed the tray on the desk and made quick work transferring things onto the nearest bedside table.

And for some reason, the man was apologizing as fast as he moved: "I'm afraid that there are portions of the full meal not ready yet. I am so sorry, dinner was to be at eight—"

"It's all right." Darius sat up, his nostrils flaring. "Do I smell hors d'oeuvres?"

"Yes, sire." Lids were lifted. "Roasted brie with almonds. Fresh crackers. Pâté that I made this afternoon. And, at your request, beef franks in puff pastries. Now, with your permission, I shall go attend unto the roast beef and the potatoes?"

"Yes, please do."

As the butler bowed and bolted for the stairwell, she asked, "Why doesn't he accept a little help?"

"He would view it as a failure on a mortal scale. He's just like that. Very old fashioned and formal about his duties—and if you push the point, you'll get the look."

"Oh, so he'll get angry?"

"No, worse. He'll tear up." Darius put a hand on his heart and closed his eyes like someone had died. "You don't want that. I'd sit on a nuclear bomb before I have to pass that *doggen* another tissue."

"*Doggen?*"

"Butler, I mean." Darius shook his head. "I'm telling you. The last time I tried to do a load of my own laundry was in the seventies and I'm still not over it. Because neither is he."

She laughed a little. "How intense. And I see he also speaks that language. What exactly is it?"

"Just a European dialect."

When there was an awkward pause, she glanced toward the bits and bites, and her stomach growled. "Are those really pigs in a blanket?"

He smiled. "I believe that's the vernacular term, yes."

"You know what?" She scooted forward toward the side

table and its display of goodies. "Forget the entrée. This is what heaven looks like to me."

As she popped one into her mouth, she heard Darius say softly, "I couldn't agree more."

When she glanced over at him to make another joke . . .

. . . he was staring at her, not the food.

CHAPTER TEN

I feel like our roles need to be reversed."

As Darius tossed the statement over the conversational threshold, he was nonetheless powerless to change the dynamic that had been so firmly established. Anne had installed him up against the pillows, which she herself had stacked, and now she was putting a plate together at the bedside table for him. Next up, she was going to feed him from her hand—which was something that tantalized him.

And also frustrated the crap out of him. He needed to wait on her—

Under her breath, she started humming something, and he closed his eyes so he could put all his senses into listening to her.

"What's that song?" he asked roughly.

"You'll laugh."

"Tell me."

"Grover Washington Jr."

She turned to him with the plate. "Just the twoooo of us . . . we can make it if we try . . . just the twoooo of ussss . . . you and I . . ."

"I love it," he murmured as she settled on the edge of the bed next to him, tucking her legs under herself. "I'm claiming it as my new theme song."

As she blushed, she seemed to try and cover up her reaction. "What do you fancy first?"

"Whatever you choose to give me."

"Pig in a blanket it is. I highly recommend them."

As she picked up one of the bundles with her delicate fingers, he took her wrist. "No, first you." When she went to argue that she'd already had one, he shook his head. "It's a thing for me. You have to come first from the plate. I am second, after you."

He gently redirected the hors d'oeuvre to her lips, and when he nodded, she opened her mouth and took a bite. Watching her chew, he felt his blood stirring, and tried to keep a lid on all that stuff.

For now.

"You finish it," she said as she took what remained and presented it to his lips.

The morsel was the best thing he had ever tasted, outside of her tomato soup and her toast. And that was the way they played the plate: One bite for her first, then one for him second. In the silence, in the quiet stillness of the bed-chamber the King slept in only from time to time, Darius and his woman formed an accord, proof that words were not needed when energy flowed between two people.

When everything had been consumed, she turned back to Fritz's display on the bedside table. "I'm going to save some room for dinner. So this next plate is all for you, and that is that. I don't want any arguments."

Her dominance made him tingle in places that were usually dormant—and even though he was inclined to push back, submitting to her had its own rewards, didn't it.

When she was satisfied with her choices, Anne pivoted around again. "So how long have you been working for your boss?"

As he debated how to answer that, she fortunately put a cracker with brie on it into his mouth, and he took his time chewing.

"I've been under him for . . . well, it feels like ever since I've been alive."

She laughed a little. "So he's that hard to work for."

"Yes." Darius frowned. "But he's had a hard life. So hard, and right from the beginning, too. His parents were . . . they were killed in front of him when he was a young—a child."

As Anne gasped, he wondered what the hell was coming out of his mouth.

"Oh . . . God," she said. "That's terrible."

"It was brutal. And he's never been right since, you know?"

"How could someone be? Was he raised by other family? Or did he go into foster care? Did they find who did it? Did they go to jail?" She stopped herself. "I'm asking too many questions, aren't I—"

"No." He captured her free hand, the one that had been feeding him, the one that wasn't holding the plate. "Never. You can ask me anything."

It was his answers that he worried about.

"What happened to your boss afterward?" Her eyes held his own. "I just . . . I mean, I know he ended up in Caldwell, unless he started out here?"

For a moment, the past crowded in on him, muscling past his focus on her. "Sometimes I'm not even sure he's on the planet. He's mad at the world, consumed by revenge, frustrated with everything—I mean, he's needed by people he doesn't want to rely on him, he's choked by a legacy he's rejected, and on top of all that, he's . . ."

A killing machine.

That part Darius kept to himself.

"The big problem," he murmured as she fed him another "pig in a blanket," as she called them, "is that he's taking other people down with him. More than anything, that's what keeps me up at night. Sometimes you're in a role you inherited whether you want it or not. It's not fair. It's not right. But life isn't fair and it's not right, and yes, there are times when you lose a lottery you didn't want to enter. The trouble comes when . . ." *A whole species.* ". . . when whole families rely on you, so your future and your choices become theirs by default. I don't mean to minimize any of his suffering, but goddamn it, you do what you have to. You fucking take care of your business because that's just where you were put in this life."

Darius shut his mouth on a hard-and-fast. He hadn't expressed any of this to anybody, and now that he was letting the pent-up emotion out, he could feel a momentum getting started—and he didn't want to say too much.

"I can tell that you love him." As his eyes returned to hers, she nodded. "It's in the tone of your voice."

"Well, actually, that's the other problem . . ." Darius took a deep breath and swept his palm down his face. "Lately, I feel like I hate him."

Dropping his hand, he braced himself as he looked back at her. Except Anne wasn't showing judgment at the revelation. She was just patiently accepting him.

Then again, she did not know the full story—

"I think it's okay to hate someone you love." As his eyebrows went up, she shrugged. "Or rather, you can hold both emotions at once. One doesn't invalidate the other because they don't mix. It's like . . . oil and water for the heart. Incompatible and yet in the same container."

He searched her face. "I have so much guilt for how I feel . . . and I can't talk to anyone about this."

"I understand. It's a hard thing to admit to yourself, and people don't always understand, especially if they're looking at it from the outside." She pushed some crackers around the plate. "My father was an alcoholic. Not a mean one, mind you. He loved my mother and me, he just drank too much sometimes because . . . well, he was the life of every party and there is no turning that off sometimes." She smiled a little. "I remember watching him when they'd have people over. I would stay up late just so I could peek around the corner and listen to him tell stories. He had this one that everybody always asked to hear again, even if they'd heard it a hundred times. About our old dog Mike and the Thanksgiving turkey."

Darius rubbed his thumb over the palm of her hand. "Something tells me that doesn't end well for the bird."

"Or the pooch." Anne chuckled. "Poor Mike had the worst diarrhea. My father added a doggie door to the kitchen after that night—and honestly, as I state the facts of the story right now, I'm realizing it wasn't just what happened . . . it was the way he told it, you know?"

As she clearly dwelled in her own past, there was a special light in her eyes and her face, but he watched both fade, the sunshine eclipsed by darkness.

"My parents got into a car accident coming home one snowy night from a dinner out." Her breath shuddered as it left her now. "I was fifteen and allowed to stay alone, stay up late. I was excited they were gone because I got to make my own meal and feel all grown up." There was a long pause. "The police knocked on the door just before midnight. I was sleepy on the sofa in front of the TV, but not worried. My father could keep them out late, you know. It had happened before."

When she didn't go on, Darius closed his eyes. "What did the police tell you."

"My—ah, my father . . . was okay, but in the hospital. My mother was killed instantly. No seat belt." The sound she made could have meant a lot of things, all of them sad. "That night is why I don't have a car, actually. To this day, I don't drive. I don't want to be responsible for . . ."

Jesus, he thought. And he'd hit her with his own.

"Anne, listen, if this is too hard, you don't have to—"

"In the aftermath, my father was inconsolable." As she spoke over him, he knew that she was deep within herself.

"Me? I was crushed, but I also felt lucky I had a parent left. Except then . . . about two weeks later, he was charged with vehicular homicide because he'd been drunk at the time." Another pause. "He never told me he'd failed a sobriety test at the scene. He never . . . said anything about that. And you know, the night the accident happened, I'd told myself he wasn't, that he hadn't been drinking. I'd told myself it was December and the roads were icy and it wasn't his fault . . ."

Darius shook his head, and kept the cursing to himself.

"My father was sentenced to ten years in prison. Pre-trial, he was offered a plea deal, but he refused to admit guilt—in part because of me, I think. He would have gotten five years if he'd just taken what was presented to him, but he didn't want me to hear him admit to it." She shrugged. "I guess that's how I learned that you didn't have to be a mean drunk to be destructive. He killed his wife and my mother, and then ruined my life along with his own—and for what? A couple of jokes? A few pats on the back, some belly laughs? I would have taken a boring wallflower and kept my family any day of the week, thank you very much."

He imagined her so young, left to fend for herself in the world. "Where did you go?"

She took a deep breath, and exhaled slowly. "My grandparents on my mom's side raised me, and even though they didn't want me to, I tried to go see him several times. He refused the visits. He died about three years in of an overdose. He just couldn't live with himself."

Abruptly, she refocused on Darius. "So this is why I say . . . you can love someone and hate them at the same time."

Reaching out, he tucked her hair behind her ear. "I don't know what else to say other than I'm sorry. And . . . yes, you do know exactly how I feel."

Anne put the plate on the bedside table. Then she took his hand in both of hers.

"You know something?" she said.

"What."

"I didn't realize how lonely I've been . . ." Her eyes returned to his. "Until now."

Darius sat up slowly, struck by the realization that it was as if she were reading his mind—while thinking the same thing he was.

"Me, too. Anne . . . that's how I feel, too."

◆   ◆   ◆

It wasn't the amount of time spent with someone. It was the resonance of the moments you shared.

As Anne stared into the face of a stranger she'd known for such a short time, she felt like they'd been in each other's lives forever. She was also keenly aware of how much she kept from other people. In sharing her story with Darius—and not just the facts, but the feelings—she had lowered defenses that were so integral to her, she'd forgotten they existed.

"Anne . . ."

There was a lot in the way he said her name, and even though the logical part of her brain was telling her to go slowly, everything else inside her was clear that she had found in this man what she hadn't even been aware of searching for. The relationship with Bruce, if she could even call it that, had been performance art masquerading as an office romance. Spurred on by the likes of Penny and the other women on the support staff floor, she'd followed a path set by others: by the misplaced envy of those around her, by Bruce, with all his upward mobility . . . by the expectations that women needed to be married by the time they were twenty-five or their expiration date was triggered.

But there was no one else in her ear now.

It was just her and this man who was looking at her like he'd found something that surprised him as well.

"I want to kiss you," she whispered.

"Yes," he purred.

Darius's broad hand brushed her cheek and then lingered at her chin. And then he didn't have to draw her forward. She moved to him on her own, leaning into him, tilting her head.

The first contact was gentle, and his lips felt foreign in a shocking and tantalizing way, everything so soft and velvety. And in spite of his size, which seemed to quadruple before her very eyes, she wasn't threatened at all. On the contrary, she wanted to keep going from this electric starting place. She wanted him on top of her, his weight pressing her down into the mattress, her legs split around his hips, their bodies no longer clothed . . .

Darius inched back. "Is this okay? I don't want to push you."

Exploring his lower lip with her fingertips, she smiled. "If I'm honest, I've wanted to kiss you from the second I met you."

"Even in the back of that car, on the way to the hospital?"

"Okay, maybe the next night in my kitchen, how about that."

His hooded eyes flashed under those thick lashes. "Works for me."

When he eased forward once more, she met him halfway again, and their mouths re-fused. The plying sensation, the heat, the live-wire charge of the kissing disappeared the whole world, and she wanted the amnesia. She was starved for this removal from everything, from Bruce, from Thurston and his check, from Charlie in the back hallway, from Miss Martle and the beautiful receptionist with the coffee offer. She wanted no more of the bruises and aches that were dogging her, no more of the sense that she was working five days a week and paying her mortgage and not really getting ahead.

Her life had been a lonely dead end, and then everything had gotten scrambled in a bad way.

But kissing Darius felt like something truly good was happening in her life—and the hope and excitement were what had been absent from everything, including from the beginning with Bruce.

As they continued to learn each other's mouths, Darius's hand snuck around the nape of her neck, and things deepened, his tongue licking into her. God, what was that cologne he was wearing? It was the best thing she had ever smelled—

With a sharp jerk, he moved back and looked to the door. Which seemed to have magically shut itself.

"Fritz will be bringing down dinner soon," he said in a raspy voice.

"Oh, sorry—"

Without missing a beat, he took her lips like they were running out of time, and then he pulled her onto his chest, demanding something she was impatient to give him. The exploration over. Now it was bonfire time, the sexual burn engulfing them.

And suddenly, it wasn't just that the world went away.

The whole galaxy disappeared.

Wanting even more, Anne stretched out and urged him onto her, his upper body rolling in on command, a hint of the heft of him making her breath get tight—or maybe that was the raw need clawing into her core. The fit of him against her, his pecs pressing into her breasts, his shoulders so broad, his mouth insistent . . . it all felt inevitable, as if everything from the moment of impact in that street to this incendiary instant right now was on a single string of destiny, drawing them together.

Entwining them.

When he moved back now, it was slowly, with regret. "I could do this all night."

"Me, too."

His eyes were the most vivid blue she'd ever seen, and they got even more intense as he stroked her hair back with a delicate touch. That huge, powerful body of his was coiled with anticipation, but he held himself in check, chaining all that she could sense inside him.

She wanted him unleashed.

"Listen," he said quietly. "I know that you're just coming out of something that was at best complicated, at worst downright abusive. Me? I haven't had a serious relationship in . . . well, longer than I can remember. I guess what I'm trying to say is that I am really attracted to you, and I hope you'll give me a shot when you're ready to think like that again. Even if I'm just a rebound, I'll take it."

As she could only stare up at him, because she couldn't believe the good fortune of it all, he flushed and laughed awkwardly. "Too much? Too soon?"

She shook her head. "No. Not at all."

"Are you sure?"

"I was already wondering how to ask for a second date without coming across as desperate."

His chuckle rumbled in his chest. "Well, frankly, I'm impressed I waited this long—I was tempted to drop that speech over the soup in your kitchen last night."

Anne had a quick memory of him in the ER, sitting in the little chair next to her folded clothes and her one shoe, the shuffling hustle-and-bustle on the far side of the draping a dire kind of backdrop to what had felt, even then, like a movie with an epic romance. And then she remembered him standing outside her kitchen, on her little porch, her missing loafer in his hand, his face shadowed, yet full of what she now recognized as something she herself was feeling . . . namely the fragile hope that this was the beginning of something special.

In a life that seemed otherwise dreary.

She wasn't even going to worry about how this was happening or why. She hadn't asked those questions about Bruce, when all along she'd been unsure whether she had any true feelings for him.

So why the hell would she ask it now when this felt so right?

Putting her hand lightly on Darius's face, she let herself get lost in his hungry stare. "You're not a rebound. In fact, I feel like . . . you're the one I've been waiting for."

His smile was less an expression, more a glow from the soul. "Anne—"

At first, the sound that interrupted the urgent whisper of her name was so quiet, she couldn't place what it was. But as Darius's head wrenched around to the door, she realized the rhythmic beat was someone coming down the stone steps. Fast. And the footfalls were heavy, so it was definitely not the butler with dinner.

Before she could say something, the oak panels were shoved open without a knock or a hello—and even though she was prepared to not see the ancient butler in his formal black-and-white uniform . . . she was most certainly not ready for what stood in between the jambs.

The vicious-looking man was dressed in black leather from head to toe, and she knew without seeing what was under his jacket that he was armed. *Seriously* armed. But whatever weapons he was carrying on his body were not what scared her.

His icy pale eyes were the stuff of nightmares, cunning and cruel . . . utterly ruthless as they took in Darius and her, together on the bed.

Were those tattoos on his temple?

"Don't you knock," Darius said in a nasty tone of voice.

As he moved to shield her with his torso, he sounded like a totally different person. Looked like one, too, his brows drawn down over a stare that was outright aggressive.

Anne had to tilt to the side to look around his thick biceps.

The other man took out what appeared to be a hand-rolled cigarette and put it between gleaming white teeth. "Didn't know I needed an engraved invitation to come down here." A gold lighter spit out a little flame, and after he used it and clipped the top shut, he resumed speaking on the exhale. "Then again, you're not the type to be caught *in flagrante delicto*. At least not in the past."

Only one of his hands was gloved. In black leather, of course. The guy probably thought cotton or wool was too effeminate—heck, maybe chain mail was too girlie for him.

"I'll meet you upstairs," Darius said tightly.

"Not going to introduce me?"

"No, I'm not. Now get the hell out of here."

The black-haired man pointed behind himself with the cigarette. "Across the hall. I'll be waiting."

As the door to the room was closed with a smacking sound, Darius shut his eyes briefly. Then he sat up. Staring across at the heavy oak panels, he seemed to age before her very eyes, years multiplying until they were decades. Centuries.

Until his shoulders dropped, and his brows drew together out of exhaustion.

"I'm so sorry," he said remotely.

"Who is he?"

"Same night." He shook his head. "The same damn night."

"What?"

"V hasn't been here in how long?" Darius rubbed the back of his neck like he needed a chiropractor. "And he shows up on the one night you're here."

"Do you work with him?"

"In a manner of speaking." Darius glanced over. "I'll go get rid of him."

"Okay, but I can leave if you have something you need to—"

"Please. Stay."

Anne repositioned herself against the pillows, plumping one up to support her head. "All right."

The tension in his shoulders eased. "I won't be long, I promise."

"Take your time. I'll be right here."

Darius nodded, as if they'd struck some kind of deal. And then he marched out of the bedroom with such a stride, she almost felt badly for the man in black leather.

As the door was re-shut, she crossed her legs at the ankles and stared down the bed with its red-and-black satin duvet. Reaching out for the hors d'oeuvres, she helped herself to another pig in a blanket.

It was lukewarm.

And now tasted like cardboard.

But that was less about the food and its temperature . . . and more about whatever was happening across the hall.

CHAPTER ELEVEN

Darius hit the door to his bedchamber like it was an opponent, punching at the heavy weight before marching into his private quarters.

Over at his desk, Vishous, son of the Bloodletter, had taken a seat and was leaning back in the carved chair, his boots propped up on the blotter, a Cartier ashtray balanced on his abs.

"Surprise, surprise," the brother drawled after a puff of Turkish tobacco. "Interrupting you on a date."

"Fuck you," Darius said as he shut them in together.

The brow by the tattooed temple lifted, those diamond eyes gleaming with cold amusement. "I don't think I'm the one you want to screw. But you know me, I'm up for anything."

Darius's fangs tingled as they dropped down from his jaw. "Don't push me. I'm not in the mood."

Vishous's nostrils flared—and then he suddenly didn't look so self-satisfied. He was dumbfounded. "Wait a minute. Are you . . . have you bonded with her? Really?"

A shaft of anxiety shot down Darius's spine and landed in his partial erection. Surely he couldn't have— "I'm not dignifying that with an answer."

"You don't have to."

Darius stalked over to his bathroom and turned the light off. Just to give himself something to do—other than homicide. "Why the hell are you here. Instead of out stealing candy from babies and kicking puppies."

"I've turned over a new leaf." Vishous tapped his hand-rolled. "I'm now full of peace and love. A hippie."

"No more black wax, then?"

That eyebrow jogged. "So people have been talking about me again."

As exhaustion tackled Darius from behind, he felt like screaming in frustration, but lacked the energy. "Look, I'm not interested in your games or this bullshit back-and-forth—"

"There's been another induction ceremony."

Darius cursed. "Not again. Where."

"Farmhouse. About ten miles out of town." The other brother inhaled and talked through the smoke, as was his way. "As soon as I got into the field tonight, I tracked a new slayer. Still had dark hair and eyes. Before I stabbed him back to his unholy maker, I made him tell me where he'd gotten the black oil in his veins."

"How many were turned."

"Over a dozen."

"Oh, *shit*." Darius pulled a hand through his hair. "There was one last week, too."

"The Omega's on a roll." Vishous stabbed his cigarette out in the little porcelain basin. "I'm heading to the site now."

Darius shook his head, well aware of where this was going. "Why? It's already done. The Omega will be gone, the inductees, too—"

"I don't think so. The *lesser* was merely an hour or two past his induction. There could be others still recovering from the ceremony." The brother's voice lowered. "And you know how much I like to exercise—"

"You can't go alone."

"I wasn't asking for your permission."

"Well, I can't go out tonight. You need to get one of the others to back you up."

The brother cocked a brow. Then nodded toward the door. "Where did you find your little friend across the hall, by the way—"

Darius jabbed a finger at the male. "Watch your mouth."

"Watch your distractions."

"Distractions?" He went over to his desk, planted his palms, and leaned into them. "Are you saying I'm not completely committed to what's left of this race?"

"I'm not the one with a human under him—"

"I keep a light on for our fucking King. I built a house for all of us that no one in the Brotherhood goes to, much less lives in. I am the thread between the Old Country and this shit existence in the New World. And you have the *gall* to suggest I'm slacking because one night—one *fucking* night—I dare to have a personal life? How many females have you fucked in the last week."

"Females? I'm not sure. But I know there were seven males. No, eight if you count that blow job I got about two hours ago. And as for picking your date over that duty you talk so much about, don't bitch at me. I'm just a mirror for your choices." Vishous tossed the ashtray onto the blotter and sat up, planting his boots on the floor. "If I die tonight, your self-imposed guilt is your problem, no one else's."

Darius closed his eyes and tried not to lose it. "Do you know when the last time was that I . . . when the last night I . . ." He cleared his throat. "When I had a *moment* of peace. Just one fucking moment to myself? All I think about is the fucking war, and our fucking King, and our fucking species—I need a goddamn night off!"

As his voice got louder and louder, he didn't bother holding anything in—even though, of all the Brotherhood, the one you never wanted to show any emotion or weakness in front of was the fighter in front of him. Vishous was the smartest brother, a warrior with an intellect honed like the daggers he sharpened, a male who had no mercy for anything or anyone. Including himself.

Whatever you showed him of your underbelly would go into his toolbox, and it would be used at some future time. To his benefit.

But Darius couldn't give a shit about that right now.

"I'm tired of fucking everything tonight." Except for the woman across the hall. "And I don't have anything left to give you, or the Brotherhood."

Vishous got to his feet. But instead of laying on the sarcasm, he kept his voice level. "This is wartime, D. There's no peace for any of us. So when it comes to going off-duty, you're never going to get a quarter from the likes of me, sorry."

Oddly, the apology part seemed sincere for once.

"Is this ever going to end," Darius wondered out loud.

"Yes."

"Because of that stupid *Dhestroyer* prophecy? Jesus Christ, that old yarn is nothing but folklore." He glanced to his closed chamber door. "But I'm still not going with you tonight."

When Vishous's unrelenting stare didn't change focus, Darius rolled his eyes. "What. Just say it. Although the shit talk better not be about her."

After a moment, the brother moved around the desk. "I didn't come here to get you to hold my hand when I go check out that induction site."

As a sudden feeling of dread hit Darius like a tank, he tried to keep his face in a mask that gave nothing away. "Why did you come, then."

Even though . . . he knew. Vishous's reputation preceded him not just when it came to snarkiness and sexual matters of an unconventional nature. There was also a lot of talk about his second sight, his visions of the future.

They were only ever of death.

"Well, get on with it," Darius said hoarsely. "Tell me what you saw."

"Sometimes people don't want to know."

"Then why give me a choice."

"Because sometimes they want to know."

Darius had the strangest sense that the pronouns had changed because the brother was distancing himself.

"So what's it going to be, D. What do you want to do."

In the silence that followed, the only thought that went through Darius's head . . . was that he wondered what Anne would choose for herself. What she would suggest he choose.

"Think about it." Vishous stepped by him. "Let me know—"

"Iwanttoknow."

The brother slowly turned. And as those diamond eyes swung around, they seemed to glow with an otherworldly light.

After what felt like an eternity, Vishous said in a grave voice, "I saw you engulfed in the sun, with flames surrounding you. *Click* . . ."

"Click?"

"That was the sound before the sun came for you. *Click.*" Vishous frowned and rubbed his tattooed temple. "It was like a mechanical sound. And then . . . the sun."

"So I opened a window? A door?" Darius shook his head. "Impossible. I'm not suicidal. I'm never doing that during the daytime."

"It wasn't daytime."

"Sure it was. That's when the sun's out." As he thought more about it, he exhaled in relief. "Jesus, you scared the shit out of me. And I'll be extra careful from sunrise to sundown. Thank you."

Riding a wave of buzzy emotion, he pulled Vishous in for a hard embrace. Then he set the brother back.

"And please don't go to that farmhouse alone," he told the male. "The Omega could be there."

"You just said there was no reason to go because he and his inductees would be gone."

"I lied. You know where Tohrment lives. Go and find him—better that you stay alive to fight than get yourself killed by trying to add a slayer or two more to your belt all by your lonesome." When Vishous opened his mouth, Darius cut in. "No, I'm serious. Don't do anything too risky, we need you."

"I always thought you disliked me," came the dry response.

"Of course I don't like you." Darius leaned in and spoke out of the corner of his mouth. "News flash, nobody likes you."

V leveled a hard stare. "Stop with the compliments, you're making me blush."

"But you're very useful. Not as decorative as Rhage, but very useful." Darius clapped the brother on the biceps. "Now go find Tohr. And have fun, but be safe—and don't come down here again without calling ahead first."

As Darius opened the door, Vishous said roughly, "It was raining. Before the sun . . . there was rain. And I'm telling you, it was night."

Darius regarded the brother across the distance that separated them. "Then your vision was wrong for once. That great glowing fireball in the sky only comes out in the daytime. But hey, I'll be careful—and so will you. Say hello to Tohr for me. He's such a male of worth."

✦   ✦   ✦

As time slowed to a crawl, Anne had to force herself to sit up off the pillows and stop with the nervous munching. With her feet dangling off the side of the bed, she looked back at the headboard. She wasn't sure what kind of antique wood it was made out of, but the carvings went so deep, she could put her fingers into the pattern of relief.

After a moment of inspection, she decided it was the depiction of a garden of fecund fruit trees.

She glanced down at the mattress. Was this a baby-making shrine or something?

Hopping off, there was a good distance to the floor, and she landed on the jewel-toned carpet with a grunt. To loosen up her sore hip and leg, she wandered over to the oil paintings that hung from hooks drilled into the black rock. The lake scenes reminded her of the Adirondacks, green mountains rising up from basins of crystal clear water, humans, if there were any, so small by comparison. Set in gold frames, the works of art were clearly masterpieces.

"John Frederick Kensett, Lake George, eighteen sixty-nine," she read aloud.

Not a clue who that was, but she'd been right about the luminous location. As she strolled to the next one, the gilded nameplate read "Thomas Cole." There was an Albert Bierstadt. A Thomas Davies.

She felt like she was in a museum—

Stopping, she focused on a cluster of three vases that were sitting on a pedestal table. Of all the objects in the room, at least one of the triplet didn't fit with the antique decor. The capped container was cheap and swimming pool blue. And the two it was with may have been old, but there was an equal ugliness to them.

She picked up the one that seemed like you could find in a kitchen store—

"Sorry about that—"

As Darius reentered the bedroom, she wheeled around—and in the process, lost her grip on the vase. Though she instantly tried for a regrab, gravity did its job, and as luck would have it, the thing landed not on the Persian rug, but on the bare rock floor that ringed the beautiful carpet. The shatter was spectacular, the china breaking open, shards going flying—

"No!" Darius barked as she dropped down. "Don't touch it!"

"I'm so sor—oh, my God." Anne recoiled and plugged her nose. "What is that *smell?*"

Darius dragged her back and put his body between her and the broken vase. "Shit."

Anne frowned. A black and glossy substance was oozing all over the pieces of pottery, and that wasn't all. There was something else there, something that struck her as horrifying—

"Is that a heart?" she breathed.

As her stomach rolled, she looked into Darius's face. His features were composed into a mask, but his eyes were pits of regret.

Drawing her back, he opened his mouth. Closed it. Then he looked over at the mess on the floor again. "Stay here. Do *not* go near that thing."

He disappeared out of the bedroom and shouted up the stairs. There was a pause—and then the thundering sound of him taking the stone steps two at a time dimmed as he ascended.

Anne glanced back at the black spill.

Every cell in her body began to vibrate in warning, and she moved even farther away. Yet the oily substance was strangely hypnotic, the way it pooled on the gray stone almost sensuous . . . like it was alive, like it was enticing her to—

Anne gasped as Darius pulled her back into the center of the room. And to think she hadn't realized she'd gotten that close.

"Listen, I need to . . ." he started.

There was a pause. And then he urged her all the way out of the room, out into the little hallway at the base of the stairs. Meanwhile, her eyes remained locked on the remains of the cheap blue vase, and what seemed to be a heart . . . and that blood-like ooze.

The door shut, closing off her view.

"Listen," he began again. "I hate to do this, but something's come up. And I can't—I have to go. There's just—I hate this, but if I don't go with my bro—friend, rather, he's going to be in danger, and as much as I'm trying to convince myself it's not my problem—I'm worried no one else will think it's theirs."

Anne tried to focus on Darius's words, but every time she blinked, she just saw that glossy black oil undulating over the uneven contours of the stone floor. Like it was trying to get to her—

"Anne?"

His face took over her field of vision, so close to her own that he encompassed everything.

"*Anne.*"

She jerked herself back to attention. "I'm so sorry. I don't know what's gotten into me."

As his mouth flattened into a grim line, he shook his head. "I have to go help my friend. Otherwise, he's going to do something really stupid on his own."

"Oh." She nodded. "Sure. Of course."

"I can have Fritz take you home—"

"The butler."

"Yes, he can give you a ride—"

"Oh, no, I'll just get another cab." When he cursed, she took his hand and got with the program. "It's okay. And I understand—"

"Or you can stay here." Before she could respond, he jumped in, "You're safe in this house. Fritz loves company, and you could just wait a little bit until I come back? I really don't want this night to end, but especially not like this, me all rushing out. So you could stay here—actually, please, stay here. I won't be gone any longer than absolutely necessary."

Anne told herself to say no, thank you, and no, she'd just call a cab, and no, she wasn't going to wait, and no . . .

"All right."

Darius's expression eased, a smile replacing some of the stress. "That's great—that's just . . . thank you."

The idea that her presence meant so much to him made

her feel important. And then his lips were on hers, a warm brush.

"I'll be as fast as I can." He glanced back at the broken vase. "But you can't stay in this room. Go upstairs while I change and Fritz cleans this up?"

"Okay, I will."

She smiled a little and turned away—

Strong arms brought her back against a strong body, and Darius bent her off-balance, holding her weight easily.

"I'll be counting the minutes," he murmured.

And then he kissed the ever-living shit out of her.

When he finally set her back on her feet, they were both breathing heavily.

"As soon as I get home, I'm going to . . ." His voice trailed off, and his eyes raked her from head to foot, their intensity making her feel naked. In a good way. "You know what, I better stop that sentence right there."

Anne pretty much floated out to the bottom of the stairs. Glancing over her shoulder, she saw him silhouetted in the open doorway—and she was never going to forget the way he stared at her: He made her feel beautiful, in a more-than-skin-deep kind of way.

For a sizzling moment, she wanted to say something alluring, something that might have come out of the mouth of, say, Sophia Loren or Elizabeth Taylor.

Instead, she just smiled again and started her ascent out of the cellar. Maybe the mystery would be sexy enough. Then again . . . given how he looked at her? Maybe she was enough just the way she was.

And as Anne continued to put one foot in front of the

other, and passed by the lanterns, and felt remarkably un-weird about staying in the house of a relative stranger with the man's boss's butler . . .

. . . neither the vampire who had offered her his hospital-ity nor she herself, who had accepted the invitation, knew that her life had been saved by her decision to remain.

CHAPTER TWELVE

As Darius re-formed in a stand of bushes that had all the ocular appeal of a ball of scrap metal, he really didn't want to hear one goddamn word from Vishous about his change of mind. He was currently in a mood that vacillated between nasty and murderous, and while that was helpful on the job, it was also an incendiary pendulum on a good night, a real frickin' joy when you were working an induction scene with the likes of V.

Especially after you'd just left a woman you'd much rather be with back at home while your butler cleaned up a *lesser* mess.

Fortunately, as the brother materialized beside him, V didn't seem to be interested in any off-topic conversation about U-turns, and what a blessing from the Virgin Scribe.

Yes, Anne was important—too important, really—but the sight of that *lesser* blood on the floor of the chamber had been what shocked Darius back to his priorities.

And of course there was no way V would have gone and gotten Tohr.

Good thing Anne had been willing to stay.

"A hundred yards this way," V said as he palmed two of his guns and started off through the brambles and trees.

Talk about your unnecessary directions. Darius could already scent the baby powder on the breeze, the stench firing him up, not that he needed much help with that. He was beyond ready to fight, and praying they'd find some stragglers—and unlike his fellow fighter, he had daggers in his hands, not guns. He wanted to get up close and personal to his prey.

Maybe he'd use his teeth, too.

Moving silently, they were draped in shadow, the heavy cloud cover working in their favor and blocking out the moonlight. About fifty yards farther in, the forest thinned and a decrepit two-story structure presented itself in the middle of a clearing. With a crumbling chimney, numerous broken windows, and siding that looked as if its paint had been sandblasted off in sections, the structure listed to the left.

So it wasn't just cosmetically run down, there were issues with its very foundation.

Trying not to think about parallels to the species, Darius quickened his pace, aware that the pair of them were sitting ducks as they broke free of their cover. Closing in, the stench of *lessers* got louder and louder in the nose, until he had to rub things to keep from sneezing out his frontal lobe. And then they were right up to the rear of the farmhouse. Without any words, he and Vishous communicated using hand signals, one of them going right, the other left.

Circling around the flank, Darius monitored the busted glass frames of the windows, his hearing supercharged to pick up even the slightest movement inside. Around him. Above him.

As he came to the far corner, he put his back against the aged siding.

He waited long enough to be sure that there was no ambush. Yet.

Then he jumped out.

The front of the farmhouse had once sported a covered porch; now there was just a pile of vine-choked kindling on the ground and a collapsed roof section hanging off the eaves. The disintegration of the proverbial welcome mat hadn't stopped people from going inside, however. The overgrown circular drive had been ripped apart by the tires of God only knew how many vehicles, the deep grooves carved through the tangled weeds and spotty dirt patches suggesting that, at least on the departure, people had been in a hurry to get the fuck out of Dodge.

Then again, the Omega didn't exactly greet his new recruits with a handshake and a fruit basket—

A flash of movement to the left brought Darius's head around. But it was only Vishous stepping free from the opposite side.

V held up two fingers, then tapped over his eyebrow. When Darius nodded, the male dematerialized to case the second floor.

Crouching down, Darius ducked under what was left of the porch's overhang and did his best to navigate through the salad of rotted two-by-fours, framing beams, and flooring lengths. A couple of times, his boots splintered what he stepped on and his crotch nearly got spanked twice.

So much for the stealth approach. Any more noise and he could have brought a marching band with him—and in retrospect, he should have dematerialized through one of the windows on the side. When he finally waded through the morass, he found the front door lying flat on the floor of the modest foyer, as if it had fallen in—or been kicked in off its hinges. And oh, God, the smell of baby powder and fresh blood and new death was so thick, it felt like a fog in his lungs, like he shouldn't be able to see through the air.

His eyes were working just fine, though . . . so he got a clear visual at all the drywall buckets stationed in the various rooms. They were filled with human blood, but the shit was also everywhere, splashed on the floors, speckling the walls . . . there were even spots of it on the ceilings.

As he moved through the first floor, he took cover behind doorjambs, corners, and the stairs, his boots leaving prints in the congealing puddles that had formed—and not everything was red. The Omega's black, oily essence was all over the place, too. Then again, no one had ever accused the evil of being a nasty neat when he was turning humans into soulless vampire killers.

Coming up to what had been a pantry, he looked through into a kitchen that still had appliances from the forties—

Creak!

Darius wheeled around, and in mid-spin, threw his dagger at a hulking shape that had snuck up behind him in the shadows.

Slap!

The instant he heard a pair of palms clap together, he knew who it was. God*damn* it. He'd rather have run into a squadron of *lessers*—

A figure stepped out into full view, and sure enough, Darius's dagger was caught between hands that were directly in front of the rib cage the black blade would have pierced. The scarred vampire behind the wartime parlor trick was thinner than he should have been by at least fifty pounds, but his big frame was nonetheless powerful—and he wasn't wearing a coat or a jacket even though there was a chill in the air. Accordingly, an arsenal was on full display, the weapons that were belted and strapped on freely visible instead of hidden.

"Zsadist."

Even though the two of them were brothers by virtue of being in the Black Dagger Brotherhood, there was no flash of recognition in the empty, shark-like black eyes staring back at him.

Then again, verticality and animation aside, the male was not in fact alive. And hadn't been for years and years.

Darius focused on the S-shaped scar that ran down that too-lean face and distorted his mouth. Then he looked at the tattooed slave band that marked the neck like an iron collar.

"You should have announced it was you. I could have killed you—"

As the male stalked forward, Darius shifted his remaining blade from his right hand to his left, dominant grip. Just in case. But the brother merely stopped about five feet away—and dearest Virgin Scribe, those bottomless-pit eyes gleamed with menace: Of all the Brotherhood, Zsadist was the most dangerous, capable of killing at a moment's provocation or impulse, and not because he was hungry or protecting something or doing a job.

Because he liked it.

And no one was quite sure where he drew the line when it came to friends and foes—

Footfalls on the stairs announced Vishous's descent, and at the base of the steps, he stopped, and didn't put his guns back in their holsters. He just stayed right there, his stare locked on what should have been backup for them, but might as well be another enemy.

"Where's your twin," Darius asked Zsadist.

"Right here," came a rough reply.

Phury stepped inside the house from the front entryway, and he was as he always appeared to be: exhausted and wrung out. Also as usual, his yellow eyes were focused only on his blooded brother. Then again, Zsadist was brutally unpredictable and some things were responsibilities whether you wanted them to be or not. Whether you had the strength for them or not.

After years of being used as a blood slave, the scarred male had no conscience or morality, anything resembling either of those things having been raped and beaten out of him by his Mistress and her guards. His rescue had resulted in Phury losing part of a leg, and Zsadist falling into the salty ocean and being mutilated for life. So they were both screwed by destiny.

It was a sad state of affairs. And a deadly one.

On that note, Zsadist's palms rotated from the vertical to the horizontal. And then he lifted the top one and presented Darius's black dagger back to its owner—who promptly took the weapon.

His vacant stare shifted over to Vishous.

And then, without a word, like the wraith he was, he dematerialized.

Darius let out an exhale. "Jesus."

"I have to go," Phury muttered. "I'm not sure how he found out about this place."

"We'll take care of everything here." Darius glanced at V, who nodded in return. "You just take care of your twin."

"Would that that were possible."

As the brother dematerialized as well, Vishous came forward, stepping around a bucket of human slop. And another. And a third.

Putting one of his guns away, he lit up a hand-rolled. "Didn't expect Z'd be the one we needed backup against."

"He must have caught a new slayer tonight, too."

"Bet that interrogation got messy."

"You're saying yours wasn't?"

"Touché."

Darius kept both daggers in his hands as he went over

to some discarded clothes. Riffling through the jackets and the shirts, he found no IDs, and yet he lingered over the pile. Something was ringing in the back of his head, some kind of instinct or reminder. Then again, maybe it was just residual adrenaline burping out of his endocrine system.

"We're going to have to do something about this," Vishous said from the kitchen's archway.

"Well, you still believe in the prophecy. Don't you?"

"I'm not talking about the Omega."

Rising to his feet, Darius glanced across the induction site—and wished they could argue over something as simple as the root of all evil. "You can't kill a member of the Brotherhood. It's against the Old Laws."

"This is the New World. And who's checking anyway."

"You just can't. Even if it's Zsadist."

Those diamond eyes narrowed, the tattooed warning at the fighter's temple distorting. "You think it's productive for you and me to be worried about whether one of our own is going to go haywire and hurt us? We shouldn't have to defend ourselves against a brother."

"You kill him, you're killing Phury, too. We lose two."

"No, we get rid of a threat that's a deadly distraction, and if that twin of his self-destructs in the aftermath, that's collateral damage for the greater good. Besides, like Phury does anything but protect that sociopath?"

"There is no greater good." Darius kicked one of the buckets, the congealing red blood sloshing up the sides. "To any of this."

And that was the problem, wasn't it.

"Is the second floor clear?" he asked.

"Yeah." Vishous exhaled a stream of that Turkish smoke. "The Omega had his fun and games with them on one of the mattresses. It looks like a scene from a snuff film up there."

Glancing around, Darius felt like he was getting nowhere in life. "Time to get rid of the evidence," he muttered.

"I don't have any bombs on me."

"I'll get what we need," he said as he dematerialized.

◆   ◆   ◆

When Darius re-formed, it was in the back of his own property, by the detached garage. And as soon as he was fully corporeal, he intended to set out for what he'd come to get. But then he looked at the rear door.

Drawn forward, he was a moth to a flame.

Through the windows, he could see into the kitchen, and this was why he was snared: Fritz and Anne were sitting across from each other at the casual dining table, plates off to one side, fans of cards held up in front of them.

Frowning, his first thought was . . . how in the hell had she gotten that traditional *doggen* to eat with her? And now it looked like she was teaching the old male gin rummy?

Anne let out a sudden laugh, throwing her head back— and Fritz smiled sheepishly as he pointed a gnarled finger at the draw pile. When she nodded, he took a card, and as he figured out where to put it into his fan, she absently sipped from her glass. Then he said something, and she clapped with approval.

As Fritz flushed with happiness, his face showed a kind of joy that Darius couldn't remember ever seeing on the butler's face.

Without a conscious cue, Darius's hand reached up and rested on the old antique glass—

The moment he made contact, the butler glanced over, as if he had sensed his master's presence—and Darius shook his head sharply. With a subtle nod, Fritz resumed his concentration on the card game.

I should go . . . Darius told himself.

And yet as he stared at Anne, he couldn't seem to move—especially as he realized . . . she was what was missing in his life. She was his greater good, his higher calling. Forsaken by his King, and disaffected by his larger purpose for the race, he knew that he could be in service to this human female. Yes, he could take care of her . . .

He *would* take care of her.

As he smelled dark spices in the cool spring air, he knew that Vishous was right and the bonding had locked him in—but that really wasn't a news flash. The difference now was that he didn't mind the shackles. Not at all.

Turning away from the window, he marveled at the way the Scribe Virgin worked, how that sacred female he didn't particularly care for or think about much had nonetheless managed to provide him what he needed to go on.

This destiny with Anne was going to sustain him.

Yes, it was.

On that note, he got his hustle on so he could return to her.

Going through the side door into the garage, he was so

distracted by thoughts of fate and the human female at his kitchen table that the sight of his ruined brand-new BMW barely registered—except then it dawned on him that the steel-and-leather projectile had set him on his present course with Anne.

To show his thanks for the sacrifice it had made, he paused and put his hand on the crinkled hood.

Then he went to the rear of the garage and picked up two gasoline tanks. This wasn't going to take long, and thank God for it.

Closing his eyes, he dematerialized back to the farm-house's side flank. Glancing up at the flaking and pitted expanse, he wondered if the humans who had shown up here during the day had had any idea what they were signing on for. Usually, the *Fore-lesser* in charge snowed them, making all kinds of false promises . . . only to serve the duped masses up like finger food to the Omega: Whenever the Brotherhood interrogated a slayer, nine times out of ten, they cried about how they'd been double-crossed, lied to, tortured—and ultimately forced to kill vampires. Except that kind of verbal diarrhea couldn't be an excuse when he and his brothers had to bury innocents. Track down their parents. Destroy lives by sharing tragic news.

Not when every time you entered that cycle of death and grief, a little piece of you died, too, because you were supposed to be the one protecting the species—and clearly you and your fellow fighters were doing a shit job of it.

Refocusing, he wasn't about to battle past the mess around the front door this time. Darius dematerialized through the fragments of a window—and what do you know. Vishous was where he'd left him, smoking at the foot of the stairs, those diamond eyes circling the desecration with a notable lack of interest.

Like he might as well have been waiting for a bus. Or maybe a pizza.

When Darius tossed one of the cans over, the brother caught the red handle easily; then he put his cigarette butt out on the tread of his shitkicker and headed up for the second floor. It didn't take long to douse both levels, the sweet bloom of the gasoline fumes mixing with the stench of *lesser* blood. The nose cocktail was both familiar and awful, and Darius got himself out as soon as he could.

Re-forming on the overgrown, torn-up lawn next to the front porch, he had to wait for only a second or two before Vishous appeared next to him. The prevailing wind was blowing at their backs, carrying the odor into the farmland to the east, so they had to move quick. Humans were known to be nosy.

Har-har.

Without a word of discussion, Vishous put a fresh cigarette between his lips, lit the thing, and took a long draw on his hand-rolled. Then he flicked the butt into the air, the tiny torch getting caught by the breeze, and carried, end over end, through one of the parlor's open windows.

The combustion was instantaneous, the fireball blowing out the remaining intact windows in the room and licking up the sides of the house's lower level, its brilliance lighting the surrounding landscape bright as noontime—

A cold rush of warning shot through Darius, sure as if someone had drawn him a road map that led to his own grave and asked him what the destination was going to be:

A second sun, not during the day.

"Holy shit!" he hollered. "We gotta move! The second floor is going to explode!"

Grabbing on to his brother's jacket, he yanked at the male. "Run, it's going to kill us! This is your vision!"

V started to argue, but then something clearly clicked in his head. With a powerful surge, both of them lunged into a retreat, but the forward momentum didn't last long. Darius's boot got locked into some kind of gopher hole, and as his weight pitched forward, a great woofing sound permeated the acreage as oxygen was sucked into the farmhouse—

Just as he landed hard on his chest, Vishous grabbed him around the waist and hefted him up off the ground— and as Darius's boot came free, the other brother ran like a bat out of hell.

Until suddenly, he didn't have to run anymore.

The second explosion was so great, it sent them both airborne, the hot breath of a dragon more deadly than Rhage's curse ushering them into flight. Propelled over the ground, Darius had an impression of scrubby weeds moving underneath his body and then the tire gouges in the driveway rushed up to eat him.

He landed on a skid, tasting dirt and getting punched in the eye with a stray rock—

Jesus, the heat of the blaze was so great, he could feel it even from this distance—

"You're on fire!" Vishous shoved him over. "Roll! Roll!"

Oh. So he was the source of the roasty-toasty.

As he struggled to follow orders, he had to rely on

Vishous for most of the rotation, his vision going sky to earth to sky to earth to sky to earth while he was pushed along, the bonfire that was still on him spinning with—

Eventually, he threw an arm out and stopped it all. Making one last quarter turn, he settled on his side—and just happened to be facing the farmhouse.

Billowing black and gray smoke curled up into the dull night sky, orange and yellow flames tickling the undersides of the clouds that coalesced over the inferno. And goddamn, he could swear that just looking at it all made his back feel hotter.

"We gotta get out of here," Vishous said. "The humans are going to come, especially if this spreads to the forest."

"Okay."

Except when Darius went to sit up, he felt like someone had draped his shoulders and spine in a cape of pain, the contours of his upper torso a tuning fork for agony.

"Shit," he breathed as he collapsed onto his side once more. "I don't think I can dematerialize."

Vishous's face appeared before his own. "Are you sure?"

Darius closed his eyes and tried to concentrate through the waves of pain. Willing himself to ghost away, to lose his corporeality, to become nothing more than a scatter of component molecules . . .

He opened his lids. "I'm . . . fucked." As V cursed, he could only nod. But then he added, "At least I'm alive, so your vision didn't come true, right?"

"Alive for now," Vishous hedged as the flames created restless shadows on his face. "My vision had rain in it. Only the explosion part was right here. This . . . is not where you end."

CHAPTER THIRTEEN

"Y ou won! Yes, you won!"

As Anne reached across the kitchen table and gathered up the cards, her gin rummy pupil was looking as if he had a sunrise in his old face. And you know, she had to smile as well. The idea that there was a place in such a grand, formal house to play a little game and snack on some finger food and have a good laugh with someone's butler?

Well, she supposed it was no more impossible than her getting hit by a BMW and meeting a man she had a true, honest connection with.

"Oh, I am most excited to have prevailed!" Abruptly, Fritz looked worried. "Is that not rude, however, mistress?"

"To win and be happy about it? It's not rude at all. It's the point!" She started to shuffle. "And if it makes you feel better, I'm taking no small amount of pride in my teaching ability—"

The back door opened and a huge figure dressed in black entered—except it was not the one she'd been waiting to see, not the blue-eyed man who had kissed her as if she were the most precious thing he had ever held in his arms.

It was the other man. The one with the cold, pale eyes, and the tattoos at his temple, and the jet-black hair.

The butler immediately stood up from his chair, all levity and delight gone. "Am I summoning the van, sire?"

"Yes. *Now.*"

As Fritz headed into a back closet, Anne slowly got to her feet. "What's happening. Is Darius all right?"

The other bodyguard looked through her, not at her, as if she were nothing that mattered to him—so she was surprised when he replied. "We're going to bring him home."

"Is he alive?" she croaked.

"He's going to be okay. He just can't—" The man stopped as the butler came back with keys in his hand.

"I'm coming with you." She knocked over a chair as she jumped forward. "I have to help—"

The man in black leather jabbed a forefinger at her. "You are staying here. If you think I'm going to allow you into the field of combat, you're out of your mind. He'd kill me, and he'd be right to do it—"

"I'm coming—"

Annnnnnd that was how she ended up with a gun in her face. As she gasped, and couldn't believe she was staring into the black hole of a muzzle, the man growled, "You're staying here. I don't have time to change your mind in a civilized way. If you want to see him alive, you will sit your ass back down at that table and fucking wait. I'm not debating you on this."

Justlikethat, he was out the door.

The butler paused and cleared his throat, as if he wanted to make some kind of a polite excuse for the Smith & Wesson exclamation point that had just been put in her puss. But then he seemed to abandon that impulse.

"I shall bring your male home to you, mistress," he said. "I promise you. But the sire is right. It is safer for you here. Please remain."

Then he was gone as well, shutting the door behind himself.

Heart in her throat, Anne raced over and looked through a window. Within seconds, one of the detached garage's bays started to open, and then a black box van shot forward down the driveway like whoever was behind the wheel had punched the accelerator. Its headlights were off, and as it ripped by her, she could see only Fritz in the glow of the dashboard. Maybe the other one, with the gun, was in the back.

Moving quickly, tripping over her feet, she tracked the red taillights through the house, jogging down the kitchen, passing through a connecting room, jumping out into the dining room. The windows on the far side of the grand and glossy table looked into the front yard, and she raced for them, just catching a glimpse of the van as it disappeared down the hill on the road.

Leaning against the window's jamb, she stared into the

street. There wasn't a lot of traffic, only one other car going by ... now a second. And then nothing.

Except for the pounding of her heart. *Thump, thump, thump* ...

She glanced back at the formal table. Two beautiful place settings had been arranged at the other end, the china and crystal and sterling silver flatware like something out of a book on royalty. There was even an arrangement of fresh flowers, and a matched set of candlesticks, and silver salt and pepper shakers ...

It was the promise of a lovely evening that would not be fulfilled.

Because Darius must have been hurt in some way. Seriously.

As worry threatened to consume her, time slowed down, but not in the way it had when he'd been kissing her. This crawl of minutes was not something to relish, not a brush of the forever that was found in the magical moments when two people explored a sexual charge. This was torture. She felt as though she was going to be here for the rest of her life, waiting for bad news.

What the hell had happened—

Combat.

From out of her panic, the word burst into her brain, and brought along with it the preamble "field of."

The man in leather had used the term. But why were bodyguards going into a field of combat? That was for military people in active war zones. And where the heck was a war zone in Caldwell, NY?

Maybe she'd misunderstood.

As the silence of the mansion bore down on her, there was no one she could call for advice, and not just right now but also tomorrow, the day after, in the future at large. She had no family, no real friends.

Like Penny at the law firm was an option? And Charlie had been helpful with the Bruce problem as it related to work, but she was not about to go to him with her personal life.

A third car went by, the glare of its headlights illuminating the undersides of the trees that crowned the road. She imagined the sedan was a Mercedes. Or maybe another BMW like Darius's boss's. Maybe it was even fancier, something with an exotic name and an astronomical price tag—

They shouldn't bring him back here if he was hurt badly. Darius needed to be taken to a hospital, especially considering his collapse earlier . . .

It was hard to pinpoint exactly when she realized that she wasn't alone. The awareness was so gradual, it was as if someone had turned up the temperature in the room degree by degree, the warmth rising gently, imperceptibly. Eventually, however, that which was not noticed became readily apparent, and Anne straightened from her lean. Turned her head. Searched the well-lit dining room, from that twenty-five-hundred-foot-long table, to the sideboards with their gleaming silver accessories, to the hearth with its carved marble contours.

"Hello?" she said.

With a frown, she checked the street again . . . except no, that was not where the sense of a presence was coming from.

Someone was in the house.

"Hello."

As her heart started to thunder again, her ears rang in alarm. The mansion had struck her as deluxe and elegant from the moment she'd walked in . . . but suddenly, it seemed like a labyrinth of hidden spaces concealing threats.

Walking off from the window, she passed through the archway of the foyer—

Anne gasped and put her hand to her throat.

Across the way, in the peach-colored parlor with its portrait of a lady over the mantel and its flanking floral silk sofas, a figure . . .

. . . was hovering *above* the Persian carpet.

Draped in head-to-toe black robes, with a face that was completely covered, whoever it was didn't have feet. At least not that Anne could see. Instead, it seemed to be floating on a bright white energy source that poured out from beneath the hem of those falls of midnight fabric.

Anne should have been terrified. But she was not.

Somehow, it was impossible to be afraid. As strange as the . . . whatever it was . . . was.

"Hello . . ." she whispered.

As if summoned, her feet moved of their own volition, carrying her across the foyer to the lovely flower-scented room, her involuntary promenade halting just inside the carved arches of the ladies' parlor.

Greetings, a female voice said in her head.

"My name is Anne," she mumbled for no good reason.

Yes, it is, the figure confirmed.

"What are you—"

No questions. I do not entertain inquiries of any sort.

"Sorry." Anne cleared her throat. "Am I . . ."

Well, she didn't know what to say if she couldn't ask anything. So she just shut the hell up. Clearly, this was a dream—maybe the whole night was a dream? Either way, she knew deep down in her consciousness that the figure standing—*hovering*—before her was a foundational mystery, something god-like and powerful, something that defied explanation to such a degree there was no reason to try to put words to its definition or existence.

He has had a crisis of faith, the figure announced telepathically. *In his heart and his soul. And he is important to me. He keeps them all together, you see; he is the glue that binds the fragments of what once was a whole.*

"Darius," Anne breathed.

You were not what I had in mind, hardly a solution I would ever have chosen, especially for him. But even I must at times accept the whims of Fate as determined by my father, the Creator. The figure came forward, wafting toward her. *And as you shall affect the course of things, therefore I shall affect the course of you.*

The sleeve of the robe lifted and a glowing hand emerged.

Anne jumped and looked down at herself. As a strange feeling curled in her abdomen, she covered her lower belly with her palms.

You already love him, the female voice intoned. *Do not try to talk yourself out of it. And your body is ready for the future.*

"What are you—"

No questions, child. I shall not remind you again.

There was a long moment of silence . . . and then Anne had a sudden conviction that she understood everything, a kind of universal awareness opening up in her mind and her heart. And yet she was totally confused.

Do not talk yourself out of it. You are upon your destiny, child, and you shall carry within your womb the future Queen.

"Oh, God," Anne croaked.

The destiny of the species shall be borne from you, and then I shall welcome you unto the Fade. So shall my will proclaim, so shall it be.

Although the figure had arrived gradually, it departed in a snap, the presence vanishing before her very eyes.

As Anne blinked in bewilderment, a gonging started going off and she spun around. The grandfather clock against the wall was chiming the hour—and she couldn't understand what it was reporting. Nine o'clock? But that wasn't possible. She and the butler had started playing cards at just after seven p.m. and it had been around seven forty-five or eight when that other man had come and said Darius was injured.

After which, she had walked to the front of the house and watched the van leave, and then minutes later, she had discovered she wasn't alone.

It was as if that . . . thing . . . had sucked time out of the world by its presence.

"I am losing my mind—"

A door opened in the back of the house, and she heard voices.

"Anne?" came the sweetest sound she had ever heard.

For a split second, the dreamscape and reality collided,

and like her accident, things were injured—specifically her sense that there was any logic to any part of this. And then she didn't care about what was reasonable or not.

"Darius!" she called out as she wheeled around and started to run to him.

◆   ◆   ◆

It was not exactly the reunion Darius had wanted. As he and Vishous turned sideways so that they could shuffle through the back door of his house, he wished he were coming in under his own full steam, walking tall and straight.

As opposed to draped on his brother like Vishous was a crutch who lived and breathed. And smoked. And cursed.

"Darius!" came his name from somewhere up ahead.

"Anne, I'm—" His breath caught as all his third-degrees protested him raising his voice. A little more weakly, he finished, "In here."

His woman's footfalls were fast and slappy, racing to him from the front of the house—and then there she was, skidding to a halt as she saw him, her pale face terrified, her eyes going even wider.

All he could do was drop the arm he had around Vishous's shoulders and put his hands out—and the next thing he knew, she was on him, tackling him and asking was he okay, and how could she help him, and did he need a doctor.

It was a greeting unlike any he had ever had, so heartfelt, and kind, and . . . loving.

Except as she made contact with the burns on his back, he jerked with a hiss.

Jumping free, Anne clasped her hands over her mouth and talked through them. "You do need a doctor—"

"No, it's not that bad—"

"The healer is coming," Vishous cut in.

Darius glared at the brother. "No, Havers is not—"

Vishous made yapping signs with his free hand as he went over to the phone and picked up the receiver.

"Vishous, I don't need a doctor." The middle finger that paused in its dialing and came back at him was vulgar and unnecessary. "Excuse me, but I do not—"

Anne stepped in front of him. "Let's sit you down."

"I'm fine—"

Unfortunately, his balance took a breather at that point, and as he listed, he grabbed on to what was in front of him. Which was her. As she grunted, she managed to keep him from smacking the floor on his second dead faint of the night, her body bracing against his heavy weight and then easing him down until he was sprawled faceup in front of the refrigerator.

Not good. The faceup shit was not good.

Wheezing from the pain, he rolled over, and he knew the exact moment when she saw his back.

"Oh, my *God!*"

Well, weren't they a match made in heaven. She was covered with contusions, and he was sporting fire damage. Voila! True love.

Throwing out his hand, he took her palm in his and pulled her in close. As their eyes met, he said, "Just stay with me. It looks worse than it feels and it'll be gone by morning. I fed a week ago."

Her face registered confusion, but his eyes were fluttering and he had to concentrate to just stay conscious. So he couldn't begin to guess what had disconcerted her.

"Talk to him," Vishous ordered as he cupped the receiver's bottom. "Just . . . for chrissakes, just talk to the fool—hey, yeah. I need the healer to come to Darius's. Right now."

Anne opened her mouth. Closed it. And in the silence, Darius was vaguely aware that he'd given something away, shared something that he shouldn't have. But he couldn't remember what he'd said—and then he let that worry go: The next thing he knew, Anne stretched out with him and put her head on the crook of her arm. Staring into his eyes, she stroked his face.

"Hi," she said.

"Hi." He smiled through the pain. "You know, we really have to stop meeting like this. In the middle of a catastrophe, that is."

Her fingertips were light on his jaw. On his hair. "I couldn't agree more. But I'm glad I'm here."

"So am I." He lowered his voice. "I didn't think things were going to turn out like this."

"You smell like gasoline."

"I'm sorry—"

"No, no, don't apologize—" She glanced up and frowned. Then sat up. "Oh. Oh . . ."

When Darius followed the direction of her attention, he could only shake his head and wonder how things could *possibly* get more complicated: Havers, the species healer, had entered the kitchen in a rush. With his black bag of medical crap, and his trademark tortoiseshell glasses and bow tie, he

looked like a college professor in search of a lectern, all offi-
cious and competent—yet Darius had never liked him.
Maybe it was the bad blood with Wrath, who was supposed
to be mated unto the male's sister, but who had refused to
claim her.

Or maybe, it was something else. Like the guy was an
aristocratic prick.

"I'm fine," Darius announced as he braced himself for
some kind of physical exam.

Damn it, this was *not* how he'd wanted any of the night
to go—

Abruptly, he became aware that the healer was staring
at Anne, not him or his injuries. Before Darius could get
aggressive, however, Vishous stepped in to solve the yes-she's-
a-human-but-it's—

"None of your business," the brother snapped. "Now
treat him before I make you."

What a mess, Darius thought.

That was the last cognition he had as Havers knelt down
behind him, examined the BBQ that was now his back—
and started cleaning all that raw meat. So yeah, not a lot of
time for musing as he became busy trying not to throw up
from the pain.

The last thing he wanted was to look like a pussy in
front of the likes of Anne.

He was supposed to be the protector . . . not the protected.

CHAPTER FOURTEEN

Anne stayed through the whole thing, lying on the kitchen floor with Darius, holding his hands as he went through the brutal debridement process. The smell of faded gasoline, burned flesh, and now astringent was something she was never going to forget. In fact, the experience was so singular that she didn't dwell on the weird apparition and the strange way the doctor had looked at her and that, as first dates went, this was not on any scale, anywhere.

Or wait, had her trip to the ER technically been their first date?

Who was keeping track, anyway.

Boy, Darius was tough, though. He refused all pain medication and just gritted his teeth through what was clearly agony.

And now . . . the "healer" was packing up his supplies, and speaking to Darius, not that Anne could understand what was being said—

She frowned and looked back and forth between them. It was that language again . . . that Darius had spoken with the doctor at the ER, that he'd mumbled when he'd stared up at her on the bed.

Shifting her position into a sit once again, she continued to hold Darius's hand, and tried to take in the words to see if there was anything in them she could understand—and it was then that she realized the doctor had refused to ac-knowledge her presence in any way.

Physicians had crap bedside manners, didn't they.

Fortunately, the man departed shortly thereafter. In the aftermath, everybody who was left just stared at Darius.

"With all those bandages, you look like someone quilted you," the bodyguard with the icy eyes announced as he lit up yet another cigarette.

He had gone through quite a number of them, which suggested that, gruff exterior aside, he had not been unaf-fected by Darius's suffering. The good news, she supposed, was that the smoking had given the butler a job, something that the older gentleman had seemed grateful for. Fritz had literally stood at the man's elbow with an ashtray in his palms, becoming nothing more than a stand for the thing. It had worked for the both of them, however, the soldier and the butler, side by side, as if they'd known each other for a century.

"Thanks, Laura Ashley," Darius muttered to his friend. "Now give us a help up, so that I can get her to her feet."

The gloved hand was extended and Darius was pulled off the floor.

And that was when Anne noticed properly that he didn't have his shirt or his jacket on.

Good . . . *Lord*. His body was packed with the kind of muscle that Olympic athletes cultivated, everything from his powerful shoulders to his pecs to his ribbed abdomen a display of male beauty and strength.

"Anne?" Darius murmured as he offered his palm to her. She looked away. Looked back.

Then she clasped what he'd put out and got gently drawn up off the kitchen floor. He asked her something, maybe like "Are you okay?" and she murmured a yes, even though she hadn't quite tracked the question. Then he was turning to the man in leather.

Darius said something in that dialect, and then there was a pause. For a moment, it looked like the two men were going to embrace, but then they seemed to move past that to shake instead.

"Take care of him," the other bodyguard said as he inclined his head to her.

Then that was that. He just walked out the door. But what did she expect? A farewell cruise goodbye—à la *Love Boat* where they all stood on the back stoop and waved hankies at the departure?

"I'd really like to go to bed," Darius said with exhaustion as he propped himself against the counter.

"Then let's get you upstairs," she offered. "Before I go home."

There was a hesitation. And then he nodded. "All right."

Abruptly, the butler seemed flustered, but Darius just shook his head. "I think that would be great." He extended his arm. "Come here so I can lean on you."

Holy . . . smokes.

As she fitted herself against him and they started walking, their bodies somehow puzzle-piece'd even though he was so much taller and broader. And wow. His cologne. While they went along, she could smell nothing of the horrible stench from before. Maybe the aftershave was more of an herbal wash that the doctor had used?

Whatever it was, she felt like she was getting drunk off it.

"Boy, he really didn't like me," she murmured as they passed through the dining room.

"Who?"

"The doctor."

Darius looked down at her. "Don't worry about him. He's a knob."

"I take it that is not a compliment."

"Nope, not in the slightest."

As they arrived at the foyer and turned to the stairs, her steps faltered, and he stopped along with her. Turning her head, she stared into the parlor—and the hairs on the back of her neck came to attention.

"Are you okay?" he said. "I know this has been a lot."

Tell him what happened, she thought.

"No, it's not that. It's that I . . ."

Except it was so strange. As she focused on the space in front of the fireplace, she wasn't sure exactly what she'd seen there. Her recollection of some kind of mysterious figure in black was a distillation that was murky and unclear, and things became foggier and foggier as she tried to remember with greater clarity.

To the point where it was as if her memories were disintegrating.

"Anne?"

She opened her mouth, but wasn't sure what to say. Wasn't sure whether she'd seen anything at all. Maybe it had been a dream that had been spliced into reality . . . and she'd just lost track of time?

"Ah . . . it's nothing," she said as she reached up and touched the Band-Aid at her temple.

It was probably a good idea to remind herself that she'd had a head injury recently.

"Let's get you upstairs," she said.

As they hit the carpeted steps, Darius's bare torso became a serious distraction—and so was the fact that for some reason, he seemed to get stronger with every extension of his legs . . . to the point that, by the time they got to the second-story hallway, he was barely relying on her at all. Except no one could heal that fast. No one.

"Where do we go?" she asked.

"It doesn't matter. We'll just pick any guest suite."

"So is your room somewhere else?"

"Yes, but here is good."

He opened the first door they came to, and as the corridor's light pierced into the darkness, she was not surprised at the glimpse of formal decor—and then he hit a switch just inside the room, and she got another eyeful of antiques and silk wallpaper and window dressings that were like ball gowns.

Where was his room? Maybe he didn't want to take her there ... but why?

"Can you tell me what happened tonight?" she asked as they stepped inside, one after the other.

There was a pause. "It's a long story."

"I understand if you can't." No, she didn't. "Was anybody else hurt?"

"No." His expression grew remote. "No one else was."

Taking a deep breath, she found herself tensing up, as if she were about to be knocked off her feet—and not in a good way. "I'm not going to read about whatever it was in the newspaper tomorrow, am I."

"No, you're not."

"I need to know ..." Crossing her arms over her chest, she looked away and saw nothing of the bedroom. "Is it illegal, what you all are involved in? I don't mind you keeping your privacy, but if it's drugs, or something like that, I can't—"

"It's not that, I promise." He put his hand over his heart. "We violate no laws, and we don't hurt anybody unless they're an imminent threat to our lives or the life of our ... boss. And I know this sounds ... ridiculous ... but I'm going to have to use a movie line on you."

"Which one? And it better not be from *The Godfather*. I really don't want to hear anything about guns or cannoli right now."

"We're not the Mob." He shook his head. "And the line is . . . the less you know, the safer you are. Seriously, Anne, this has nothing to do with the civilian side of things."

Her brows lifted. "So you're with the government? Exactly who is your boss?"

"I can't tell you, I'm sorry. You're just . . . going to have to trust me."

Covert ops in Caldwell? she thought as she eyed him up and down.

"All you really need to know," he said softly, "is that I will never hurt you. Ever."

Anne thought about what his burns looked like. "Are you safe?"

"No, but I'm well-armed and well-trained, and I don't take stupid chances."

Abruptly overcome, she put her hand up to her mouth and blinked away tears. "You know what? In the next life, I'm coming back as an inanimate object. This human thing is just way too intense for me."

"Anne—"

"No, I don't want . . . to talk about anything like that anymore. I feel like my life has been spotlit for drama for way too long."

Clearing her throat, she glanced down at the intricate, jewel-toned rug with a desperation that she couldn't hide—and then she did what she could to wrench herself out of the tailspin. Walking around helped a little, and she decided that on that theory, she needed to go run a marathon.

Stopping in front of a dresser that had an inlaid design of flowers on every drawer, she reached out and traced the outline at the top level. "At least your boss has terrific taste in decor," she said roughly. "Everything around here is like a stage set for an old Katharine Hepburn movie."

"Yes, he does have a nice house."

Aimlessly, she went over to check out the bathroom— okay, wow. The last time she had seen that much marble had been . . . well, never, actually.

Turning to face him, the yearning in his eyes was undisguised, and she teetered on the edge of an abyss. Then she realized he must be in pain, standing there with his back in the shape it was.

"You probably wish you could have a shower, don't you," she murmured, eyeing the dirt and the sweat and the smoke smudges that covered his chest.

He whispered something under his breath, something that sounded like, "It's not the shower I want."

But then, more loudly, he said, "Yeah, I wish I could get clean."

"I'm sure it's not allowed with your bandages, but how about I wash you on the bed? You know, with a hand towel? It won't be as good, but—"

She lost track of what she was saying as she looked up into his face again.

Stark hunger—and not for hot water or food or drink— drew features that were now familiar to her in strange and exciting lines. And this triggered something for her, something in the back of her mind . . . that was just out of reach.

As Anne frowned, he rubbed his face like he wanted to scrub off his own nose. "Sorry. And you don't have to do that for me if it's too much."

Shaking her head, she went to speak—and promptly forgot what had been on her mind. Something had happened downstairs when he'd been gone, something significant and shocking . . . and as that fog came back to her, she watched from what seemed like a vast distance as her hands went to her lower abdomen—like they were cradling something precious.

"Anne?"

Opening her mouth to respond, she fought against the amnesia, knowing she had to tell him about what she'd seen, what had been said. Reaching down deep into her memory, she tried to pull whatever it was to the forefront—and it was almost there, nearly within grasp. It had been in the parlor, when she'd been alone in the house. Someone had come, and had . . .

"Are you okay, Anne?"

She shook her head. Then corrected herself. "I mean, yes, I'm fine. Sorry. I don't know what's wrong with me."

Darius cursed. "If you want to go, I don't blame you."

No, she thought. She didn't want to leave. Even though Bruce should have taught her a lesson about trusting strangers . . . she had to stay with this man who stood before her. In fact, being here with him now was . . . important.

And besides, Darius had almost died tonight, and she had almost died two nights ago. Life was so very fragile, and that made a person not want to waste time.

"Let's get you over to the bed," she countered in a husky voice. "I'll take care of everything."

◆   ◆   ◆

Funny how his back didn't bother him much anymore. And not because it had completely healed up already.

It turned out all he needed as a painkiller was the prospect of Anne's hands on his bare skin.

As Darius stretched out faceup on the king-sized bed, it was a damn miracle. He couldn't feel anything of the agony that had nearly left him passing out down on the kitchen floor—and this was even after he allowed the full weight of his torso to sink into the mattress.

But was she sure she wanted to do this?

Tilting to the side, he looked through the open door into the bathroom. The female he was so desperate for was at the sink, running water until it grew warm, getting towels and soap, finding a bowl somehow. From time to time, the mirror caught her reflection, and what he saw in her face made him want to kick his own ass. She seemed way too tired to do anything other than curl up in her own bed and sleep for twelve hours straight. She was determined, however, and maybe it didn't reflect well on his character, but the idea that she was actually going to touch him?

Well, he was seriously disinclined to argue with her agenda.

And on that note—even though nothing seriously sexual was going to happen, not at all, not when she was running a hot hand towel down his naked chest, nope, nope, *nope*—he shut the door out into the hall with his mind. Then he willed the overhead light off and flared up the lamp on the inlaid bureau across the way. If the night had been a couple of degrees colder, he would have lit the fireplace on a mental cue as well.

Except he'd kind of had it with flames this evening, and even more . . . he hated what he was keeping from Anne. He really did.

Running a hand down his face again, he thought back to Vishous's vision. The brother was positively eerie with the prognostication stuff, but fortunately, at least when it came to tonight, he'd been wrong. Darius hadn't died. Almost, but ultimately, no.

They'd both most certainly seen the sun, though. That second floor set of fireworks had been an explosion and a half.

So Vishous had been wrong. Sure it hadn't been raining, but . . . maybe the vision had served its purpose. Thanks to what the brother had seen, V had been primed to do the saving thing, catching Darius and carrying him after he'd gotten his boot stuck in that hole—which was kind of ironic, all things considered, given that Darius had gone out there in the first place to make sure the other fighter made it out alive.

Then again, he supposed that was the interconnected nature of fate, everyone's individual choices, and if-this-then-that's, colliding in a way that only felt random to the participants in their separate timelines. Destiny, if you believed in the Creator's master plan, provided that the sum of events wasn't chaotic at all. On the contrary, everyone's billiard balls were set up precisely in a triangle, and the stroke of the cue was done by a world-class player who knew which pockets would receive which rolls.

Everything was inevitable. Even free will—

"So I found a porcelain bowl in there." Anne came out of the bathroom. "It was full of wax fruit—I hope Fritz doesn't mind that I emptied it out? And God, do you smell this soap? It's like a garden—there was French writing on the wrapper. It's all so fancy in this house."

Anne was talking fast while she came across to the bed, and he couldn't decide whether she was nervous or just truly fascinated by everything she was discovering under his roof.

His *boss's* roof.

Fuck.

As she put the basin down on the bedside table, he took a deep breath and wished that Fritz stocked the house with unscented soap: Even though he was glad she liked the perfume, in order to catch her scent, he had to sort through the flowers of it all.

"You're on your back," she said with disapproval.

"I'm feeling a lot better."

"That doctor is a miracle worker."

When she sat down on the mattress, her eyes went to his bare chest, and as they lingered on his pecs, he thought . . . yup, he was suddenly feeling much, much better.

"Your boss has nice towels." She took a small one and dipped it in the warm water, then wrung the thing out. "These are so soft."

When she put the washcloth on his upper arm, he closed his eyes and tried to keep the erotic shudder to himself—

"Sorry, am I hurting you?"

He captured her wrist as she went to remove the cloth.

"No, please. Don't stop."

As the words came out of his mouth, something told him he was going to be saying them a lot. If she'd let him.

"Okay," she whispered.

Anne was impossibly gentle as she went back and forth to the bowl, the little towel warm as she stroked it over his biceps, his skin cooling when she returned to the soapy water to rinse things out. As she moved up to the base of his throat, he found himself arching back and offering her his vein—and her lack of response to the instinctual movement was a reminder of the reality that he refused to dwell on.

By the time she started with his pecs, his lungs really were burning, and speaking of s'mores, he had totally forgotten all about his back. Then again, he was obsessed with her face. He focused on her eyes, her lips, her neck, partially because in the soft light, she was the most beautiful thing he'd ever seen . . . mostly because the sight of her hand upon his flesh would have sent him right over the edge—and he was already in a debate with his dumb handle.

He didn't want her to know how aroused he was, but things below the waist were getting harder to hide. The good news? As the essential thickening at the center of his hips intensified, at least she seemed too absorbed in not dripping water on the bed's coverings or the floor to notice.

Or maybe her preoccupation was deliberate. He couldn't tell.

With a quick jerk of the hand, he pulled the drop of the duvet over his pelvis, just as Anne stretched across to his other arm—and yes, he could have moved toward her to help her reach that biceps, that forearm . . . but then he would have missed the sensation of her leaning on his chest—

Without any conscious thought, he captured her wrist again.

It was not to stop her.

On the contrary, it was to ...

As her eyes met his, he knew that he had crossed a line, but he couldn't help it. And he asked her, without speaking, the question that was tingling in the air between them.

In reply, her stare dropped to his mouth ... and she answered him in the same way, silently. Intensely.

And it was a *yes*.

"I don't want to waste time," she said hoarsely. "And I'm done with having no horizon."

"I feel the same way. I want to be out of purgatory ... I want to live."

"Yes," she whispered. "*Yes*."

Shifting his hand to the nape of her neck, Darius drew her to him—and when they were close, he held her there. Just in case she wanted to change her mind. She didn't. She was the one who finished the distance, and their lips meeting once again was the most natural thing in the world.

Yet she was the one who ended their connection.

He kept his disappointment to himself as she returned to the bowl—

Anne came back with the little towel, pushed the covers off him, and placed the cloth on his abdomen. As his six pack tightened reflexively, he looked down his body. On the far side of her hand, behind the fly of the cargo pants that really needed to come off because they were dirty and carried a whiff of gasoline and house fire and *lesser* blood . . . his erection was oh, so obvious.

And she saw it, too, her stroke over his stomach stilling.

She had to know what she'd been doing to him, though.

Opening his mouth to say something, he promptly lost his voice as she swooped that hand towel right across his waistband. And went back. And forth.

At his hips, his cock punched at its confines.

Without another word, she went back to the bowl—and this time, she left the terry cloth in there. Turning to him, her eyes locked on his.

"I think I've washed everything I can get to."

"Mm-hm," he said. Because he didn't trust his voice.

"I'll just . . . take care of your pants then."

Darius closed his eyes and arched back into the pillows. "Oh . . . God . . . yes."

He kept his lids shut because there was no way in hell he was going to make it through the sight of her undoing that button and that zipper—not without coming all over the place. And as it was, just the sensations of tugging and pulling were enough for him to have to fight for control: With every shift, his erection was getting friction, and his mind conflated and confused the sensation until it was her hand on him, not the underside of the fly—

Darius moaned as he felt a cool rush and a delicious release of the constriction.

Anne's exhale was the sexiest thing he'd ever heard. "I want to touch you—"

"Please," he groaned as he rolled his hips.

As his eyes popped open, there was no closing them, not with what he saw, not with what she was doing: Her hand circled his erection in a grip, and the sight of her fingers on his shaft, below his head, holding him . . .

Darius bit his lip—then realized his fangs had dropped down. Hiding that shit quick, he concentrated on Anne. And what a thing to focus on. She started in slowly with the stroking, and with a surge of lust, he pulled her to him so he could have her mouth. Entering her with his tongue, he imagined it was her core that he was licking into, and after that, he didn't think much. It was all about what she was doing to him, the up and down on his arousal, the slick kissing, the softness of her breasts against his pecs as she rested on his chest.

Except then he had to stop her. Covering that talented hand of hers with his own, he groaned. "I'm going to come."

"Good—"

Before he knew what he was doing, his body moved on its own, rolling over in a surge and taking her with him so that he pinned her with his weight. Staring into her eyes, he was breathing like he was running for his life as he moved her hand out from between them. And just so she was sure it wasn't because he didn't want her, he growled and kissed her harder, sweeping his arms around her—except he kept his hips back, and when he finally eased off her mouth, his voice was nothing but a rasp.

"Not until I'm inside you." As her eyes flared, he shook

his head. "There's no rush. I'm more than willing to wait. But I will not come until I'm inside you."

For a split second, he thought he might have come across as pushy.

But then she bit her lower lip, closed her eyes . . . and arched into him as if she were imagining him mounting her properly, entering her, filling her up.

"Yes," she moaned. "Darius. Inside me . . ."

CHAPTER FIFTEEN

B ack when Anne had been down in the kitchen, teaching the butler the difference between a flush and straight, she had found herself wondering how the night would end.

Darius coming home with those burns had not been it, for sure—but beyond that, she wasn't entirely surprised to find herself with him more than half naked and her so hungry for him that she wasn't thinking about anything other than the sex. This stopping, though, and its reason, was unexpected—

You already love him. Do not try to talk yourself out of it.

The mysterious voice came from somewhere inside her, and for a moment, she couldn't understand what it was, why she was hearing it. Yet the words were familiar, as if they'd been spoken to her all her life.

They were also the truth and they galvanized her.

She *was* in love with him. And she didn't want to end this here.

As the realizations hit, she instantly negotiated with the conclusions: Too early, too soon after Bruce, too much . . .

None of that was persuasive. And if Darius didn't want to orgasm before he was inside her? Well, there was a solution to that.

Aware that she was being impulsive, but driven by a need she was not going to argue with, Anne untucked her shirt, and didn't waste time with the buttons. She swept it up and off her head. And yeah, wow. The way he looked at her breasts in the modest cups of her nothing-special cotton bra? It was like it was the first time he had seen a naked woman.

"Anne."

As he sat up, his abdominal muscles were ridges under his skin, and the sight of his arousal lying up his stomach, so thick and hard, made her desperate in a way she hadn't ever been about anything: His sex was her obsession in an instant, a lock-in that she didn't want to get free of, a choice that was inevitable—and not because of any outside force, but because of an inner conviction that there was an eternity for her in this moment, this chance to be with him.

And time wasn't forever for mortals.

"You're beautiful," Darius said as he reached forward.

His hands trembled as he caressed her through what covered her, and then his lips were on her throat, her collarbones . . . her sternum. Spearing her hands into his hair, she

held him closer to herself, and he nuzzled at her as he un-
clasped the front of the bra. When her breasts were bare to
him, he licked and sucked on her, the sensations magnified
to such a point that she felt the contact all over her body, not
just on her nipples.

Splitting her thighs, she welcomed him to her, his erection a hard length that rubbed against her core through the
tangle of her skirt. Desperate to be totally naked, she felt
like everything was moving so fast, and yet it was too slow.
She wanted him inside her now, she wanted that orgasm
from him filling her up, she—

"Daaaaaaaaaaaaaaaaarius . . ."

Darius's head ripped up and looked at the door as she
did the same.

Down somewhere on the first floor, someone was singing: "Daaa-aaa-rrriuuusss . . . Dariusss, Da-da-dariiiiusss!"
Pause. "Da! Da-da-da-d-da-d-d-daaaariusssss . . . where are
you and I need a Baaaaand-Aid!"

It was the "Banana Boat" song. And Harry Belafonte
definitely sang it better.

"Dariussssssssssssssssssssssssssssssss, Da-da-dariuuuuuuuu-
uuuuuuuusss!"

"Oh, my God." Darius dropped his head between her bare
breasts. "No. Just no. This night can't be doing this to us."

"Who is it?"

"The scourge that never stops eating." Darius pulled the
covers off the other side of the bed and wrapped her in them
as he got to his feet and yanked his pants back up. "I'm surprised he's looking for Band-Aids, but I guess you can put
ketchup on anything. I'll go get rid of him—"

"Annnnnd I'm also hungry," came the booming voice. "Dariuuuusssss, Da-da-dariuuuuss—"

Riding a string of F-words, the man whose name was being used to butcher an otherwise very fine song zipped himself up with all the force someone would use to deadlift a hatchback. And as he went to the door, the fact that his strong back was covered with bandages was a grim reminder of where the night had gone.

The roller-coaster ride of surprises was continuing, evidently.

He glanced over his shoulder at her. "I swear, it's not usually a madhouse around here."

"It's okay."

"Just give me a minute." He put a hand up. "And no, I'm not going to leave this house again. I'm injured out, for one thing. For another? No one but you and Fritz are going to want to be around me. Trust me."

Darius was shaking his head as he left, that singing flaring in volume as he jerked things open, then dimming again as he closed her in.

She lasted about a second and a half.

She had to know who else had stopped by for a visit. And a proper-name-a-cappella.

Scrambling, Anne pulled her bra back into place and fastened it. After she contorted herself in order to get her shirt back on, she jumped off the bed and headed for the door. Out in the hall, she finger-brushed her hair into some sort of order on her way to the stairs—

Anne stopped as soon as she could see over the balustrade.

Down in the foyer, just inside the wide-open front door, Darius was standing with a man who . . . was like nothing Anne had ever seen before. The guy was so handsome, she almost couldn't focus on him, his blond hair thick and swept back from his beautiful face, his eyes so turquoise they were neon, his body so chiseled that even fully clothed, he seemed both naked and full of sex appeal—

His eyes locked on her. And the smile that was sent her way could have lit up the world.

But it was funny, Darius was the only one she truly saw.

"Hi!" the man said as he waved at her. "What's going on? How you doing?"

Next to him, Darius put his head in his hands. But the blond man was so welcoming, so irrationally happy to see her, she couldn't help but like him. He was like a big, beautiful golden retriever.

Anne was halfway down the stairs when she realized his right sleeve was stained with blood. And by the time she was standing by Darius, she noticed that there was another wound on his side.

"Are you okay?" she asked as she wondered whether they were going to have to get that Harvard professor with a doctor's bag back.

The man made a *pshaw* motion with his hands. "Right as rain. Not a big deal, just need to plug the holes—and have a sandwich." He looked at Darius. "You have bread and some cold cuts, right—oh, hey! Fritz! I'm starved, can you—"

"Oh, yes, sire!" the butler said from the dining room with equal enthusiasm. "Right away! I have lamb and beef, and roasted potatoes—"

The blond man leaned in and wagged his brows at her. "Actually, I lied about the sandwich. Of course, I'm looking for a whole meal. Big surprise, I know." More loudly, he called out, "Fritz, if you've got dessert, too?"

"Baked Alaska," came the cheerful reply.

"Ammmmmmmmmmmmmmmmen." The man lowered his head and placed his palms together as if he were praying. Then he smiled and winked at her. "I knew I could count on that butler." With another shot of volume, he said, "I'm coming, Fritz—maybe we do both the beef and the lamb? *Boeuf* and turf? Moo and chew? Except I think that's moo-and-baaa, but it's not really funny enough . . . hey, does anybody know what rhymes with cud—wait! I got it! Meat and bleat!"

With a flying peace sign, he took off after the elderly man, all but skipping, in spite of his wounds.

"Thud," Darius said under his breath. "Thud rhymes with cud, and it's the sound of my head going through a plate glass window from frustration."

"Technically, that would be a crash."

"Excellent point. And before you ask . . ." Darius started to shut the front door. "Yes, he works with me, too—"

The heavy panel was caught just before it met its jamb by a strong hand. "Hey, can I use your phone?"

At the sound of the male voice, Darius's head dropped in obvious exhaustion. Then he took a step back to let whoever it was inside. "Anybody else in the clown car tonight?"

The man who came in next had professional soldier written all over him, from his erect carriage to his short hair and his tired, navy blue eyes. Like the others, he was dressed in black and wearing a loose jacket that she knew was less about the night's temperature and more about what kind of weapons were under it—

Stopping short, he looked over at her, his stare doing an up and down that was judgmental, but not in a hostile way; more like he was cataloging her attributes in case he ever needed to ID her body. And his focus was so intense, she felt like he was going back through her family tree.

With that over, he touched his brow and inclined his head, as if he were wearing a formal hat. "Ma'am." Then he glanced back at Darius. "So can I use your phone? I want to call Wellsie so she knows I'm okay."

"Yeah," Darius murmured. "You know where it is."

"My car's blocking your driveway."

"At this point, that's the last thing I'm worried about. And just as an FYI, I'm not leaving this house tonight."

"I see you got a nice tan on your back."

"I forgot my sunscreen, what can I say."

The soldier walked off toward the kitchen while Darius leaned outside and double-checked the entryway. Like he was wondering if there was another wave coming.

As he shut the door, he took a deep breath.

Before he could speak, she reached out and took his hand. "Hi."

His eyes shifted to hers and he smiled a little. "Hi."

She traced his face with her eyes. Then brushed his mouth with her thumb. "Listen, I have to go to work in the morning."

"I know. I'd like to drive you home?"

"I can take a taxi—" She squeezed his palm to cut off an argument. "You have a lot going on here and you're hurt and I . . . I'm going to take a taxi."

He frowned. "I want Fritz to drive you then, okay? I won't feel right otherwise."

"Okay. Deal."

There was a long moment as they stared into each other's eyes. And then she was smiling even more and so was he—because they both knew it wasn't ending here. This was just a pause, a speed bump that slowed things down.

"Tomorrow night," he said softly.

"Yes," she whispered.

As he glanced toward the dining room, to the voices in the rear of the house, she knew he wanted to kiss her—and when he looked at her once again, she stepped into his body. Being careful not to touch the bandages up his back, she rested her hands on his hips and tilted her head.

With a gentle caress, Darius cradled her face, his thumbs stroking her cheeks. "I don't know how I'm going to make it till tomorrow."

"Me, too."

"I'll come to you. At nightfall, I'll be at your house, knocking on your door. And no one will find me there."

"I'll be waiting."

The kiss started restrained, but that didn't last. The next thing she knew, he had bent her back and she had her fingers in his silky hair and that amazing cologne of his was the only thing she could smell—just like he was the only thing she could feel.

Anne wanted it to last forever. She really did.

Unfortunately, the eternity she got was not the one she asked for in her heart.

◆   ◆   ◆

Darius walked down his driveway as the box van backed out, his eyes trained on Anne, who was in the front passenger seat. Shoving tight fists into the pockets of his stained cargo pants, he used all the strength he had to fight the urge to follow them ... to go through her house and check that it was safe ... to stand guard as she slept regardless of the daylight toasting him to a crisp.

Just to make sure she was okay—

"Holy crap, you've got it bad."

As the wry female voice registered, he mostly kept his wince to himself while he pivoted around. Wellsie, beloved *shellan* of Tohrment, son of Hharm, was standing off to the side on the grass, and the redhead was clearly amused—as well as ready to call him on his shit. This was not unusual. The female had always been a straight-talking vampire, her tongue sparing no one any recitation of their stupidity. She was also as loyal as any fighter, just as fierce, and warm as a summer night.

In Black Dagger Brother circles, she set the bar for the standard for a mate, and was probably the reason no one else had had a female's name carved in their back—

In a quick flash, Darius pictured himself kneeling before the Scribe Virgin, his brothers using their black daggers to mark him with the name Anne, salt water being poured on the open wounds to seal them in his flesh permanently ...

"Hello?" Wellsie said, waving her hand in front of his face. "You still in there, or has love boiled your brain, Darius, son of Marklon."

"You know," he murmured, "if it were anyone but you, I'd deny it."

"That your brain is boiled or the love part."

"Both."

She inclined herself in a bow. "I appreciate your honesty."

"Like you wouldn't know if I were lying."

"In an instant." As they both turned and strolled up the driveway, Wellsie looped her arm through his in a friendly way. "Tohr says she's a human."

"He met her for only an instant."

"It doesn't take a fingerprint analysis to know someone's not one of us." She stopped him and put a hand on his shoulder. "It's not a criticism by the way, from Tohr or me."

"Yeah, you guys aren't like that."

"We just want you to be as happy as we are."

"Has Tohr finally started cleaning up after himself after all these years?"

The female glanced through the kitchen windows, and stared at her *hellren*. "We're working on that. I tripped on a battering ram the other day and stubbed my toe. It didn't go well for him."

"At least he doesn't snore."

"That's only because I put a pillow over his face when he does."

"And people say there's no romance after mating."

As Wellsie let out a laugh and headed for the back door, Darius intended to go inside with her, but his feet didn't listen to the command. He just stood there, looking into his house.

The table that was usually empty was scattered with playing cards, and food that Fritz had put out, and the rolls of bandages Rhage was wrapping his arm in, and now Tohr's elbows as he leaned in and said something to the brother.

"There's safety in numbers," he heard himself say.

"Nah, there's something even better." Wellsie glanced back at him. "There's *family* in numbers. Maybe it'll still happen, Darius. You never know."

Wellsie had been out to the mansion he'd built up on that mountaintop, had walked through the rooms to see the furniture arrangement, the rugs and paintings, the billiards tables . . . as well as the kitchens and the laundries, the basement and the garage. They'd gone through the whole layout, the pair of them, and not because he'd been showing off.

He'd thought maybe she would understand the yearning he had for the Brotherhood to be united under the same roof. After all, she and Tohr had set up housekeeping with each other because they'd wanted the same thing he did: A proper home. A place of solace and refuge and safety. Where those who were loved and valued above all others were never far.

He'd hoped she'd get her *hellren* on board. Tohr was the most strategic of the brothers, the one who appreciated the virtues and necessities of organization, discipline, and structure within a community of fighters. He was also the most levelheaded of all of them. Surely, if he saw the value in cohabitation, he could get the others to sign on, too.

Nothing had come of it, though. Probably because Tohr also recognized how hopeless the situation was.

"It's going to happen, D," she murmured. "You just need to keep the faith."

Darius stared at the males around the table, and mentally added others. Wrath. Vishous. Phury. It was hard to edit in Zsadist, so he left that out. And then he tried to picture them all with *shellans* they loved, and young at their feet and in their arms. Maybe throw in a cat or a dog.

Maybe a cat *and* a dog.

"I'm beginning to think it's just a fantasy," he said roughly.

"All dreams start that way. I always knew my mating was going to be arranged, but I fantasized I would somehow have a love match . . ." Wellsie shrugged. "And now here I am, living the reality I wished for, and how sweet is it? I'm going to spend the next five or six centuries by Tohr's side, having a young and raising them—and then we're going to go to the Fade together and sit on a cloud for eternity sometime far off in the future. It's going to be great."

Darius laughed and shook his head ruefully as he went to get the door for her. "You and Tohr have always had it together. Out of all of us, you guys really have it going on."

"So how did you get burned." She sniffed the air and tapped the side of her nose. "I can smell it."

"Vishous and I had a little barbecue."

"Fun, fun. Did they serve you with chips and beer?"

"Yup, and I would have invited everyone else"—he opened things up—"but it's hard to find them."

"Like I said, just keep the faith," the female intoned as

she stepped by him. "And hey, if things work out with that human, I have a mating dress she can borrow."

The second the female entered the kitchen, Tohr's head whipped up and his eyes locked on his mate. The change in the male was immediate. Tohrment was always composed ... except when he saw Wellsie—and the change wasn't subtle: Joy transformed him, making his eyes glow with warmth, his spine straighten with purpose, and his lean, harsh face suffuse with a flush.

And it was at that moment that Darius knew for sure what his own feelings were.

He loved Anne.

He had bonded with her.

Seeing Tohr's reaction to his mate's presence was like looking at himself in the mirror: He did the same thing whenever he was around his woman.

After all, happiness was universal, even if its canvas of features was different.

God, he couldn't wait until nightfall. He really couldn't.

CHAPTER SIXTEEN

T he following morning, as Anne walked up the broad
steps to Beckett, Thurston, Rohmer & Fields's sky-
scraper, she felt like she hadn't been to work for a
year or two. Everything from the art deco elements of the
facade to the revolving doors to the lobby full of men and
women in suits and office clothes felt like a flashback in a
movie.

In the space of a night, she had rewired her life. And
now it was as if this working-girl thing was all a memory
rather than her actual existence.

Riding up in the elevator, she replayed scenes from being
with Darius, and as she blushed, she stared down at her
flats. Around her, men talked about baseball scores, and
weekend getaways with the wife and kids, and stock prices.
It was all a foreign language, and not because she had no in-

terest in the Yankees, and had no wife or kids. Also, no money in stocks.

She was physically present, but not mentally so.

And she smiled to herself as she fought her way through the suits to get off on the firm's bottom floor.

In a daze, she relied on her feet's muscle memory to get her to her desk—and here it was, the familiar chair, the familiar office plant . . . the in- and out-boxes as she'd left them the previous evening. Standing over the elements of her nine-to-five industry, she put her hand on the coat stand and stared at her nameplate.

ANNE WURSTER

The letters were drilled into a fake-wood slide mounted in a horizontal holder. And for some reason, it was as if they were a "Hello, My Name Is" sticker with somebody else's first and last written in.

As she stood there in a daze, whispering voices percolated all around her. And phones rang. And someone passed her by and doubled back.

"Did you hear?"

Anne looked at Penny. Blinked. Tried to focus. Today, the girl was in bright yellow, a shade of marshmallow Peep that brought out the brassy undertones in her hair in a rather bad way.

"I'm sorry, what?" Anne blurted.

"About Charlie." The woman leaned in as if she were trying to be discreet, but then didn't turn the volume down on her voice. "He died last night."

With a jolt of disbelief, Anne shook her head. "Who died?"

"Charlie Byrnes. The junior partner. You know him, right?"

"He *died?*"

Penny nodded in a way that was just one degree off from excited, the yellow plastic disks she was wearing as earrings swinging. "It was on the news. He was murdered. At his apartment. It was ... awful. They found him because the blood came through the ceiling of the flat below him and the building super was called. He'd been stabbed *so* many times."

Anne put a hand over her mouth. And then added the other one. "Oh, *God.*"

"It's just terrible." More nodding, which led to more swinging. "The partners are going to get us all together at ten. Don't know what they're going to say. I mean, what else is there to say?"

As a wave of dizziness came over her, Anne fumbled around and sat down in her chair—

The instant her bottom hit the seat, something felt all wrong and she leaned to the side. Reaching under her hip, she pulled out ... an eight-by-eleven envelope.

Penny was still talking, and Anne turned the thing over to see what was on the front. There was no name, no label. But the flap in the back had not only been secured with the little metal fastener thing, it had been taped shut as well.

"Anne?"

She glanced up at her office mate. "I'm sorry, what?"

"You want to come with us at ten for the assembly? All the girls and I are going together. It's in the auditorium."

"Okay. Sure, yes."

"It's a big shock, right?"

With that, Penny took off, zeroing in on another co-worker who had just arrived—like she had some kind of quota to get through when it came to breaking the story, Walter Cronkite in a wig and that god-awful yellow outfit.

Glancing down at the envelope, Anne tested the tape. It was on so tightly and there was so much of it, there was no way to get a fingernail into the flap. She had to use scissors, and she was careful as she cut open the top. Putting the shears aside, she looked in.

Then she pulled out . . . photographs.

There were nearly a dozen color pictures, all taken at a distance—yet it was clear who the subject was. Bruce. It was Bruce . . . and he was somewhere in the grimy part of down-town, meeting with someone . . . whose appearance struck her as strange. The other man seemed to be in his early thir-ties, and yet his hair was ice white. His skin, too. He was so pale, it was as if he were a ghost.

The series of images showed the progression of a covert meeting, from the approach, to the greeting, to the talking. And as she looked at each one in turn, she dubbed in what might have been said. The pale man seemed to be the one doing the persuading, the cajoling, until finally he appeared angry.

Some kind of accord was struck, however. In the last image . . . the two shook hands, as if they had come to an agreement. Unsurprisingly, Bruce had a secret smile on his face, as if he had negotiated well and prevailed.

Turning the stack of photographs over, she shuffled through them—and found a note written on the back of one in the middle.

Market and 17th Street. Unknown subject (R). Roth at CPD contacted.

She recognized the handwriting. It was Charlie Byrnes's. She knew this because of the paperwork he'd filled out when he'd hired Bruce as his paralegal.

Obviously, the photographs had been taken by the private investigator Charlie had hired to vet all the lies. But what exactly where they showing? And this had to be what Charlie had wanted to talk to her about at six o'clock last night. To think if she hadn't been early for her date, she might have gotten more information.

Now, the man was dead.

"Oh, Charlie . . ." she whispered.

Going through the photographs one more time, she wondered . . . what exactly had he wanted to tell her?

And why had he gone to the police?

✦   ✦   ✦

At the end of the workday, Anne put her coat back on, grabbed her purse, and tucked the envelope with the pictures under her arm. When she stepped out of the building, a fine spring evening embraced her gently, and she breathed in deep—only to get a whiff of pungent river mud.

Instead of heading for the bus stop, she walked west and south, striding against the tide of the other pedestrians who were heading for the open-air parking lots and the other public transport stations.

The headquarters for the Caldwell Police Department were about ten blocks over, and as she went up the steps, she felt like she needed to get some kind of ID out. Entering the building, she proceeded over to the uniformed officer at the reception desk. After signing in, she followed the directions given to her, going up one level in an elevator and hanging a left.

The homicide division's offices were down the hall, and when she came up to the door, she raised a fist to knock—

It was opened by a man in plainclothes and the instant recognition on his face was a surprise. "Oh, hey. You're here to see Tim Sulley, right? The woman who called from the law firm."

"Ah, yes. Yes, I am. My name is—"

"Anne Wurster. Yeah, he told me. Tim! You got a visitor."

"Thanks, Bud," came the answer.

Anne entered and checked out an open area that was filled with cubicles. Most of them were vacant of detectives, but all the desks were cluttered with paperwork and telephones, and she felt right at home. In a surface sense, of course. The reality that she was downtown at the police department's homicide division was anything but familiar and reassuring.

The man who got up and strode toward her was about forty, so older than she was, but he still had some youth in his face. With springy salt-and-pepper hair, and a sunburn that made him look like he'd put on theater makeup, he had an easy smile and eyes that were direct.

"Tim Sulley, ma'am." He finished pulling his sport coat on. "Thanks for coming down."

When they shook hands, his grip was firm and brief.

"Thank you for having me." What, like this was a cocktail party? she thought. "I mean, thanks—oh, just, here are the photographs. I don't know what I'm saying."

"Come this way." He took her elbow lightly and started to lead her. "And listen, you're not a suspect or anything. I'm only taking us into an interview room because my desk is a mess."

"I'm not worried."

The nine-by-twelve box he let them into had egg-carton padding on the walls, and as he'd said, a bare table with two mismatched office chairs. Things were kind of dingy, hunks missing from the soundproofing, the short-napped carpet stained. When the detective sat down, she did the same.

"So, yes, here are the photographs," she said as she slid the envelope across the chipped tabletop.

"And Charles Byrnes told you he wanted to meet with you?" The detective took the images out and started going through them. "Last night?"

"At six o'clock after work." She leaned forward and tapped one of the pictures. "That's Bruce McDonaldson. My . . . well, we dated for some months, and the night Charlie fired him, he tried to strangle me when I broke up with him."

The detective looked across at her sharply. "Tell me what happened."

With his calm encouragement, she told her whole story as dispassionately as she could, trying to sound . . . well, professional, maybe? What the hell did she know, she'd never given a statement as part of a murder investigation before. And as she laid things out verbally, Detective Sulley went through the images twice. Then he pushed them aside and sat back.

"So you think Bruce went to Charlie's apartment last night."

"I do," she said. "Charlie was the one who actually fired him. When Bruce lost it with me, he told me so. Sure, my boss, the head of HR, was with them, but Charlie apparently was the guy who told him the ruse was up, the lies were out, and he had to go. He was incredibly angry at Charlie."

The detective stared across at her for a little bit. Then his eyes went to her temple and he pointed to his own. "And how's your head?"

Anne touched the Band-Aid she'd forgotten was still there. "Much better."

She'd kept Darius and the car accident out of things— so she was braced for Sulley to bring up the other detective who had been taking photographs of the tire marks in the road outside Bruce's development.

He didn't.

When she stayed silent, the detective sat forward. "I'd like to arrest Bruce McDonaldson for assaulting you. All I need is for you to sign a statement and I'll send an officer out to him right now."

"Of course. I'll do whatever I have to, to put him behind bars."

"Do you mind if we keep these photographs?"

"Not at all. Please do." She frowned as the detective slid the images back into the envelope. "Can I ask you something?"

"Absolutely," Sulley said. "And I'll make sure you have my card in case there's anything else after you leave here."

"Do you think Bruce killed Charlie Byrnes?" She lowered her eyes. "Because if he did, it was my fault."

"I'm sorry?"

Tears speared into her eyes and she wiped them away. "Like I said, when I discovered that Bruce's paycheck had been garnished . . . I went to Charlie because Bruce was his paralegal. I was confused, upset. I probably should have told my boss in HR first, but Charlie had always seemed so approachable. Maybe if I hadn't gone to him . . ."

Detective Sulley put a reassuring hand on her arm. "It's not your fault. Trust me on that. You are *not* responsible for McDonaldson's actions."

"So Bruce did kill him?"

"I don't know. But he's certainly a person of interest now." The detective's voice became both grim and sure. "And I promise you this, if he did commit murder, I'm going to get him locked up. Trust and believe in that."

Anne took a deep breath. "I can't believe Charlie is . . . gone."

"Are you safe at home?" the detective asked. "I mean, do you have—"

Anne nodded. Then she looked down to make sure her face didn't show anything. "I'm not . . . alone."

Anymore, that was. And thank God for Darius.

CHAPTER SEVENTEEN

When Anne finally got home, she let herself in her front door, and as she closed things up, she was aware of double-checking that she'd thrown the dead bolt. Yes, she had, but damn, she wished she could barricade the thing. Moving through the dim rooms of her first floor, she turned on more lights than usual, and when she went into her kitchen, she walked to the slider and tested whether it was locked. It was, and the bar down on the floor was in place on the track.

Outside, the light was draining from the sky, and she found herself both dreading the night . . . and becoming excited by its approach.

Which was a weird straddle for her mood. But Bruce wasn't in custody yet, and all she could do was trust in what Detective Sulley had promised her—namely that the guy would be arrested as soon as they went to his place. Hopefully everything went well with that.

And meanwhile, she was ready to see Darius.

Upstairs, in her bedroom, she quickly changed out of her work clothes and had a shower. After moisturizing her legs and her face, she blow-dried her hair. As she put down the Conair, things seemed flyaway-ish, so she pumped a little hair spray on the frizz and ran her palms over the top to flatten things.

Clothes . . . she needed to get dressed in something that was . . .

Well, easily removable.

At a quarter to eight, she was back down in her kitchen, and as the darkness bled through the glass slider, her anxiety returned to the forefront. The idea that Bruce had done something unthinkable to Charlie Byrnes was—

Knock. Knock. Knock.

As Anne jumped up from her little table, she had a thought that she hadn't been aware of having taken a seat. With a pounding heart, she looked to the sliding glass door, and when she didn't see anything out on her shallow back porch, she glanced toward her living room—

"Anne?" came the muffled voice from down there. "It's me."

She ran so fast for the front door that she skidded on the hall throw rug and hit the panels with a bang. Her hands were inefficient as they skipped around the dead bolt, but soon enough, she had things opened.

Andtherehewasstandingonherdoorstep.

It felt like a lifetime since she'd seen Darius—and maybe it was the Charlie thing, maybe it was the Bruce thing . . .

maybe it was that she'd been missing him all day long . . . whatever the reason, she leaped at the man. And what do you know, he caught her as if he were in the throes of the same kind of reunion she was.

Sweeping her off her feet, Darius stepped over the threshold and kicked the door shut as he kissed her. And kissed her. And kissed her some more.

When he finally separated their lips, they were both breathing hard. "Where's your bedroom?"

"Upstairs," she groaned.

With a powerful surge, he swung her up into his arms and took the steps two at a time, carrying her as though she didn't weigh a thing. And given that she had only two bedrooms, and was using the second as an office and sewing station, he took the correct left and went directly into her private space.

Kicking the second door of the night shut, he laid her out on her mattress. "Anne, I need you—"

"Come here—"

The instant their mouths fused once again, their bodies did the same, her breasts up against his chest, their hips grinding together, his erection pressing into her lower belly through their clothes.

When he eventually sat up, she was worried he was putting the brakes on things, but it turned out it was just to wrench his leather jacket off. And as he tossed the heavy folds, the thing landed with a thud, like there were weights in it—but then she didn't wonder about what kind of weapons had hit her floor because he was taking off his shirt.

She did the same with her own, pulling the soft sweater over her head.

"Anne . . ." he said as he looked at her bare breasts.

Yup, there had been no way she was wasting time with a stupid bra.

Lowering her lids, she stared up at him through her lashes. "I figured why bother, you know?"

"Amen to that."

He was on her a split second later, ravishing her with his mouth, sucking on her nipples, stroking her from shoulder to hip. In return, she arched against him and opened her legs—

Anne cried out his name as she felt one of his hands ride up her inner thigh and cup her sex. Rubbing herself against his palm, clamping her legs together, she felt like she was melting from the inside out, her blood running hot and desperate. She told herself the passion was proof that this was the right man, finally—and then she wasn't thinking about anything other than getting completely naked.

"Is this too fast?" he grunted as he went for the fastening on her jeans.

"No." She pulled at his shoulders. Grabbed at his back. "No—"

In the recesses of her mind, something registered, something that she knew she should have paid attention to. But then it was gone as he started to take off those Levi's of hers. The next thing Anne was aware of, they were both naked and he was lying on top of her, his erection thick and hard, off to the side. As he smoothed her hair back, his eyes roamed her face.

"Anne?"

"Yes," she said, "I need you now."

"But I don't want to bruise you any more than you already are. You're still healing."

"You think I can feel anything other than you at this moment? Really?"

He closed his eyes reverently. And then his hand went between their bodies.

A hot, blunt brushing stroked up and down her core.

Do not stop yourself, a voice said in her head, one that was not her own.

No, she thought, she would not do that—

Grabbing his buttocks, she pulled his hips into her, and the penetration was so smooth, so deep, that they both cried out—and the communion was so right, so perfect, tears flooded her eyes. And that was before he started to move.

The pumping was slow at first. Steady. In and out, the advance and retreat making her feel full, but also frustrated because she wanted it harder, faster. There was wonder for her, too—at how this all seemed so inevitable, as if she were fulfilling a purpose that she had always had.

A love she had always known.

Wrapping her arms around his shoulders, she said in his ear, "Harder. I need to feel all of you—"

Darius cursed and there was a hesitation. Then he seemed to unleash something within himself, his body becoming a piston, his passion overtaking them both until all she could do was hold on for dear life. Looking up at the ceiling, her head jerked back and forth on the pillow as the bed creaked and the headboard banged against the wall. He was an animal, he was wild . . . he was taking her, making her his own, dominating her—

The orgasm swept into her, her body going stiff as rhythmic pulses radiated out from her sex. And in response, he abruptly halted.

"Oh, fuck, I can feel you," he panted. "Oh, God . . . Anne, I can feel you coming . . ."

✦   ✦   ✦

Darius told himself it was happening too fast, too hard, that it was too wild and unhinged. But Anne was with him all the way, her nails scoring his healed back, her moans the stuff of fantasy, the scent of her arousal suffusing the room and getting into his blood—

And then there was the sensation of her sex milking his erection, trying to pull a release out of him.

He fought the impulse to let go, though, fought it with everything he had, until he gritted his teeth and his vision swam and he thought he was going to lose consciousness.

Except he needed to pleasure her more first—and he did.

Finally, at the last moment, just before he was going to orgasm himself, he pulled out of her, clapped his palms on her thighs, and dived down her body.

Fusing his lips onto her sex, he sucked on her, swallowed her, penetrated her with his tongue . . . kissed her core as deeply as he had her mouth. Her body was instantly racked with another orgasm, and another, and still he kept at it, eating her until she was writhing from side to side, shoving pillows off the bed, kicking her legs, throwing her arms.

And then he could wait no longer.

Rising up from her, he wiped the lower half of his face, then licked his way up his palm, not wanting to spare even a morsel of her.

"Anne . . ." he said in a guttural voice. "Look at me."

Her lids lifted and her hazy eyes struggled to focus.

Moving her boneless legs up, he took a moment to enjoy the sight of her swollen, glistening flesh. Then he palmed his arousal and propped his free hand on the mattress.

He stroked her sex with his head until he glistened as well.

Then he stared deeply into her eyes. And plunged into her.

His hips started pumping before he gave them any kind of command—and he lasted only four strokes before he started to orgasm.

Just as he began to ejaculate into her, he pulled out again.

And marked her as his own.

Orgasm after orgasm, he flooded her inner thighs and her sex with his essence, and when she was dripping from what he had left on her, he slid back into her core and started to fill her up. Beneath him, she stretched her arms overhead and held on to the iron posts of the bed frame, her dark hair tangled, her cheeks flushed, her mouth swollen in the best way. As he continued to go for it, her breasts jogged to the beat of his thrusts, the pink tips he had suckled on hypnotizing him. And her ribs pumped. And her lips opened farther.

She watched him the whole time. While he made her his in all the ways that really mattered.

It was the single best sexual experience of his life.

Little did he know . . . it was to be his last.

CHAPTER EIGHTEEN

This is the most incredible peanut butter and jelly sandwich I have ever had."

As Darius made the pronouncement, Anne was inclined to agree with him. The pair of them were propped up in her bed, naked under the covers. Over on her bureau, her alarm clock suggested it was nine minutes after midnight, but that couldn't be right, she thought.

Had they really made love for four hours straight?

Anne bit into her own PB&J and laughed. "You know, they do say that the best way to a man's heart is through his stomach. But you're proving to have a really low threshold for quality."

"On the contrary. You underestimate your skills."

"Well, then I'm going to have to send Wonder Bread a thank-you letter. And Julia Child needs to watch out for the way I add a cup of water to that can of tomato concentrate." As she reached for her glass of milk, a twinge deep inside of herself was a delicious reminder of exactly how much exploration they had done with each other's bodies. "Personally, I think the exercise has made all the difference."

Because, really, what exercise it had been.

"What we did was so much more than aerobics," he murmured as he glanced over at her.

Anne flushed with a feeling of well-being. For all the ferocity he'd unleashed, the light in his eyes was gentle. Loving. And for some reason, that was the best part of the sex.

Okay, fine. It was second best to all the orgasms.

"For me, too," she said softly. "More than a workout, that is."

They finished their sandwiches in silence, and as she popped the last bite of hers into her mouth, she was fairly sure, if she were to turn the lights out, that the glow in her heart would be illumination enough to read by.

"Tell me," he said as he settled more deeply into the pillows, "how was your day?"

"Well." She cleared her throat. Took another sip from her glass. "More milk?"

"No, I'm fine." He frowned. "So what happened today, Anne?"

"Oh . . . I . . ."

Darius took her hand. "Talk to me."

She really didn't want to spoil the moment. But between his direct eyes and the way he was holding her palm, it was as if he had opened up a void she just had to fill with words.

When her mouth started to move, she wasn't sure what she was saying, not exactly, at any rate. But the story came out about Charlie and then her trip down to the CPD's homicide division. She also shared her fears about Bruce. And her questions about the photographs.

"I wish I could have gone with you," he said remotely.

"Me, too, actually." She finished off the milk they'd been sharing. "I just . . . Charlie was a good man. I mean, not that I knew him outside of work, but even before the Bruce stuff, he never treated me or anyone else in HR or any of the secretaries as less than. He was always respectful. And even though that detective told me not to feel bad, I can't help but blame myself. If I hadn't gone to Charlie and told him about all the lies that affected me, he wouldn't have hired the PI and found out about everything else. He wouldn't have fired Bruce and then maybe . . . but I guess it is stupid to think like that."

Darius's mouth grew thin. "So they believe Bruce killed him?"

"They're looking into it now, for sure. And Tim Sulley was not screwing around."

There was a pause. "Anne, I know this is . . . tell me, are you worried Bruce is going to come after you?"

She wanted to brush off the question. You know, so she didn't seem paranoid. Her silence as she tried to figure out how to respond seemed to be answer enough, though.

"If you're worried about your safety here," he said, "you need to come stay with me."

For a minute, she pictured that cozy kitchen, such a haven in the otherwise formal house—and then recalled

Fritz, who was so solicitous . . . and those people who, though fierce, did not frighten her.

"I wish I could."

"Why can't you?"

"It's your boss's house, right?"

"He won't care. Trust me."

"Well, I appreciate the invitation, I really do." She glanced around her modest bedroom. "But this is my home. I live here . . . I don't want to just abandon my place."

"I'm not suggesting you vacate permanently." He squeezed her hand. "You could just stay with me for a little while. Until things settle down and you're sure that bastard is going to jail for a long time."

Smiling ruefully, she whispered, "Actually, I think I'm worried . . . that if I lived with you even for a week, I won't want to come back."

"Good. Because I'm sure I'd never want you to go, either."

When she looked at him in surprise, he just stared back at her—and then his eyes dimmed with some kind of dark emotion.

Suddenly . . . she was scared. Not of Bruce, though. She was frightened by what the change in expression meant. Something was upsetting him, and it was the deep kind of upset.

"What's wrong?" she said softly.

Darius closed his lids and seemed to brace himself. "Listen, before this goes any further, I need to tell you something about me. A lot of things, actually—"

The quiet thump was so muffled that, had all her senses

not been fine-tuned with sudden anxiety, she might not have heard the sound. But as Darius turned his head toward the closed bedroom door, she was sure she hadn't imagined it.

A second, muffled bumping noise made her heart start to pound. "Someone's in the house," she whispered.

And that was when she realized—

"Oh, God, I didn't lock up!" She went to get off the bed. "I didn't lock the front door after you came in—"

Darius caught her wrist and pulled her back. "You stay here. Do *not* leave this room, do you understand? No matter what you hear, you stay here—"

"What are you going to do?"

Like she had to ask?

Surging off the bed, Darius yanked his pants back on and went to his jacket. As he took out a handgun, he muttered, "Don't worry, I'm perfectly legal."

"We should call the police."

"Give me a minute to find out what it is." He went to the door. "Stay here."

As Anne watched him go, every instinct told her to pick up the phone. Call the CPD downtown. The local sheriff. Hell, call the detective(s)—either one or both. Gonzalez or Sulley. She had both their cards . . .

Instead, she stayed where she was, frozen in her bed, an empty glass of milk clutched tightly in her hands.

The prayer she put up to God made no sense, the entreaty a gobbled-together mess of words covering a multitude of different panics. She was positively dizzy from fear.

As well as the sense that something very, very bad was about to happen.

◆   ◆   ◆

The second Darius stepped out of Anne's bedroom, he smelled it: baby powder and the stink of death combined. For a split second, his brain refused to process the reality that his enemy was in her house. Somehow, someway, a fucking *lesser* was inside, even though he had no idea how they could have tracked him dematerializing—

Down below, a shadow wheeled by at the foot of the stairs, the dark pattern thrown by someone moving through the living room, just out of view.

Darius briefly closed his eyes. Goddamn it, he'd ghosted out from an open window at the back of his house. Even if some slayers had been staking his location, they wouldn't have known where he'd ended up—

Creak.

Click.

Abruptly, things got a little darker.

Creak. Click. Creak . . .

The slayer was going through the rooms and turning off the lights, one by one—and there was no hesitation, as if he knew where the lamps and switches were located. And then a voice, soft, but carrying far enough for Darius to hear:

"Anne, oh, Annnnne. You've left out a mess here in the kitchen."

A warning rode up the back of Darius's neck. *Anne?*

How the fuck did that slayer know her name—

Something simmered just below his consciousness, something that he knew he should remember.

"I always told you . . . open jars must be capped properly and put away. Peanut butter and jelly, a loaf of bread left out? Tsk. Tsk . . ."

Harnessing every protective urge in his body, Darius focused himself and dematerialized down to the first floor. And the instant he re-formed, there was a quick shift in the kitchen, a shadowy figure spinning around to face him—

What the fuck, Darius thought as he recognized the man immediately.

And what do you know, Bruce McDonaldson had the same response, the man pulling a double take.

Except . . . he was no longer a man, was he.

"You're a vampire?" the new *lesser* said with confusion. "And what the hell are you doing in this house—"

Darius pointed his gun at his enemy. "You picked the wrong team, asshole."

And that was when it came back to him. In a quick flash of memory, he recalled being at the induction site at that farmhouse . . . and going through some of the clothes that had been left behind. He'd picked up a suit jacket and some kind of instinct had immediately fired—but he hadn't been able to place it at the time. Now things made sense.

He'd caught Bruce's scent on the coat. That was what had registered. Except his brain had refused to process the implications of it all because hey, what were the chances that Anne's ex would become one of the Omega's new recruits?

Then again, the guy had told her he was destined for bigger things. Usually that just meant snagging a better job, however, not a complete immortal rewiring by a metaphysical source of unfathomable evil.

Fucking hell, Darius thought as the slayer ducked into another room and turned off the final lamp.

From out of the darkness, a chuckle weaved through the still air. "Have you told her what you are, vampire?"

As the man—*lesser*—kept talking, Darius glanced out the nearest window. The neighbors were close. If he pulled his trigger, it wasn't going to take long for the cops to get called. Not the kind of peanut gallery he was looking for, especially when there was about to be a stinky, black-oil mess to clean up.

"I asked you a question, vampire," the disembodied voice demanded. "What have you said about yourself, hmm?"

Darius tucked the gun into his waistband at the small of his back. Then he closed his eyes and concentrated, triangulating the slayer by scent and the source of the chatter . . .

Locking on its location, he dematerialized into a shallow study. But the *lesser* was fast, disappearing around a corner, even though it was dark. But then fucking Bruce knew the house by heart, didn't he.

"You know I'm going to kill her, don't you," came the drawl. "I've got a score to settle with the bitch."

The slayer was moving again, and Darius prayed he didn't take to the stairs. But that had to be where he was headed. He had to know Anne was up in her room—

"Cat got your tongue, vampire?"

One last chance, Darius thought as he closed his eyes again. He had only one more opportunity to—

Some sixth sense directed him, his body disappearing and traveling back where they had started, in the kitchen . . .

where he re-formed right behind the now-undead. By the bread Anne had taken out to make sandwiches after all the lovemaking.

No time to waste.

As the *lesser* focused ahead on the living room, Darius threw out his arm, snagged a hold around that throat in the crook of his elbow—and choked the fuck back, locking a grip on his own wrist for better leverage. The response was a furious battle, the former Bruce McDonaldson slapping and kicking, the slayer far stronger than the man had been, but not yet fully within the power granted unto him by the Omega's conversion. That would come within a couple of days.

Assuming he "lived" that long. Which he wasn't going to.

Banging into cupboards, the fridge, the table, things clattered and fell and broke, and then Darius smelled peanut butter as the open jar of Jif landed on the floor. After that there was clanging, like they had hit pans, a scattering, too, across the linoleum—

Darius shouted as a set of teeth bored into his forearm, and in response, he spun the *lesser* around and shoved him face-first against the wall. A picture fell and crashed.

Replay of what had gone down back at that apartment. Except oh, God, this was Anne's place.

Stay upstairs, he prayed. *Just stay where you are, sweetheart—*

The lights came on overhead. And as the glare blinded them both, he cursed. Anne was standing just inside the room, a pink bathrobe belted around her waist . . . a gun up and aimed in their direction.

"Bruce," she said in a voice that wavered. "Stop fighting, I'm calling the police."

That chuckle returned. At least until Darius drew all the way back on the choking again.

"Don't kill him, Darius!" she commanded. "I'm going for the phone—"

"No—" As Darius barked the order, she stepped farther into the room. "Anne, go back upstairs—"

"Just hold him where he is—"

Meanwhile, the slayer was still chuckling as he wheezed—and then came a staggering blaze of pain that took Darius's breath away. As Anne screamed and dived out of sight, he staggered back in shock. He tried to keep his hold, his position, but something wasn't working right and it was sending him off-kilter—

Things happened fast at that point, the slayer going for his gun, the pair of them do-si-do'ing around as he attempted to retain control of his weapon—at the same time his stomach was rolling and his body wasn't behaving as it should.

"Put the gun down, Bruce! Or I'll shoot!"

As Darius looked toward her voice, his balance listed and he threw out his hand for the counter. Which was when he saw the blood running down the outside of his pant leg. Except a superficial wound like that shouldn't have made such a—

Fuck.

It wasn't a minor flesh wound and it wasn't his thigh. The blood was coming from his gut: The hilt of the steak knife Anne had used to spread the peanut butter and the jelly was sticking straight out of Darius's abdomen. When the hell . . . did . . . that . . . happen . . . ?

As his knees gave out, he landed on his ass, his hands going instinctively to where he'd been stabbed.

Standing over him, the *lesser* laughed some more and leveled his cold stare in Anne's direction as she tried to take cover behind the arch into the living room. He was still dressing like Don Johnson, everything teal and white and out of place for so many reasons, although thanks to the scuffle, his togs were all wrinkled and untucked. Add to the dishevelment those crazy eyes? You had a really dangerous, kind of well-dressed sociopath—who was armed with Darius's own fucking weapon, the one that he should have used right away and to hell with the neighbors.

To hell with the pride of a bonded male who wanted to protect his female with his bare hands.

"Did he tell you yet?" the *lesser* said to her as he pointed that muzzle at the archway.

"Bruce, I'm ordering you to put down the gun—"

"Ask him what he is. Go ahead, ask him." More with that laughter. Then he cocked his eyebrow. "Not going to? Okay, fine, have you checked out his front teeth? Have you asked yourself why you've never seen him during the day? Do you wonder why he's so secretive about what he does, where he goes, who he knows?"

"I will shoot you, Bruce—"

"He's a vampire," the *lesser* announced. "And hey, I'm just learning more about his kind, too. Maybe it's something you and I can do together. After all, I told you I would better myself—and I got my leg up in spite of you and what you did to me. In spite of that asshole Charlie Byrnes."

"Bruce, stop—"

"I killed him, you know, and Charlie didn't stand a chance against me, the pussy." The slayer took a step forward, toward her. "Guess what, neither will your vampire. And when I decide it's your time, neither will you."

The slayer's arm swung back around, the gun now pointing at Darius. "You're twice the abomination of nature I am—"

The discharge of the gun was loud as it echoed around the kitchen, and Darius threw his hands up to the center of his chest, certain it was a mortal wound—

Except the *lesser* was the one who fell into a crouch and went for his heart with both hands. Not that there was anything left behind his sternum anymore.

The former Bruce McDonaldson dropped the gun, fell to the floor, and landed on his side, clutching his pecs. And still he laughed, black blood speckling his mouth.

"The joke's on you, Anne. You can't kill me like that anymore."

Darius glanced down at himself. His abdomen was still pumping out bright red blood at the site of the stabbing, but he didn't appear to have been shot, and that was all that—

No, that wasn't all that mattered. As he looked back at Anne, horror was dawning on her stark face, her mind making all kinds of mental connections that he wished like hell he could prevent or undo. Except the *lesser* had gotten it right. Darius had lied by omission.

About what really counted.

And the fact that Darius had been on the verge of telling her everything wasn't going to matter. Not at all.

The *lesser* let out a cough. Then he wheezed as he drew in a breath. "He's a vampire, Anne. Your lover's a vampire— I can smell him on you. You fucking slut, you fucked him." Laughing, laughing . . . crazy laughter as black blood bloomed on the lapels of the slayer's bright blue suit jacket and the front of his white t-shirt. "You were fucked by an animal and he didn't tell you, did he—and you thought *I* was a liar."

Darius's dagger hand locked on the steak knife. Gritting his teeth, he braced himself for the pain that was coming.

"He's worse than I am, Anne." Bruce didn't seem to notice all the black oil coming out of his mouth. Didn't appear to care about the fact that his breathing was getting more ragged. Then again, he wasn't going to die—and clearly hadn't yet done the math that the suffering he was in was going to be perpetual. "He lied to you about the very thing he is. At least when I was human, I only lied on the surface—"

Darius yanked the blade free of his stomach, and in a single coordinated lunge, threw himself forward, raising the knife over his shoulder, every ounce of his strength trained on a stabbing motion he was going to have to make at just the right time, in just the right way.

And he did.

On a vicious strike, he hit the *lesser's* chest just to the left of the sternum with the stainless steel blade, and as he felt the knife penetrate, he prayed that his momentum was great enough to pierce the empty cavity where the heart had been—

The *pop!* was every bit as loud as the shooting had been, and the flash was as blinding as the overhead light when it had been turned back on.

In the aftermath, Darius collapsed backwards, his skull bouncing on the hard floor, a sudden nausea racking him.

Curling onto his side, he retched a couple of times. And then he concentrated on breathing.

God, the burn smell. The baby powder stench. The—

"You're bleeding."

Shifting his eyes up, he saw Anne standing over him. She looked like she'd been through a hailstorm, except for the fact she wasn't dripping wet: She was utterly wilted, her robe hanging loose from her shoulders, the gun she'd taken out of his jacket lax at her side, her face so pale he became worried she was going to lose consciousness.

But that wasn't going to happen, was it.

She wasn't in clinical shock. She was just . . . mortified.

"Yes, I am bleeding," he said. And then he answered the question that was on her face. "Yes, he is right."

Anne just stayed where she was, staring down at him like she'd lost touch with reality. Then again, she had her bare feet on the smudge mark created when her ex-boyfriend had been sent back to the Omega . . . and her current boyfriend, a vampire, was bleeding out in front of her refrigerator.

No, wait, guess he was by her oven.

And not that he was her boyfriend.

The sheen of tears that glossed her eyes was the worst condemnation of him and his actions that he could imagine.

"I'm sorry, Anne," he choked out. "I didn't know how to tell you, what to say—"

"Who do I call?" she cut in roughly. "Your house? Do I call your butler? And please, don't lie to me about some boss. You're the one who lives there. Who do I call to get you help."

"Give me the phone, I'll do it—"

"No, *I'll* make the call."

She turned around and took a receiver off a wall-mounted cradle. As her trembling finger dialed the number he'd given her on a piece of paper the night before, it struck him that she must have memorized the sequence.

And dearest Virgin Scribe, he wished he could go back to the moment when they'd been standing by the box van just before she'd left. He'd insisted she call if she needed help and she had looked up at him as if he were some kind of hero.

"Hello?" she said abruptly. "Ah, Fritz? This is Anne. Darius has been stabbed by—I don't know what it is, it's gone . . . now . . . I, well, he needs help. He's been stabbed and I can't take him to a—so what do I—"

She fell into an *mmm-hmm*. And followed that with another one. "My address is—oh, you know it already. All right. Thanks, and I hope you—find someone fast. To come here. There's a lot of blood."

As she hung up, her eyes returned to Darius, and he realized that he might have been the one who'd been stabbed in the gut . . . but she was the one who had died.

And it was all his fault.

CHAPTER NINETEEN

As Anne rehung the receiver on its prongs, she realized what was wrong. Well, okay . . . there were a lot of things that were wrong, but now she remembered one specific inexplicable.

Darius's back.

When he had taken off his shirt upstairs, and she had put her arms around him . . . there had been no bandages. And as he had left her room to go see about the noise, there had been nothing marring his smooth skin. No burns. No scars. Not even a blemish or discoloration. Nothing.

As if he hadn't been lit on fire the night before.

She hadn't noticed it at the time. And there had been so many other things she had dismissed or been too distracted to track: The deference the butler had paid him. The way Darius had, in fact, never smiled widely or flashed his front teeth. The vague disclosure about what he did for work. And then there had been those other men who had shown up—

And that broken jar with the black inky stuff that had smelled . . . exactly like Bruce just had. Right before he'd up and disappeared, right in front of her eyes.

What the *hell* was happening in Caldwell.

"Vampire," she said weakly.

"It's not what you think."

"You're right, because I thought you were . . ." As she threw up her hands, she noticed she still had his gun in her palm—and shouldn't that have shocked her? Well, it didn't. It was barely a blip on her radar considering everything else. "I thought you were like me."

"I am."

"You are not. Not in any way." She laughed in a bitter fashion. Then closed her eyes. "And you lied to me, too. God, I'm such an *idiot*—"

"Don't say that—"

"What do you call a woman who traded in someone like Bruce for . . . whatever the hell you are? And to think I was worried about a wife and two kids? *Jesus*. I had no idea the real problem was fucking Dracula."

As he cursed under his breath and dragged a hand through his hair, she fanned the air in front of her nose. "This stench is the same as what was around the vase I dropped at your house—and that is your house. Isn't it. *Isn't it!*"

Her voice was getting louder, but like she cared about that?

"I'm sorry," he said.

"You're *sorry*. You keep something like this from me? I mean . . ." As her anger crested, she knew she had to get control of herself, and took a deep breath. "Even after what I told you . . . about how Bruce lied to me—and oh, my God, what the hell did he turn into? What happened here? What—"

At the very moment her thoughts spun out into total incoherence, two men showed up in her kitchen. As in . . . literally appeared from out of nowhere right in front of her.

No, wait, they're two vampires, not men, she reminded herself. *Never men.*

Weaving on her feet, stunned past all comprehension, she decided surely this had to be a dream.

Except it wasn't. And holy hell, she knew the two— *vampires*—who were in her kitchen: One was that doctor type, with the bow tie and the white coat and the tortoise-shell glasses. The other was the guy with those tattoos at his temple.

"While you treat him, I'm going to go take care of the neighbors," the one with the diamond eyes said to the physician. "Their lights are coming on, so they heard something or saw the flash of the *lesser* being sent back to the Omega. I'll neutralize them—"

"Don't you dare kill those people!" Anne hollered hysterically.

"Excuse me?" the man—*fucking vampire*—shot back.

"My neighbors!"

"Oh, relax." He gave her a bored look. "I'm just taking their memories so a flank of cops doesn't show up on your front doorstep and ask you questions you can't answer. Sound good to you? Great. I'm *so* glad you approve—now give me that fucking gun before you shoot me by mistake."

Anne blinked. Looked down. Saw that she had pointed the weapon directly at the vampire. "This cannot be real."

As the doctor knelt by Darius and opened his bag, a gloved hand reached forward, and she didn't fight the disarming. Had she really shot Bruce? Had she really been about to shoot—

"What's happening?" she asked the man. Vampire. Whatever.

When he let out an exasperated exhale, she figured he was going to ignore her. But then he shook his head. "It doesn't matter. It's not permanent for you."

She thought about what he'd said about the neighbors.

"My memories," she whispered, "are mine. You have no right to take them."

"Just talk to him," the vampire muttered as he nodded at Darius. "He needs to stay conscious and he'll do anything you tell him to."

And then the guy disappeared from right in front of her.

In the aftermath of the departure, Anne went over and picked up one of her chairs that had been knocked to the floor. Sitting down, she hung her head and felt Darius stare at her as he was treated. The doctor started talking about operating, but Darius argued with him, the two going back and forth, getting heated.

At least the whole stay-conscious thing seemed to be handling itself.

And finally, she had to look over—

What she saw made . . . no sense. Or should have made no sense.

Before her very eyes, the stab wound appeared to be knitting itself back together. To the point where she could watch the skin closing, as if in a special effects movie.

In spite of everything else she had seen, the cognitive dissonance caused by this phenomenon was so great that her mind retreated from what was before her eyes. Unfortunately, what it escaped to was just as upsetting: Bruce had been right about one thing, wrong about another. Yes, Darius was worse than he had been, but as shocking as the basis of this newest bunch of lies was, the reason she was so affected by them was because she had fallen in love.

With someone of another species.

Dear God in Heaven above, how was this her life.

◆   ◆   ◆

"I'll be fine," Darius said as he shoved Havers's disinfecting efforts away. "I'll call if I have any issues."

Assuming he didn't bleed out right here and now. Which was probably the biggest medical risk he had, right?

As if that "grave" outcome was a serious possibility, Havers hesitated, his bag wide open, all those treatment supplies the kind of thing that he seemed compelled to use like the gauze and tape had an expiration date. And great, now there was some more discussion about surgery, although not that much more—which wasn't really a surprise. As much as Havers took his job seriously, he was a member of the *glymera*, and as such, he wasn't comfortable slumming in a human's house.

He was probably going to pull a Silkwood when he got home. And didn't the disrespect make thoughts of scalpels appeal.

"It does appear to have missed your vital organs," the healer hedged.

"Lucky me," Darius muttered as he looked over to Anne.

She was just sitting in her chair, her shoulders slumped, her eyes barely blinking. Every once in a while she glanced over, but it was as if she couldn't stand the sight of him. Not that he blamed her.

When Havers finally left, Darius pushed himself up higher on the oven door and moved his legs out straight. The fact that there was black and red blood on her linoleum was as stark a commentary on their relationship as it could get.

"I didn't tell you," he said roughly, "because you wouldn't have believed me. And if you had, you wouldn't have given me a chance."

It felt like forever before she responded. "Was any of it true."

Not a question, more a rhetorical that was spinning around in her head. Still, he felt compelled to answer. "I do have a boss who is impossible. That wasn't a lie."

"Well, aren't you a hero."

And of course, the biggest truth was that he loved her. But he knew that was the last thing she wanted to hear. "I'm so sorry I lied to you."

"I am, too. I really am."

The words slipped out before he could stop them: "I love you—"

"Don't say that, ever," she snapped. "Not around me, at any rate."

Fuck. "I didn't mean to hurt you."

She pushed her tangle of dark hair back and drew the lapels of the pink robe tightly to the base of her neck. "You know what the crazy thing is? Not that this all isn't insane . . . but the most crazy thing is that I literally cannot believe I am here again, the truth exposed and biting me in the ass. The only thing I can say to your benefit is that at least your hands are not around my throat. But I still feel like I can't breathe—"

"I'm sorry—"

"*Stop* with that. And I need you to leave. Right now. I don't want to ever see you again." She gestured to her head with a limp hand. "My mind can't handle any of this, and I just need tonight . . . all of this . . . *you* . . . to be over. I need you to have never existed."

Darius closed his eyes. Reopened them. "I can make that happen . . . I can take your memories."

When her brows flared, he touched the side of his own temple. "I can make this all disappear. You won't think of me ever again, it will be as if I never, ever . . . existed."

Anne opened her mouth. Closed it. Then the silence stretched out into infinity.

With an abrupt jerk, she shook her head. "No, I don't want to forget you. I didn't learn my lesson with Bruce, so God sent me you, just to make sure I finally get it. And I have. No more letting people in. I'm done with that."

Darius scrubbed his face again. Wow. Who knew the only thing worse than her eager to wipe her memories of him . . . was her wanting to enshrine him for the rest of her life as a curse. And God, he wanted to say something, anything, that would help her.

So he spoke words that got him right in the heart: "I'll go now."

As he went to try to push himself up off her floor, Vishous picked that moment to materialize back into the kitchen. And when Anne jumped in her chair, Darius cursed.

"He's leaving," she said thinly. "Help him with that, will you."

She got up and turned away. "Do me a favor and lock the front door behind you. Even if it's just the knob, at least it'll keep some things out. Hopefully."

Patricia Anne Wurster did not look back as she shuffled off for her stairs.

And as Darius listened to her go up to the second floor slowly, he felt like he was bleeding out with each of her footfalls.

"Are you okay?" Vishous asked softly.

Darius put his palm up in the air. "No, I'm not. Give me a hand, will you?"

"Can you dematerialize?" his brother asked.

"It doesn't matter, just get me out of this poor woman's house."

Vishous dragged him off the floor, and then Darius limped to the front door. The fact that it was slightly open suggested that Bruce had, in fact, come in that way. But who knew. Who cared.

About anything.

Pausing at the base of the stairs, he looked up at the closed door that was at the top on the left. He pictured her in her bed, curled on her side, holding herself.

Or maybe she was stripping the sheets.

Burning them?

"Did you take her memories?" V demanded. "Just now?"

"No." He looked at his brother. "And you're not going to, either. Are we clear."

"That's not the way it works—"

Darius fisted up the front of V's jacket. "Well, it's how it fucking works this time. You leave her alone. We've done enough damage."

There was a split second as he waited for V to correct him with a "*You've* done enough damage." Or maybe point out that if she couldn't remember, how'd she know anything had been taken from her? But the brother just shrugged and stepped out over the threshold.

After a moment, Darius followed, and he closed things up behind them. His fingers lingered on the knob—and then he willed the dead bolt into place.

Limping down onto the walkway, he stopped and turned back. Shrouded in darkness, he stared up at the bedroom's windows. The venetian blinds were lowered, but the lights were on. He had no idea what she was doing up there. Well, he could guess the generalities . . .

As it dawned on him that he was never going to know any more details about her life, it was as if she had died. Or he had.

"It was only a matter of nights," he said hoarsely, "but it's going to have to last me a lifetime."

And then something dawned on him.

He looked at his brother. "Your vision. It really wasn't about the farmhouse, was it. That wasn't the second sun."

"We don't need to think about that right now—"

"Because it wasn't raining last night." He leaned forward. "It wasn't raining. In your vision, you said it was raining, right?"

"Yeah. I did."

Numbly, Darius glanced back at the bedroom window. "That's what you saw, the rain. Before the click, before the second sun."

"Yeah."

Darius took a deep breath. "Good. It means there's still an explosion out there, waiting for me. Now, I just have to find it."

Closing his eyes, he didn't expect to be able to dematerialize—but for some reason, maybe because getting off Anne's property was the very least he could do for her, he managed to spirit away.

Then again, maybe it was because as a bonded male without his mate, he was in so much pain, he didn't even feel his stab wound.

Pity that suicide got you locked out of the Fade.

So thank the Virgin Scribe for Vishous's vision.

And sooner rather than later on the fireball, please.

CHAPTER TWENTY

On the Monday morning after Anne's life went into the blender of fate, she emerged onto Beckett, Thurston, Rohmer & Fields's top floor at eight thirty a.m., stepping off of the elevator along with two associate attorneys. When both of the men pared away and went down the service hall Charlie had called her into, she had a moment of deep sadness as she glanced toward where he had been standing when she had spoken to him for the last time.

Then she turned in the opposite direction and walked forward.

The lovely model/receptionist was not at her desk, and that made things easier. Although it ultimately wouldn't have mattered if the Brooke Shields look-alike had been there with her sincere smile and another offer of coffee.

Anne would have kept going, with or without permission.

Passing through the waiting area, she continued by the conference rooms . . . and came to Miss Martle's desk. As the woman looked up with a frown, Anne put her palm out.

"It's all right, I'll let myself into his office."

"I *beg* your pardon."

Anne ignored the noise and walked around the desk, opening Mr. Thurston's closed door with a quick punch of the handle. The man himself was just coming out of his private bathroom, his suit jacket off, his hands vigorously working a monogrammed hand towel like they weren't just wet, but stained.

He stopped dead when he saw her. Just as Miss Martle rushed in and started blustering.

"I'm here to talk to you," Anne said in a low voice. "Privately."

Mr. Thurston's eyes narrowed. And then he assumed a pleasant expression that was so fake, she wanted to kick him in the shins just to see if he could make it stick.

"That will be all, Miss Martle," he said, cutting through the woman's indignant tirade.

"But she forced her way in—"

"*That is all.*"

Like the trained guard dog she was, once she'd been given a direct command, the older woman backed off, even though it was clear she disapproved of the whole world at the moment.

When the door was closed, Mr. Thurston tossed the hand towel back toward his sink. "Have a seat, Miss Wurster."

"No, thanks, I'll stand. I'm not going to be here long."

"Oh? Eager to get back to the job that pays you so well?"

She waited until he sat behind his desk, and the fact that he took his own sweet time made her feel like he was moving slowly on purpose.

"I'm here to sign your release," she said.

Instantly, his smile became far more sincere, especially as he went to open a drawer. "Well, isn't that good. I still have your check—"

"You're going to pay me fifty thousand dollars. And then I'll sign."

The partner froze where he was, the drawer halfway out. "I am sorry, what did you say?"

"Your firm failed to protect me from another employee."

Mr. Thurston's eyes gleamed with elegant menace. "You were in a relationship with the man. Your poor personal choices are hardly our problem."

"I never would have met him if you hadn't hired him. And your human resources department failed to perform proper due diligence prior to offering him employment."

"May I remind you that you *work* for human resources, Miss Wurster."

"Not in hiring, I don't."

The senior-most partner steepled his hands and assumed an air of utter superiority. "We are not responsible for what he did—"

"How many other employees have you not vetted, hmm? Maybe there are some with criminal histories you don't know about, or false diplomas, fake names, messy backgrounds—and how would that look? You know, if someone like a newspaper or a federal agency happened to come in here and do some actual digging on not just the staff, but the attorneys themselves? How certain do you feel about what would be found?" She leaned in. "Or maybe the question is . . . how lucky do you feel, Mr. Thurston?"

The cast to his face became so dark, it changed the color of his eyes from platinum to storm cloud. "Don't toy with me, little girl."

"Oh, I'm not toying with you. I ended up in the emergency room and needed X-rays because your employee attacked me. What kind of headline is that going to make? Tell me, how much confidence do you think your blue-chip clients are going to have in your father's"—she pointed to the oil painting—"firm after they learn a violent man with no relevant law experience was playing paralegal on their cases?"

"Our clients are very satisfied with our attorneys," the man snapped. "And they don't know you at all."

"They don't have to know me. All they'll have to do is read the papers or watch the news. I'm just a little girl, right? Well, nobody likes it when people hurt little girls, even if they think we're stupid and can't take care of ourselves." She shook her head. "Trust me, you and your firm don't need this public relations nightmare, and it is going to be one. I'll make sure of it."

There was a long pause. Then the man sat back in his chair and smoothed his dark red tie over his bright white button-down shirt. As his hand made the pass over the silk, a gold cuff link flashed.

"Extortion is a federal crime, Miss Wurster."

"This is not extortion. You made me an offer first. This

is a negotiation, and the implications of negative press are your reality, not a threat I'm making."

The smile that came back at her made a blizzard look warm and inviting. "You'd do well not to try to school me in my area of expertise. And in light of this conversation, I'm not giving you a dime. What I will do is make sure you never get a job in this town again—"

"Bruce McDonaldson killed Charlie Byrnes." Anne refused to let the tears that surged fall. "And I went down to CPD headquarters and met with a homicide detective just to make sure the authorities know this. The news will be coming out soon. Tick tock. Better practice what you're going to say to your clients in front of the mirror in that private bathroom of yours."

Surely some bluffing was allowed, she thought. And what do you know, when she really needed one, she had a poker face.

As the man on the other side of the desk got very, very quiet, she thought about Bruce . . . and what he had become. How he had "died." She'd tried not to dwell on any part of that over the weekend—and sure enough, her brain instantly began to overload with all the panic and confusion she'd suppressed.

Forcing herself to refocus, she kept her voice level. "Fifty thousand dollars, Mr. Thurston. Right now. And then you won't have to worry about that ugly murder stuff being compounded with what happened to me. Isn't that going to be a relief considering how much is going to be on your plate? Phew. Wow, soooo much better."

There was another long pause. "I don't have some checkbook, you know. I can't just get a pen and—"

"You're the senior partner of this law firm. Call someone and have them bring a money order to you." Glancing behind herself, she went over to the sofa and sat down. "I'll wait."

◆   ◆   ◆

It was three o'clock by the time Anne arrived back at her house, and as she got out of the cab she'd taken from downtown, she had a number of bags to carry inside. The driver helped her, and she tipped him ten whole dollars.

While he drove off, she shut herself inside, locked the dead bolt, and inspected what she'd bought: Two suitcases. Some fresh clothes and underwear. A new purse. A camera.

She didn't know how long she was going to be gone. Where she was going to go. Whether she would even come back.

Well, she supposed she had to return at some point to deal with the house. But she'd worry about that later.

Up in her bedroom, she got her toiletries together, and avoided looking at the bed. She'd stripped the sheets and thrown them in the laundry the night Darius had left— and as the memory of him was easily called to mind, she took note that she hadn't been erased.

Or whatever they referred to it as.

Over the weekend, she'd expected them to return and do the duty on her—and still did. The only thing she had to go on was that as of right now, she could still recall everything: from the car accident, to the ER visit, to . . . all the things that had happened afterward.

This was the other reason she wanted to get out of town.

Even though it was incredibly painful to think about

Darius, she was still resolved when it came to not wanting to be robbed of her recollections of him. She'd come to view the slideshow of images as her punishment for trusting another stranger after one had just lied to her.

Looking back on it all, she couldn't believe she'd let herself fall so far, so fast. What had she been thinking?

Then again . . . it hadn't been about thoughts. It had been about feelings. And nothing proved the relativity of time better than infatuation backed up by a heady dose of lust. It was literally how love affairs worked, duping you into believing that the intensity of emotion equated to you having known the person forever. And as long as she could call on her memories of Darius and hold the evidence of her stupidity in her mental hand . . . then maybe she wouldn't do it again. Ever.

So yup, anywhere but Caldwell was her destination. She had no ties to anyone, nobody to miss her, no pets, no complications. No job. It was time for a fresh start. A new chapter. A . . .

As her mind drifted, she headed back downstairs and hated that she couldn't concentrate properly. Then again, she hadn't slept for three days, and there was a strange benefit to the exhaustion. Thanks to being a zombie, she didn't have any energy to spare on getting worked up about the future, and this was kind of liberating. Her lack of fear, regardless of its source, made her feel in charge, somehow.

Glancing around, she ended up staring through to the kitchen. There had been a helluva mess in there to clean up after Darius had left, and the burn mark on the floor from where Bruce had been . . . where he'd . . .

"Oh, God." She put her hands to her face and held her cheeks like her skull was in danger of blowing apart. "Oh . . . God."

The thing about trauma, especially when it was fresh, was that it took over everything the instant the door to it was opened. Between one blink and the next, she saw the chairs knocked over, the pans scattered on the linoleum, the peanut butter jar on the floor, the jam spilled like blood on the counter.

The actual blood, red and black, smudged all over the place.

She'd cleaned everything up. But that was only on the surface.

Just like her composure was only on the surface.

As she felt her thoughts threaten to fragment into insanity, she pulled herself back together with the reminder that at least if she was by herself, no one could hurt her, ever again. And this was a good and necessary thing. In truth, and though he would never know it—because she would never see him again—Darius had the venerable distinction of being the worst pain she had ever lived through. Which, given her history, was really saying something.

He'd been out of this world since the moment she'd first met him.

Hadn't he.

CHAPTER TWENTY-ONE

Nine Months, Twenty-four Days, and Eight Hours Later . . .

On the night Anne died, she was at least three weeks past her due date. And that was all she knew for sure. Well, that and the fact that she was utterly terrified.

Then again, how many pregnant women were all, *I got this, no big deal?*

Still, as the time to give birth approached, she assumed that most expectant mothers found themselves with at least a mixture of fear and joy. She had only the fear, had only ever had the fear. There was no question whose it was. So the tension and the horror about what was growing inside of her had been her traveling companion while she'd been away from Caldwell, and yes, she had considered terminating the pregnancy—pretty much throughout the entire first trimester. She'd even made an appointment at a clinic . . .

But at the last moment, she hadn't been able to go through with things.

What she had followed through on were her travel plans. She had seen most of New England and the Midwest, and had only returned to Caldwell two weeks ago because even her resolute denial couldn't override the reality that she was waddling like a duck, couldn't tie her shoes, and felt like she was going to pop.

Being back at home had been even harder than she'd expected, proving that her memories hadn't faded and neither had her sense of betrayal. She still hadn't reached out to Darius after the night she had told him to go, and she was not any closer to understanding what he was, what Bruce McDonaldson had turned into, or what had happened after she had watched a man get stabbed by a steak knife and disappear with a flash and sound of a Roman candle—

"Ohhh," she groaned.

Putting her hand on her swollen stomach, she grimaced through the pain. And then she checked her watch. Two minutes apart.

Things had moved fast with the labor, and she knew she was running out of time if she was going to get help. Nonetheless, she waited on her couch in her living room through two more contractions—and then she finally launched herself to her feet and lumbered for her purse. Gathering her keys, she left out the front door and walked to the Ford Taurus she had bought after completing a driving course in Plattsburgh and finally getting her license.

Squeezing behind the wheel was a thing, and she had to take a breather twice on account of the contractions. But then she was driving off, her hands gripping the steering wheel so tightly her knuckles were white.

Traffic was light because it was after ten p.m. and this was the suburbs—and yet she was terrified she was going to get into an accident. Then again, that was how she always felt. She made herself conquer the fear, however.

She was done being afraid of anyone or anything.

Done with being treated like a little girl when she was a grown adult.

Done with the casual misogyny she had always accepted as just part of the way the world worked.

And what do you know, it turned out she was treated as she demanded to be treated, and now it was with respect. If one thing good had come out of all of this, it had been finding that measure of strength.

The St. Francis emergency room entrance and parking lot were just as she remembered. Which shouldn't have surprised her, but did. Then again, she felt like she had last been to the facility fifty years ago, with Not-Danny DeVito.

And a man who would change her life for all kinds of bad reasons.

She glanced down at her stomach. Well, and one reason she already loved with every fiber of her being.

Pulling into the closest space she could find, she got out and dragged herself toward the revolving doors. On the far side, she wobbled over to the reception desk and waited until the woman looked up at her over a pair of reading glasses.

"Hi, may I help you—"

"Dr. Robert Bluff. I'm here to see Dr. Bluff."

"I'm sorry, ma'am. This isn't a doctor's office where you

can ask for a specific provider. This is the emergency room—"

"I know where I am. I want you to page him, right now. And if he's not on shift, you're going to call him at home. And if he's on vacation, you're going to bring him back from wherever he is. He's the only one who's going to deliver my baby."

The pushback was immediate, but also unperturbed, as if lots of weird demands had been tossed over the receptionist's proverbial transom. "Ma'am, I'm not sure I was clear enough. You can't just—"

"Page him, right now. Or I'm having this baby in front of you and all the nice people in those chairs over there."

The woman hesitated. But as Anne just stared her right in the eye, her hand reached out to the phone. After a couple of buttons were pushed, the receptionist said, "Dr. Bluff, you have a . . ."

"Patient," Anne said.

"A patient at the front desk. Paging Dr. Bluff, please come to reception."

As another contraction hit, Anne held on to the desk's edge and swayed. Just as she was about to have to go sit down, the sharp, burning sensation eased, thank God—

The sudden rushing feeling that hit her next was not unexpected, she supposed. But as the insides of her legs ran with a hot fall of liquid, she guessed it was better for her water to break here than in her car—

Dr. Robert Bluff marched out of the double doors of the treatment area, his face annoyed as if some protocol had been breached. But the instant he saw her, he did a double take.

Anne lifted her hand. "My water broke. Sorry—"

"That's not water," he said as he rushed forward. Over his shoulder, he shouted, "I need a wheelchair, right now!"

With a sense of dread, Anne looked down at herself— and what she saw was incomprehensible. Her inner thighs were bathed with blood, so much of it that a brilliant red pool was forming at her feet.

Throwing out a hand to the doctor, she grabbed on to his sleeve. In a low, urgent voice, she said, "You remember me, from before. I was here with one of your kind. You know what I'm talking about."

The man's—vampire's—eyes bugged out.

"It's his," she said softly. "The man—male—I was with. This is his baby, and you're the only one who can do this."

Dr. Bluff glanced around. Then he whispered, "I'll take care of everything."

The wheelchair arrived in the nick of time. Right as her knees gave out, she collapsed back into the seat, and she was grateful that Dr. Bluff insisted on pushing her out of the waiting area himself—and it was just as well she left. The patients and families who were in line to be seen were all looking over at her in horror, and as she was swept through the double doors, she was willing to bet the jogging orderly with the rolling bucket and the mop had been called on account of her.

The next thing she knew, she was being transferred onto a gurney in a room that had four solid walls and a lot of equipment.

Trauma bay, she thought. She was in a trauma bay.

Dr. Bluff worked fast with his nurses: IVs were started, questions about allergies and medicines were asked, basic assessments were taken. And when he pressed a stethoscope to her belly and listened, she prayed for a—

"The baby's alive," he said grimly. "I have a heartbeat."

Anne's relief was part of the complicated tangle of emotions she had been stewing in ever since she'd missed her period and learned she was carrying Darius's child. She had no idea what she was bringing into the world. But it *was* hers, and she'd made peace with that.

It was the only thing she'd made peace with.

"Nurses, step out, please. I need a moment."

The women in uniform seemed a little surprised by the order, but they did as the doctor demanded. And then Dr. Bluff was looming over Anne, his face drawn in tight lines.

"You're bleeding profusely. I believe you probably have a placenta previa, something that is very common for pregnancies that are—that are complicated in the way yours is. Here's the problem. If I give you human blood, and the young is a half-breed, as you say? It will kill the fetus immediately, although the transfusion may save your life."

A strange coldness came over her. "And what if you don't give me blood."

"You're going to die."

As she heard the words, her mind refused to process them. "I'm going to . . ."

"It's your life or the young's—and if you pick the latter, I can't promise it's going to survive anyway. But I will promise you will not make it."

Time slowed to a crawl, and Anne was grateful for the distortion as her mind seemed to be refusing to process anything. *Think, think, think . . .*

The image that came to her, the memory, was so sharp, so clear, it was as if it had been implanted in her mind by some other force: She was back in the rear of a car, cradled against something warm and vital, her body sprawled against . . .

"Darius," she said weakly.

"Would you like me to call him?" Dr. Bluff asked.

Anne shifted her eyes to the chandelier above her. The light was bright and she blinked in the glare.

As a strange, prevailing coldness began to seep into her body, she felt herself start to tremble.

"Would you like me to call him?" Dr. Bluff repeated. "It has to be now, if you want him here . . . we're already out of time."

CHAPTER TWENTY-TWO

When Darius finally got the call he'd been waiting for, praying for . . . it came in no form he
had ever expected and definitely one he didn't
want. Instead of Anne's voice, reaching out to him, it was
that of a male whose face he could only vaguely recall. And
instead of his female breaking her rightful silence and somehow forgiving him . . .

"You need to come immediately," the doctor from a lifetime ago was saying in a hushed, urgent tone. "St. Francis
emergency room. I'm losing her. You don't have a lot of
time."

Darius's hearing went in and out. "Anne?"

"Your mate. She's in labor, and she's losing a lot of blood.
If you have anything you want to say to her, you better get
here right now."

Click.

The line went dead.

Darius took the phone away from his ear and looked at it. "Sire?"

He glanced across his kitchen at Fritz. His butler was polishing silver at the sink, and had paused in all his elbow grease.

"Sire? Whatever is wrong?"

Blood loss . . . ?

"Ihavetogo."

Tossing the receiver in the vicinity of the phone, Darius raced out his back door and dived into the shadows. When he closed his eyes, he sent up a prayer unto the Scribe Virgin that he'd actually be able to dematerialize—and the incantation must have worked because in spite of his panic and confusion, he managed to ghost out—

And re-form in the parking lot of the ER where he had first brought his Anne, all those eons ago.

The fact that he came back to his form right under a streetlight wasn't something he gave a lot of thought to: After nine months of nothing, after nine lonely months of despair and self-blame, after nine months of suffering, he just wanted to see Anne. To hold her. To hear her voice. The black hole of her absence, which he more than deserved, had begun to feel perpetual. But God, he didn't want the relief like this. Another accident, another dire injury . . .

Running in through the entrance, he skidded to a halt in front of the reception desk.

"Mr. Wurster?" the woman asked.

When he nodded, she hit a buzzer. "Go through the double doors, follow the trauma signs, she's in bay one."

Darius took off again, hoping he could still read once he got through those doors. Fortunately, his literacy stuck with him and the signs were in brilliant red, but more than that, there was the smell of fresh blood. Lots of blood.

He ripped open a glass door—

And there she was.

His Anne.

With a moan of helpless agony, he rushed over to her bedside—as, from out of the corner of his eyes, he saw blood dripping off the table she was on. Jesus, the mattress underneath her was stained red. So were the sheets. There was actually a bucket underneath, one that was filling at an alarming rate.

It reminded him of the ones at induction sites.

Dr. Bluff, that half-breed, was on the other side of her, holding her hand. And as the male started to talk, Darius couldn't hear anything.

"Anne?" he said in a cracked voice.

Her lids fluttered open, and she turned her head toward him. There was an oxygen mask over her mouth and nose, and she batted at it. When Darius went to remove the thing, the doctor had stuff to say about that, but the two of them ignored him.

She looked like she had aged twenty years. Fifty. And she was white as paper.

"Darius," she said in a whisper. "You have to take care of her."

"Who? Take care of who?"

"The baby." Her eyes started to roll back. "The baby . . ."

Darius's hearing phased in and out for a second, everything going dead quiet before coming back.

In slow motion, he turned his head and realized . . . her belly was swollen. "Young?" he said numbly.

Dr. Bluff cut in. "She's having your young. I told you over the phone."

"My young?" Why was everybody speaking in a foreign language? "My . . ."

Anne grabbed his hand in a powerful grip. "You take care of her. Swear to me. You will watch over her and you will make sure she's safe. You owe me that—you owe her that."

"Anne . . ." As one of his eyes starting twitching so badly it strobed everything, he tried to remember how to speak. "How did this happen?"

Oh, come on. Like he didn't know? That final night, when he had come to her . . .

"I should have told you," she said roughly. "But I didn't . . . I couldn't."

"You have nothing to apologize for." Compared to his transgressions? "Shh. Don't worry. We just need to get you some blood. Right?"

As he looked at the doctor, the male shook his head.

"No blood," Anne said. "It'll kill her."

With dawning horror, Darius glanced down to the bucket. Which was almost half full. "No. No, it won't. You'll just get some—"

"It's her life or the baby's," Dr. Bluff said. "That's—"

The glass door burst open, someone in a white coat and blue scrubs entering in a rush.

"Not now," Dr. Bluff snapped. "Privacy please."

As the other physician glanced at Anne, and immediately shook his head sadly as if he'd recognized there was no good outcome to be had, Darius stamped his boot. "Then we do something else. There has to be something else we can do—"

While the glass door shut again, Anne's eyes watered, tears slipping onto her temples and dropping off into her beautiful dark hair. "I'm dying, Darius. So I can't take care of—"

"You're *not* dying. You're right here with me." He glanced over at the doctor again. "She's here. She's not . . ."

"She's chosen not to have a transfusion," Dr. Bluff explained. "She's choosing the young over herself."

Darius looked back at Anne and started shaking his head. "Have the transfusion—"

"It will kill her—"

"I need you—"

"I can't kill our baby. I can't . . . I *won't*."

Things began to beep fast and alarms started to ring. This time, when medical staff bolted in, Dr. Bluff just put his hand up to stop them from getting close. He didn't tell them to leave.

"Darius . . ."

Something about the way Anne said his name cut through the sudden chaos, the smell of all that copper blood disappearing, the humans in their hospital garb becoming invisible.

"Take care of her." Anne's eyes were luminous in her

graying face. "If you want to make amends with me, that's how you do it. Watch over our daughter. Make sure she's safe. Love her enough ... for the both of us."

"No, no, no ... Anne, I love you ..."

Her eyes stared up at him, luminous, but dimming. "Tell me you didn't mean to hurt me."

"I didn't. I love you, I still do. I just didn't know how to tell you without having you be afraid of me. Or disgusted."

"I've missed you."

Pain flared in his chest. "I have missed you every night and all day long—"

She gasped and then her eyes started to roll back. "Oh, God ..."

CHAPTER TWENTY-THREE

Darius's mate died seven minutes before his daughter was born via cesarean section, in trauma bay number one of the St. Francis Hospital's emergency room. It wasn't until twenty-four minutes after the birth that he got to hold the young, the tiny, wriggly pink thing all swaddled in a soft white and red and blue blanket.

Sitting down with what remained of his beloved, the chair under his butt was hard, but that didn't matter. Nothing mattered.

As he cried, his tears landed on the young's face.

As he cried, the body of his mate grew cold on the treatment table before him.

The medical staff had departed from the bay, and when Dr. Bluff eventually came back, the vampire had the smarts to move slowly and speak softly.

"Do you want to cremate the body?" the male asked.

"Yes," Darius replied, even though he didn't know what he was responding to.

"I've put the young in the system, and gotten her a social security number. That'll help with what comes next."

Did anything come next? Darius wondered. Maybe he just stayed in this plastic chair forever, holding the infant and trying not to see all the blood.

"Thank you," he mumbled.

"You know, she may not be a vampire," the doctor offered. "If she's a half-breed, she may not need to be exposed to your side of things."

Darius looked up. "Don't you mean ours."

"No, I don't. I made my choice a long time ago and I'm urging you to do the same for your daughter. If you leave her in the human world, she won't be hunted."

"I'm not letting my young get raised by—"

"Think about it. Can you keep her safe in your world? From the Lessening Society? It's much safer here. On the other side."

He thought of the two estranged young he had already lost to the war. And lied to himself: "No, it isn't."

"Yes, it is. And I know what you are. I found out who you are. If the *lessers* discover a member of the Black Dagger Brotherhood has a young, they will find her and take her just to get to you. And when you go to try to retrieve her, they will kill you both—after they make you watch your daughter die in a horrible way."

With the sound of a wounded animal, Darius squeezed

his eyes shut and cradled the fragile being he and his beloved had brought into the world. The idea that anything could ever hurt her made him both weak and powerful.

"I will hide her to keep her safe," he countered dully.

"From the Omega? Really? At your house, wherever that is? Where fighters go in and out every night and slayers stalk the shadows. She'll be safe there?"

Darius blinked. "Yes . . . she will."

"*You're* going to keep her from all that, from the evil who has engineered an army of undead just to kill us because of what we are." Dr. Bluff walked through the bloody mess on the floor over to Anne, whose body had been covered by a fresh white blanket up to her neck, whose face was frozen and growing more inanimate by the moment. "Truly, you're that powerful."

Darius looked at his love's expression. Anne seemed so peaceful, like she was sleeping, and he prayed she was in the Fade . . . prayed that she had made it to the Other Side— and wished he knew whether humans were allowed there.

If not, he would see her in her Heaven. Someday, somehow—

He thought of Vishous's vision. For the last nine months, he had prayed for that fireball, but it had yet to come and now he was glad. What would have happened to his young now if he were dead? She would have been lost to the human world. Or maybe Bluff would have saved her somehow. Or maybe the male would have let her die.

Either way, Darius never would have known about his own young.

"You can watch over her from afar," Bluff said roughly. "Keep her safe that way. You have a *doggen*, right? He could keep tabs on her during the day."

Darius looked down at his daughter's angelic face. Her eyes were closed and her little bow of a mouth was parted as she breathed in a quiet pant, like she was already growing so fast.

"I'm not looking for your advice."

"You should take it. Like I said, there's a reason I'm on the human side—and I'm still alive."

Dearest Virgin Scribe. Darius had thought that the pain of losing Anne while she was living had been bad. But now she had died and he knew an even greater grief. While facing an even more overwhelming loss . . .

It was as his agony exponentially expanded that he realized, as much as he hated the doctor being right, he was going to have to let his young go.

"How did Anne know it was a daughter," he murmured numbly.

"I don't know."

"What will happen to my young?" he asked as he stroked his daughter's soft cheek.

But neither the doctor, nor anyone else, knew the answer to that. It was more a statement of his stark terror at the future.

When a soft cooing noise came back at him, it was like a knife to the heart, and then her eyes opened and she seemed to focus on him.

Dr. Bluff said quietly, "I will make sure she gets into the right situation. I swear it to you. Your mate was my patient and I lost her. I owe her independently of you and I sharing a common species."

"What if my young goes through the change?"

"If she does, she'll be an adult. You can approach her then. And she may not."

"I can't lose her."

As Darius said the words, he didn't know who he was talking about: his mate, who had never been his, really, or the daughter who would never get the chance to be with her father.

If she was lucky.

After all, he had made a vow to his beloved and he would not shirk that or his duty to his progeny. And sometimes, the best path in life was the absolute hardest.

"Okay," Darius choked out. Then he switched to the Old Language. "*The daughter of mine blood and heart shall be raised human. Yet upon my honor, I shall never, ever be far from her. And may the Scribe Virgin save the soul of any who would e'er harm her . . .*"

CHAPTER TWENTY-FOUR

One week later, Darius took the ashes of the only female he had ever loved up to the mountaintop mansion he had built north of Caldwell some sixty years before. As he re-formed by the barren, dry fountain in the courtyard, he looked up at the great gray monolith.

Tracing the darkened diamond-paned windows with his eyes, measuring the rooflines, counting the floors, he didn't have the mental energy to picture the interior, all the untouched furniture draped in sheets, the unslept-in beds likewise covered, the unused porcelain and silver and crystal sitting on shelves, ready to be called into service.

And yet remaining untouched.

He was bored mourning that old pipe dream.

Besides, now he had two real people to grieve, not just

some piece of real estate he had built for a community that didn't buy into his utopian vision.

"This is home," he said in a hoarse voice. "Or at least I had hoped it would be."

Of course there was no reply. Which was what happened when you spoke to an urn.

Still, he took the container that he'd been clutching like a football, all tucked in against his ribs, and held it up. As if Anne could see anything.

Which was stupid.

Lowering it back down, he rubbed his thumb on the cold metal. The repository for his beloved's ashes was made of brass and had a screw top, and he had picked it up—along with what remained of his mate—just after nightfall from Dr. Bluff, who had more than lived up to his promises. Elizabeth, which was what Darius had named the young, had been given over to a nurse and taken home, and he and Fritz were already staking out that property.

So the young was not alone in the human world—

The wind brushed up against him from behind, shoving at his body, as if nature itself wanted him to get on with what he had come to do. Taking the cue, he dematerialized up to the roofline, to one of the peaks in the very front of the mansion's roof. The gusts were even stronger with the additional elevation, and he had to steady himself by gripping a lightning rod.

When he looked down to the courtyard, he had absolutely no impulse to pitch himself off. He had to stay alive; he had a purpose now. He lived for his and Anne's young.

He had done so many wrongs to his female, and as she

had said, the only way he could make up for any part of it was to do exactly as she'd asked. The fact that watching over their daughter was a sacred duty he would have performed anyway didn't matter.

He was going to do this for his Anne.

"I promise you," he said to the Milky Way overhead. "I will keep her safe."

Regarding the twinkling stars in their curtain of velvet night, he thought about how cold and vast space was, and how, in the scheme of things, his little plot of suffering wasn't even a blip on the universe's radar. But the truth was, as every snowflake that fell in winter was a precious miracle, so, too, was each mortal's minute galaxy of existence.

We are our own suns, he thought, *drawing life out of darkness in the form of emotions and meaning out of randomness by virtue of our connections.*

And so, when loss came—and it always did—and the center of that world lost its light, the tragedy was of unfathomable, universal impact.

Even when it only impacted one person.

Or . . . vampire.

Unscrewing the lid, Darius's heart was in his throat. "I'm not going to let you down, Anne. I promise."

Hitching a breath, he wept openly as he tipped the brass urn over—

The wind caught the ashes and carried them off, to the beautiful view of the mountains, to the moon . . . to the stars. As he watched them go, he pictured his mate's beautiful face as she smiled up at him, her eyes sparkling, her hair flowing.

So alive that he'd felt like they'd had forever. Just because he loved her that much.

When all was empty, he screwed the lid back on and tucked the urn into a crevice behind the peak.

"I love you," he said to the sky.

Because as far as he was concerned, his *shellan* was out there somewhere in the cosmos, witnessing him do the right thing. At least he hoped she was. Surely the Scribe Virgin would welcome her into the Fade.

But who knew.

He stayed a moment longer. And then another. And another. Like he was waiting for something . . . a response, or maybe a sign. Meanwhile, beneath him, the mansion he had built with such hope, and which he sustained with such disappointment, slept in the manner of the inanimate that was unclaimed, empty as always.

Though the vacancy had always struck him as a waste, now he couldn't imagine anybody living there, ever.

Then again, it was no longer a potential home. It was a mausoleum.

And the living part of him had just been buried on its rooftop.

Forevermore.

EPILOGUE

Present Day

Elizabeth, née Randall—beloved *shellan* of Wrath, son of Wrath, revered *mahmen* of Wrath, son of Wrath—entered the Audience House via the back door with her son on her hip. As soon as she stepped inside, she smelled fresh pastries, and Little Wrath, or L.W., as he was known, clearly approved of them as well.

Normally composed in a way that could at times freak her out, he extended his arms and made grabby motions—and naturally, the uniformed *doggen* who was baking the delicacies dropped everything she was doing and rushed over with a porcelain plate.

"Sire," she said to the young, "it is my pleasure."

The female bowed low, presenting the Danishes as if they were gifts, as if L.W. were fully grown and sitting on the throne that his father occupied.

"And for you as well, my Queen," the pastry chef added shyly. "May they please your palate."

When the female straightened, her eyes locked on the Saturnine Ruby that Beth always wore—even though the thing weighed a ton and she was constantly worried about knocking it on something and she'd never been a jewelry person. The citizens and the staff wanted to see it, though. Needed to. It was history that reached forward into the present, and she and her family were an intrinsic part of that continuity.

"Thank you," Beth said. "You know I love the cherry ones."

"Indeed, I do, and it is my pleasure to make them with mine own hand."

As Beth took the plate with her to the front of the house, L.W. snagged one of the pair, and she had to admit, he was already a precise eater, just like his father.

"Mama?" he said as he held it out to her.

"Mmm." She paused and took a bite. "Thank you."

"Mmmmmmm."

Sticky fingers. Sticky mouth. Sticky face.

Who cared. The kid was adorable, and you couldn't cheat him of his happiness—especially because he was so serious most of the time. If there was one thing she worried about, it was the gravity that blanketed him. It was as if he already carried on his shoulders the weight of the species, as if he knew what his future would entail. Sure, the King was democratically elected now, but maybe L.W. was seeing into the decades or centuries ahead somehow. Maybe he was destined to be as his father was, revered by his subjects.

Responsible for them, too.

She wasn't sure she wanted that for her son. But it wasn't up to her, was it.

"It's up to you, big man," she said as she resumed walking out to the front of the house.

After centuries of refusing to lead, Wrath, the sire, finally decided to assume his legacy and take the throne. And that was why this house, which was far away from the mansion on the mountain where they all lived, had been called into service for the civilians who sought out audiences with their King.

"Hi, Miha," Beth said to the receptionist in what had once been the ladies' parlor.

The female looked up from the schedule book. "Mistress! And the sire!"

The way Miha's face lit up as she looked at L.W. was a reminder of how much the species needed hope for the future. And how much they loved their leader—and his son and *shellan*.

At first, the reverence had been hard to get used to. Then again, when she had finally learned the truth about what she was—and the fact that she wasn't human—there had been so much to recast and reset that she'd had a lot of experience with awkwardness. And really, was it that bad to be loved?

Better than a poke in the eye with a sharp stick, as the saying went.

"We're just here to see Dad." Beth hiked L.W. up a little higher and tried to keep the plate steady. "And for the grub."

As L.W. waved his gooey treasure around, she tried to move her hair out of range—

"Would you like me to take that porcelain for a minute?" Miha asked.

"You know, that would be great. I'll be back for it."

"Also, how about a napkin?" Miha took one out of her desk. "I don't have wet wipes, I'm afraid."

"That's awesome. Thanks."

Accepting the precisely ironed damask square—because Fritz only ever did everything in his houses correctly—and turning over the sweets, Beth smiled a goodbye and wiped her son's face as she walked across the foyer. When she came up to the set of closed double doors, she wondered if it wouldn't be better if she held off interrupting—

The panels whipped open.

What was on the other side was not a surprise, yet it wasn't easy to see, either. As usual, there were a number of Brothers and fighters standing around, all fully armed, and also as usual, they looked over at her with brotherly respect and love. But the vibe in what had once been the formal dining room was tense. Which was par for the course as well and nothing she was ever going to get used to.

V. Tohr. Z and Phury. Rhage and Butch, along with John Matthew and Qhuinn and Blay.

"*Beth.*"

As her name was spoken with a barking authority, she turned to the fireplace. Two armchairs had been set up facing each other, the vacant of the pair for the civilians who came with their celebrations, grievances, and conflicts, the other filled to overflowing with her *hellren*. Seated in what became a throne whenever he was on it, Wrath was an enormous presence in his leathers and his muscle shirt, his waist-length black hair falling from its widow's peak, his blind eyes hidden behind wraparound sunglasses, his guide dog right by his side on the floor.

"What's wrong." The King jumped to his feet, the surge startling the golden, who followed his master's example in confusion. "What—"

"Nothing's wrong." She motioned with her hands for him to calm down even though he couldn't see her. "I was just driving into town to meet Sarah over at her and Murhder's house, and I thought I would stop by."

"Dada," L.W. called out.

Those dark brows dropped down low. "Who's guarding you both?"

"It's fine—"

"No one is with you?" he demanded. Like he was prepared to relieve Vishous, who coordinated security details, of the Brother's remaining testicle. With a rusty spike.

"I'm just going to Sarah's—"

"But what if you needed something or—"

"Wrath." Instantly, the King shut up, in a way that he only ever did when she said his name in that tone. "We talked about this, remember. I let V know what I was doing, as we agreed, and then I got in my car with our son and headed out like a normal person."

As she glanced at Vishous, the goateed fighter nodded and flashed his Samsung forward. "Yup, she hit me up. And I got her on my phone. I'm tracking her all the way."

"I'm not a prisoner and neither is your son."

After a full minute of glowering, the great Blind King sat his ass back down, and if he were any other living thing, you might say he sulked a little, his lower lip pooching out, his brows sinking even lower. Of course, given that he remained a straight-up killer, even in his retirement from fighting, nobody would have thrown that kind of observation around.

"Come here, *leelan*," Wrath muttered.

As Beth walked the length of the long room, L.W. reached out with his Danish, and Wrath's face softened as he clearly focused on the scent of his son. Meanwhile, at his feet, George lay back down and thumped his tail, snuffling and smiling in the way goldens did.

"Someone's sticky," Wrath said.

"Very."

The great Blind King reached out, flashing the tattoos that ran up his inner forearms, his lineage displayed in the symbols of the Old Language. "My *leelan*. My son."

He didn't care that L.W.'s hands were covered with cherry filling and glaze. He didn't care that his Brothers were in the room. He didn't give one living shit about anything other than his family—and as soon as Beth was in range, he picked her up off the floor and settled her in his lap like she weighed nothing.

As she repositioned their son, she wrapped an arm around Wrath's huge shoulders and was reminded of how powerful he was. Even though her male was barred from going into the field, he kept in top shape, sparring with Payne in the gym, lifting, running on treadmills. He continued to work with his throwing stars, and stab targets, and shoot guns. And as ever, he was always in charge of the

Brotherhood, the household at the mansion, the species at large.

Yet he had a gentle side.

L.W. rarely giggled, but as Wrath went for the Danish and smacked his lips, the peal of happy laughter seemed to fill the whole house.

And it was the strangest thing.

Her vantage point changed even as her position didn't. Suddenly, she felt as though she were looking at the three of them—four of them, counting George—from a distance, regarding what was up close from far enough away that it was as if she were a bystander.

And what did she see?

A family. A strong, anchored, united . . . family.

Emotions percolated and Beth glanced away so that she could clear the sheen from her eyes without doing something obvious.

And that was when the past came back.

Instead of being in the dining room as it was now, emptied of most of its furniture, nothing left but the pair of armchairs, and Saxton's desk in the corner, and the sentries who guarded her *hellren* . . . she saw things as they had been when she'd first stepped into the house: The long, glossy table set with fresh flowers, crystal, and porcelain. The lovely carved chairs with their silk seat covers. The sideboards with their sterling silver serving platters and curling candelabra.

And there she and Wrath were, on their first date, clustered at one end of the table, the electricity and the anticipation charging the air between them.

Like eating peaches.

"Leelan?" Wrath whispered. "Why are you crying?"

Running her hand through his long jet-black hair, she couldn't put words to the complex feelings swirling in her chest.

"I'm just . . . grateful," she said quietly. "For my life now— and everything that started the night I met you. Everything that is right and good . . . started with you."

Wrath wrapped his hand around the nape of her neck and inched her forward to his lips. As they kissed, more memories bubbled up, of them in their mating bed up on the third floor of the mansion, of the people and families they lived with, of this wonderful, fraught, funny, scary existence they shared.

"Well," her *hellren* murmured against her mouth. "For me, it all started with you, too—"

"Fuck!"

At the barked curse, she and Wrath pulled apart—

—just in time to see John Matthew collapse onto the Persian rug in a seizure.

◆   ◆   ◆

Underneath the Audience House, there were two subterranean bedrooms, and the Brothers ended up carrying John Matthew down to one of them because the civilians were already starting to arrive, and nobody needed to see one of the King's private guard with his eyes rolled back into his skull and his extremities flapping like he was hooked up to a car battery.

And naturally, Beth wasn't going to leave until the male was done being assessed.

For one, he was his half brother. For another, maybe there would be something she could help with.

"Well, he does have a history of seizures," Doc Jane hedged as she packed up her doctor bag.

"Do we need to do an MRI or something?" Xhex, John Matthew's mate, leaned over the bed and brushed back his hair. "He's not coming around like he usually does."

The female had arrived within moments of being summoned, and the panic on her hard face had been difficult to witness. Beth had been through a couple of emergencies with Wrath, and she knew the special kind of terror that came with your *hellren* being hurt or in danger.

And the female was right. Usually John Matthew would be better by now. Instead, he was still lying against the pillows, all logy and out of it, his eyes closed, his breathing shallow. But he had been able to answer simple questions like what year it was, who was the human president . . . what was Rhage's favorite meal.

Everything had been the correct response to that last one.

"What are we going to do?" Xhex asked.

As Doc Jane sat back on her heels and crossed her arms over her white coat, her forest green stare narrowed on John Matthew like she was surveying the inside of him with some kind of special second sight.

"Let's talk out in the hall," she eventually replied.

Xhex nodded sharply and walked around the bed. As she passed by Beth, she gave L.W.'s chubby hand a little squeeze.

"I'm so sorry," Beth whispered.

"It's okay," the female said, even though it wasn't okay.

Doc Jane murmured something to her patient, and then she stepped out, too, the heavy door to the chamber closing behind them both.

Left alone with the Brother, Beth once again hitched L.W. up a little higher on her hip and then stared at John Matthew, willing him to be okay. He had always been such a mystery, born in a bus station with the Brotherhood's star somehow marking his chest, adopted by Tohr and Wellsie just before his transition by a stroke of pure luck. And then, after Wellsie's tragic murder, and Tohr's disappearance, the other Brothers and their mates had taken the boy in and trained him up.

Now he was a bona fide member of the Black Dagger Brotherhood himself, a powerful fighter, a vicious protector, and a proud, bonded mate to a female of worth.

Beth had always felt a special kinship with the male, not just from their blood connection, but because he had come from the outside world, too, and been narrowly found just in time.

As she had been.

Without Wrath's vein on the night of her transition? She would have died. Likewise, if John Matthew hadn't been brought to the Brothers by Bella? He would have died.

And the King wouldn't have a mate.

And neither would Xhex.

It was as if things had fallen into place exactly as they had been meant to all along, that which had seemed implausible while it occurred, presenting as inevitable in retrospect.

Beth focused on her son. L.W. was back in what she thought of as his all-business mode. Even though he was too young to understand everything—understand anything, really—his pale eyes, which had turned green, unfortunately, were over on the bed, on the prone warrior whose lids were shut tight and whose breathing remained shallow.

As she considered doctors and biological accidents of fate, she knew her son was probably going to go blind, just like his sire.

With a wave of anxiety curdling in her gut, she turned away and went for a walk around. It was on her second pass by the desk that she stopped. Frowned. Felt her own chest get tight.

Over the years, she had been down here from time to time . . . and yet she had forgotten why the chamber was so significant to her—

No, she hadn't forgotten. The relevance had never been lost; it had just been eclipsed by regular life.

But seeing all of the images of herself now was a reminder of who had lived here. Who had watched over her.

Who had loved her from afar.

Her father, Darius.

The collection of photographs was extensive, the angles, exposures, and eras all different, just like the frames. But the subject was always her. Taken as a collective, it was a catalog of the eras of her life, from her early childhood and teenage times when she was at Our Lady of Mercy, to her college years at SUNY Caldwell, to when she'd gotten her job at the newspaper.

She had never met her father, but she had no doubt that he had taken care of her. Protected her. Loved her. The photographs were proof. The stories from Fritz were proof.

That he had put her in the path of Wrath to save her life . . . was proof.

"Mama."

As L.W. pointed at one of the black-and-white close-ups, she cleared her throat and said roughly, "Yup, that's me."

Closing in on the image, picking up the sterling silver frame, she remembered that particular softball game at Caldwell High—she'd been pitching, and the picture had been snapped when she'd been on the mound. She'd been sixteen, and determined to win, her eyes sharp under the bill of her cap, strands of her hair drifting into her flushed face. She had a feeling the picture had been one of her father's favorites, as it was set right at what would have been his elbow when he'd been in the antique chair.

She had seen a painting of Darius and knew she looked a lot like him.

She had seen a photograph of her mother, who had died in childbirth, and knew she looked a lot like her.

It was funny, even though they were both gone, she felt as though they were never far. And hey, she was a vampire, so why couldn't ghosts be real—

Beth.

As she heard her name, she wheeled around to the bed, even though she knew it wasn't John Matthew speaking out loud. For one thing, he was a mute. For another . . .

What. The. *Hell.*

John Matthew's eyes were open and he was staring at her, but something wasn't right about his face. Not at all.

Even though his features were the same as they had always been, they were somehow different, the eye shape, the angle of the jaw, the arch of the brow, not his anymore. And where were his pupils? Only the whites were showing—

Beth.

That voice. That deep voice . . . which she had never heard before, and yet which seemed . . . so very familiar.

Drawn toward the bed, she said something that made no sense, but was undeniable: "Dad?"

Standing over not-really-John-Matthew, she stared in wonder at what seemed to be looking at her. Was it really . . . her father? It certainly appeared as though what she knew of Darius's features had been laid over the other male's.

Maybe she'd had a seizure, too. Or maybe this was a dream?

I think it's time for me to go, the voice in her head said. *I think . . . you're okay.*

"Dad . . ." she choked out. "How are you here?"

He's beautiful. Just like his mahmen.

"Oh, God, *Dad."*

The next thing she knew, she was lying across a powerful chest, crying, and L.W. was reaching for the face that seemed partially an illusion.

I love you, Elizabeth. I always have. And your mahmen, *she loved you so much she gave her life so you could live.*

"I love you, too—"

My job is finally done, my vow completed, my destiny here served. You're safe and you're happy, and you're loved as you deserve to be. That is all I've ever wanted for you. Stay with your Wrath. Love him and your son with your whole heart. And know that I'm not leaving you, I'm just going to be watching from above from now on.

Beth inched back, ignoring her tears. "I don't understand this."

You don't have to. All you need to know is that your parents love you very much and always will.

The apparition lifted his hand and brushed L.W.'s cheek. Then he touched Beth's hair.

"This isn't real," she said hoarsely.

It is, and I'll prove it. Go back to the mansion I built for the purpose it is finally being used for. Go to the topmost peak in the front roof. You will find a bronze urn there. Your mahmen's ashes were put in it after she was cremated. I scattered them over the mountain, letting the night wind draw them to the stars. That is how you will know this is real. I have to go. I love you—

There was a jerk of John Matthew's body.

And then, "What the *fuck*."

Beth looked up in alarm. Xhex had come back in from the hallway and she was standing in the open doorway, staring at her mate like she'd seen a stranger.

Because . . . well, maybe she had, too.

"I don't know what just happened," Beth said numbly.

When she glanced back down . . . John Matthew had returned, his eyes rolling into place, the pupils struggling to focus as if he'd woken up from a coma. And as his mate hustled over and took his hand, he looked at Xhex.

The female was pale to the point of being stark and she was shaking her head like she was utterly dumbfounded.

"Your grid," his mate said. "Your grid . . ."

As a *symphath*, Xhex could apparently sense things other people could not, and Beth had heard about the way they categorized a person's emotions and consciousness. Not that she completely comprehended it.

"The shadow is gone," the female murmured as she stroked her mate's face. "It's just . . . him now."

Beth's eyes went back to the displays of photographs on the desk and she held L.W. a little tighter. Was it possible her father had found a way to stay with her after his death?

What a miracle that would be, if it were true.

"I have to go back home," she heard herself say urgently. "Right now."

When Xhex looked up, she started for the door. "I need to know if this is true. I have to know for sure."

Except she already had her answer. In her heart, in her soul, she was absolutely certain that when she got back to the mansion her father had built so that the Brotherhood and their mates and families could all live together under one roof, so that they could be safer together, so that they could support each other through the good times and the bad, she was going to dematerialize up to the rooftop . . .

And find the urn her father had put up there.

And know that he had always been with her.

Her mom, as well.

In truth, she had had . . . the very best parents in all the world.

◆   ◆   ◆

Curiously, it had not been hard to leave his daughter.

As Darius arrived in a hazy landscape of white nothingness, he was at peace in a way he couldn't remember ever having been before. The thing about parenting was, even though you never felt you had done enough or done anything really well, there was a time to let go . . . there was a moment when you finally had to release your young to proceed out on their own. And if that time presented itself when you knew what you had brought into the world was in a good place? It was easier than you thought.

Granted, his parenting had always been distilled through another: first, his loyal butler, and then, after a miracle, John Matthew. But he hadn't let such barriers get in the way of his love or his duty. And Beth was truly living her best life . . .

After debating the when of it all for so long, he had not been prepared for tonight to be the night necessarily . . . except something about seeing his daughter and his grandson sitting on the lap of the great Blind King, with Wrath's powerful arms wrapped around the two most precious things in Darius's world, had made him realize that for better or worse, there was nothing more for him to do.

She was, literally, in the very best hands.

And it was time for him to leave her.

Just as the confirmation struck his heart, a white door appeared directly in front of him, and he took a deep breath and recognized what was being offered to him.

The Fade awaited on the other side of it.

Yes, it was time. Yet he had had to straddle the divide to communicate directly to his daughter just one time. Only once. And thanks to the Virgin Scribe, Elizabeth had known it was him, and she had responded in the way he had always hoped she would if they stole a moment together.

She loved him. Even though she had never known him.

So now . . . he could go in peace. All he had to do was reach out and open things.

Still, he hesitated at the door that had come for him.

Staring at the mystical portal, memories flickered through his mind, the images of the past from as long ago as over twenty years to as recent as the night before. As he watched the slideshow, he wondered dimly if he were dying now for real, if the whole life-passing-before-your-eyes thing was turning out to be the final truism he learned on earth.

Except no, he had died in actuality a couple of years ago. On a rainy night. When a second sun had consumed his mortal body.

Vishous's vision from over two decades before had proven to be correct. A car bomb and its brilliant blast of light and heat had blown him and his newest BMW to high heaven, and he had died. Then again, V was never wrong, was he—although in this case, the brother hadn't been completely right, either. Or maybe he just hadn't been shown what came next: the Scribe Virgin coming to Darius and offering him a deal, a token of faculty traded for the chance to be with his daughter, to make sure she was safe.

To live up to his role as father, and his vow to the female he loved.

Of course he'd taken the bargain.

And so he had stared out from behind another's eyes and watched over his young.

Until now.

Focusing on the door, he told his hand to reach out. When his arm didn't move, he repeated the command.

But he was too afraid of what was on the other side. If

Anne wasn't there—or if she was, and she didn't want him—then eternity was just going to be an infinite suffering, all the worse for being never-ending—

Click.

The sound seemed both utterly foreign and entirely prosaic, the kind of thing that happened countless times in a night, the inner workings of a door unlatching.

His thought, as the portal opened before him, was that this wasn't how it was supposed to work. He was supposed to open the—

"Anne?" he choked out.

From out of a swirl of fog a figure appeared unto him, and for a moment, he worried that he was wrong, that it wasn't her, that—

"Hi."

The familiar voice was just as good as the smile he had seen only in his memories and his dreams: Sure enough, yes, *yes*, it was her, it was his beautiful, dark-haired female.

Anne was standing on the other side of the threshold, a white robe draping her, her body whole and healthy, her face radiant and shining with something that he had mourned as he had never thought he would see it again.

Love. Pure, abiding, soul-deep . . . love.

As she held her arms out to him, Darius exploded into action, leaping over the divide, jumping at her.

Their embrace was solid, even though she seemed to be part of the ether, and as he held her tight, and felt the warmth of her, and smelled her scent, he closed his eyes to savor the way her arms wrapped around him.

They stayed like that for an eternity, and if this was all

that the Fade provided? He was soooooo good with the way the Scribe Virgin had set up the world.

So good.

Except Anne pulled back.

And as he opened his mouth to tell her something, emotions ramrodded him as he looked into her eyes. From out of a choked throat, he asked the one thing that mattered most:

"Did I do a good job?" he said in a guttural voice as he started to choke up. "God, did I take care of her well enough—"

Anne captured his face in her hands. "Oh, yes, Darius. You did a perfect job. You did just what I asked and more than I could have hoped for. You were a magnificent father and protector. Thank you—*thank you.*"

His breakdown was over twenty years in coming, and as he collapsed into her arms and wept—for her, for him, for their Elizabeth—his one true love smoothed his back with her hand. It was all he'd wanted to hear, the confirmation that he hadn't let her down, not in this one job she had given him.

Not in what had been his most important mission.

"You did just what I asked," she repeated, over and over again. "You loved her as no other father could possibly have done better."

When he finally calmed down, he lifted his head and scrubbed his face. Then he focused on his Anne.

The love she had for him was emanating from her, a sun of warmth and healing. And when she said the words, his world slid into a completeness that felt like it had been preplanned, perfectly engineered, created just for him, in spite of his lonely, mournful suffering:

"I love you, Darius."

The shudder that went through him was gratitude and awe mixed into one. "I love you, oh, Anne . . . I've always loved you."

"I know."

As she rose up onto her tiptoes, he leaned down, and their lips met reverently. And then . . . not long thereafter, with passion.

When Darius came up for air, he couldn't keep the smile off his face. Especially as he felt the worries and pain of the mortal coil begin to dissolve, peace fulfilling his soul after his work upon the earth was done.

Abruptly, he had to laugh at his good fortune—giggle, was more like it.

Slipping an arm around his beloved's shoulders, feeling the warmth of her body, scenting her, he had to go there as he regarded the endless horizon: "Ah . . . so, what's this place about? They have anything that resembles a bed we could use for a couple of hours. Nights? Months?"

Anne's laughter was free and easy and like the air he'd needed when he'd been alive: necessary to him. "Yes, as a matter of fact. And so much more."

"Oh? Tell me all about it."

"Well." She put her arm around his waist as they started walking off together. "There's Milk Duds. And fettuccini alfredo—like in that old movie with Al Brooks and Meryl Streep? We've got milkshakes and pies and chocolate, too, all with no calories. Any film or TV show you've ever wanted to watch, and book you wanted to read, and place you've wanted to go. We have beaches and forests and deserts and mountains. Art and architecture. Fashion. We have everything you can imagine and things I can't even describe."

"You're going to have to teach me all about it."

Anne grinned up at him. "My pleasure, and it seems only fair."

God, she was so beautiful. "How so?"

She stopped, and reached up to his face again. "Because you taught me the most important lesson of them all."

"And what was that," he asked tensely.

As a spear of worry went through his chest, she allayed any fear he'd ever have.

"That love conquers all."

Darius started to smile again and so did she. And then he did the most natural thing in the world.

Or the afterlife, as it were.

He kissed his beloved mate until neither one of them could breathe, and wasn't that just what eternity needed to be all about?

"I'm so looking forward to forever," he murmured against her lips.

"Me, too, Darius . . . now that you're by my side again. Me, too."

ACKNOWLEDGMENTS

Thank you to all the readers who have asked for this story. I'm so grateful for all your support and love for this world we have been immersed in for so long. This origin tale was so satisfying to get onto the page. Without your pushing, I don't know whether I'd have written it down.

I'd also like to thank Meg Ruley, Rebecca Scherer and everyone at JRA, and Hannah Braaten, Jamie Selzer, Sarah Schlick, Jennifer Bergstrom, Jennifer Long, and the entire family at Gallery Books and Simon & Schuster.

To Team Waud, I love you all. Truly. And as always, everything I do is with love to and adoration for both my family of origin and of adoption.

Oh, and thank you to Naamah, my Writer Dog II, and Obie, Writer Dog-in-Training, who work as hard as I do on my books! And also to Frank, because . . . Frank.

Do you love fiction with a supernatural twist?

Want the chance to hear news about your favourite authors (and the chance to win free books)?

Christine Feehan
J.R. Ward
Sherrilyn Kenyon
Charlaine Harris
Jayne Ann Krentz and Jayne Castle
P.C. Cast
Maria Lewis
Darynda Jones
Hayley Edwards
Kristen Callihan
Keri Arthur
Amanda Bouchet
Jacquelyn Frank
Larissa Ione

Then visit the *With Love* website and
sign up to our romance newsletter:
www.yourswithlove.co.uk

And follow us on Facebook for book giveaways,
exclusive romance news and more:
www.facebook.com/yourswithlovex

PIATKUS